The
Tin
Cookie
Cutter

Barbara Briggs Ward

The
Tin
Cookie
Cutter

BARBARA BRIGGS WARD

The Tin Cookie Cutter

Published by Wheatmark®
2030 East Speedway Boulevard, Suite 106
Tucson, Arizona 85719 USA
www.wheatmark.com

ISBN: 978-1-62787-721-3 (paperback)
ISBN: 978-1-62787-722-0 (ebook)
LCCN: 2019907453

Bulk ordering discounts are available through Wheatmark, Inc. For more information, email orders@wheatmark.com or call 1-888-934-0888.

The
Tin
Cookie
Cutter

Chapter One

CHRISTMAS WREATHS DISPLAYED ON THE FRONT porch of an Amish farmhouse caught Claire's eye—not because of their red bows against off-white clapboards, nor the fact that Claire was a photographer. Rather it had everything to do with thinking about Christmas—something she hadn't done in years. With a long list of things to do, Claire told herself she'd only stay a few minutes as she turned off the snowy country road and pulled into the farm.

Noting narrow tracks in the snow like those of a buggy going from a barn to the road, Claire followed them down to the two-story structure. That's when she noticed a pick-up truck parked further away next to a smaller building. There was no sign of anyone around.

An open area between haylofts in the main barn allowed Claire to go inside where the snow had gathered in heaps. A buggy was sitting toward the back. Nailed to old boards were harnesses and horseshoes, chisels, and other tools, along with bells on leather straps. Claire was able to smell varnish and shellac, wood that had been sawed, wood that had been shaved, boards that had been painted, and sacks of grain that had been stacked side by side. Walking further inside, she could hear horses stirring behind a closed area. Peeking through a crack in the wall, Claire saw one shaking its mane and another swishing its tail. For a brief second she was certain she saw reindeer way in the back in the shadows.

On the other side of that open area was another door. Claire turned the knob but it was locked. The door had a small window with what looked like a burlap bag partially covering it. Getting up on her tiptoes Claire was able to make out a large anvil similar to what her grandfather kept in his barn. Against both walls were wooden bins full of wooden toys. One oversized bin held sleds and rocking horses. In the center of the room were long wooden tables. A few had pencils and hammers and what looked like patterns sitting on them. One wall was all cans of paint. The other held a chalkboard where it looked as if names were written with times and dates.

Claire could have lingered longer in that barn. It brought back memories of playing with her cousins in her grandfather's barn where they'd vowed they would always remain close. Of course they weren't aware of life and how things change. Eventually Claire's grandmother died from a stroke. She was going on twelve when her grandfather sold the farm.

While she wanted to get inside that room with the wooden toys, Claire realized her presence was being watched. She'd been taking photos of the Amish professionally ever since divorcing Eric five years ago come January. One of the first things Claire realized was the importance of respecting their privacy. In return she gained their trust, which earned her access to their homes. Claire learned how to tell their story without revealing their faces. Even though Claire had been down the road right outside the door countless times, she'd never noticed this farm. It was as if it came out of nowhere just when she needed it to be there.

Walking out of the barn, Claire noted footsteps in the snow. She'd missed seeing them earlier. Claire thought they might belong to whoever owned that truck. Thoughts of that someone out in the freezing cold hurried Claire along a shoveled path leading to the front porch, where the wreaths with red bows were hanging from nails. Walking up the steps, she noticed there were two sizes. Each was a combination of balsam and cedar. Claire didn't see any price tags. It didn't matter. She knew she wanted to buy one.

Standing on the porch as wisps of snowflakes twirled through the air like ballerinas, Claire was reminded of dance recitals she'd been a part of growing up. The woman directing the program didn't put up with excuses. She refused to consider Claire being somewhat overweight as the reason why she was clumsy in her tap shoes, clumsy in her satin ballet slippers. It was an offhand remark Claire's father made to her mother about Claire maybe needing the next size purple tutu a day before performing in the annual recital that turned that recital into her last. She quit dancing despite wanting to learn more.

Claire often wondered how her father would have reacted to her photography. Not the awards but the work itself. She wondered the same about Eric, whose departure came out of the blue one beautiful July evening as they were on their way home from dinner. That's when Eric told her she was boring; told her she could have the house. All he wanted was out of their marriage. Claire didn't fight him. She wasn't surprised. In a way his departure was a relief. Their relationship had changed a few years earlier after he'd told her he didn't want children. That came as a shock to Claire. He'd said the opposite when they were dating. Convinced she'd never have the family she'd hoped to have, Claire bought the equipment needed to build her business.

With the wind coming at her, Claire zipped her coat up as she noted the sound of a little one running around inside the house. When she knocked on the door she heard giggling. A few minutes later the door opened and there stood a rather tall man wearing a heavy flannel shirt over a turtleneck with jeans and a wool scarf wrapped about his neck. A navy knit hat fitting close to his head made it easier to notice his deep brown eyes and bit of a beard as he came walking through the doorway.

"Well, good morning," he said with those brown eyes smiling. "You seem surprised to see an English man."

Extending his hand, he introduced himself. "I'm Tommy Morgan. I'm here helping out with some projects in the barn."

"It's nice to meet you, Tommy. I'm Claire Ryan. These wreaths caught my eye. Being a photographer, I had to stop."

"A photographer. Are you local?"

"I'm in the area. I focus on farmlands and the Amish. While I've gone by here before, I've never noticed this home with its intriguing setting until now."

"There is something special about the place. John and Elizabeth Miller own it. You couldn't ask for better people than the Millers."

"It has a feel to it."

"I agree. I stopped by one day about four years ago to buy some vegetables and I've been coming back ever since. I consider John and Elizabeth my friends. We help each other out all the time."

"I took a look in the barn. It reminded me of Santa's workshop with all those wooden toys."

"That's all John's work. He's been told before how his barn looks like the North Pole. While he laughs it off, their Bishop agrees. Every year about this time I come around at the tail end of one of his biggest projects to help load his goods on sleds. When John returns we'll get started, so I'd better get back to work. There's a lot to do. After all, Claire, it is Christmastime. Elizabeth is busy with the baby. Try knocking again. She's probably in the kitchen by now."

Going down the steps, Tommy turned back around. "Nice meeting you, Claire. Something tells me I'll be seeing you again soon."

With those wisps of snow pushing those little dancing ballerinas over the fields, Claire stood on the top step and watched as Tommy Morgan headed down the path. She could hear the snow crunching with his every step. Reaching the barn, he turned back around again and waved. Thinking Tommy felt her watching and feeling embarrassed, Claire waved, then did a quick knock on the door. Again Claire heard a little one running, followed by some giggling as the door opened.

The image of the Amish woman with a baby swaddled in a blanket, surrounded by what sunlight there was coming through a side window, made Claire want to capture the moment with her camera. She knew that was an impossibility so she stood there staring. With her white muslin cap framing her face, the young woman's green eyes seemed to glisten. Long lashes only enhanced them. Her skin was flawless; her smile, shy yet welcoming. She was small in frame with delicate hands.

The Amish woman didn't invite Claire in. They stood looking at each other until Claire asked about the wreaths.

"They are not for sale. They are a part of a special order."

That's when the baby started crying. It was too cold outside.

"Would you like to come in?"

"If you don't mind," Claire replied.

When the young woman opened the door a little wider Claire took that as her cue. Inside she went as the mother tended to her little one.

Chapter Two

WITH THE WIND EDGING ITS WAY along the windows of that Amish home and the floor creaking with their every step, Claire had the feeling of being back in her grandparents' farmhouse. The scent of yeast mixing with currants and kneaded dough and spices swirling from an oven reminded Claire of her grandmother's Christmas bread. It was a family favorite.

Having been inside several Amish homes, Claire was aware they followed a certain floor plan unless a home had previously been occupied by the English. While this particular home followed the floor plan, it had a few extras, like a lamb sound asleep in a basket next to a stone fireplace. The lamb wasn't the only one sleeping. Sitting in a rocking chair was an elderly woman wrapped in a shawl. Her head was down. Claire could tell she'd been knitting. Her loom was in her lap and on the floor sat skeins of yarn. The old woman's glasses were at the tip of her nose. Her cap was sitting to one side of her head. A few strands of long gray hair could be seen loose and falling past her shoulders. Claire felt awkward staring at her. She could only imagine the woman waking up and being frightened by her presence. As Claire was deciding whether or not to sit down at the table, a toddler came crawling in from another room heading toward the rocking chair. Holding on to a blanket thrown over the woman's lap, the child pulled itself up and began to chatter as if telling the elder to wake up and get ready to play. Claire sat down at the table and moved toward the little one, ready to act if the child headed toward the fireplace. But that never happened. After all the tugging and pulling, the old woman woke up as the young mother came back in the room still carrying the baby. Taking hold of the toddler, she used her foot to pull a wooden cradle out from the wall. Kneeling, she laid the baby down. Covering the sleeping child with a fleece blanket, she moved the cradle a little closer to the lamb. Then standing with the toddler still in hand, the young woman tended to the old woman who was wide awake and either ignoring Claire or she didn't notice her sitting at the table.

"I'm making some mint tea. Would you like a cup, Mummi?"

"Yes, Elizabeth. Thank you."

Turning toward Claire, the young mother extended her hand.

"Welcome to our home. I am Elizabeth. The baby sleeping is Mary. This busy little boy is Abraham. My grandmother is the knitter. Her name is Catherine. We call her Mummi."

Hearing her name, Catherine sat straight up. Tucking her hair back inside her cap she looked at Claire and waited. It took Claire a second to understand the woman expected her to speak first.

"I'm Claire. Thank you, Elizabeth, for inviting me into your home."

"I've seen you before," spoke Catherine. "I remember. You take pictures. I've seen you lots of places taking pictures."

"You're right, Catherine. I am a photographer."

With Abraham in a high chair, Elizabeth went to the kitchen, returning with a handful of crackers. Putting a few down in front of the youngster, she asked, "Did you come to take pictures?"

"I admit your wreaths caught my attention."

"I've had others stop and ask about the wreaths. I've thought about making some to sell but filling special orders takes all my time. Mummi is the baker unless she's sitting in her chair. That's when she enjoys knitting."

Getting a cup of milk for Abraham, Elizabeth added, "My husband John is a woodworker. He is quite busy this time of the year."

"I was drawn to your barn the minute I saw it. Once inside, it was obvious someone had been busy."

"Did you take pictures?"

"No. I would never do that without asking."

"Some people do."

"I always ask, Elizabeth. I respect your privacy."

"Thank you, Claire. Would you like a cup of mint tea? I can add a touch of honey if you like."

The idea of enjoying a hot cup of tea with two such interesting women was beyond Claire's expectations when stopping.

"That's kind of you."

"With honey?"

"Yes please, Elizabeth. With a touch of honey."

Claire watched as Elizabeth worked around a kitchen with braided rugs and enamel pans and a pie shelf above a woodstove where a pot full of water was steaming hot. The aroma of mint only added to the lovely aromas already in that kitchen with windows offering views of fields separated, in some places, by fence lines. In others, hedges laced in snow stretched out of sight. Claire noticed an oak hutch built into a corner with doors on the top half accented in tin. Opening one of those doors, Elizabeth chose three of the china cups hanging from hooks with saucers stacked underneath.

"Such beautiful cups, Elizabeth."

"Thank you, Claire. Each cup has been a gift. I treasure them all."

"I understand. I have a few that were my grandmother's."

Putting the china cups on a wooden tray, Elizabeth prepared the tea. Watching her was like watching a maestro intent on details. Taking the mint in hand, the young woman tore the fresh leaves into pieces. Going back to the hutch, she reached for a teapot on the top shelf. After filling the pot with hot water, she added the mint. While the tea was steeping, Elizabeth arranged cookies on a dish. Then she filled the cups with the hot tea, added a bit of honey and stirred each one. Placing the cups with saucers on the tray, she left room for the china plate full of cookies. Grabbing a few more crackers, Elizabeth walked back to the table. As she was serving the tea, her grandmother looked out the window.

"Snowing harder. Look at those sheep. The weather doesn't seem to bother them."

"Sheep?"

"Yes, Claire," Catherine explained. "Our English neighbors raise them. A few must have gotten out of their pen again. Last time that happened one got hit by a car. Guess they didn't mend the fence like they said they were going to."

Curiosity got the best of Claire. Going to a front window she noted the sheep were moving almost incognito due to the snow. Accompanying them were three young men looking like shepherds. Each carried a staff. They seemed to have the sheep in tow as they led them across the road and into a field as the sun broke through the snowflakes swirling like feathers from a pillow.

Back at the table, Claire sipped her tea as she listened to the women now sitting at the table talking about their day ahead. Claire felt as if she should add a little something to the conversation since she'd disrupted any plans they'd made.

"I didn't mean to stay. I'm sure you have much to tend to."

"You are no bother," said Elizabeth. "With the other children getting home early from school, it is nice to take a few minutes to enjoy a cup of tea. That reminds me. I told Hannah I would have everything ready and on the table for them to make their Christmas cards. Excuse me for a minute."

"The girl never sits. I try to help as much as I can. I am thankful Elizabeth and John took me in. I tangled my feet in pumpkin vines and ended up breaking an ankle. But it is healing. I am on my feet again and will be home soon."

Looking at the old woman drinking her tea, Claire asked how many children were in school.

"There are three. Hannah is thirteen. She is the oldest and a big help to Elizabeth. All the children help as they must but Hannah knows what to do without being told. After Hannah comes Frank. He is nine and Faith is seven."

When Elizabeth returned, her arms were loaded down with paper and pencils, glue and crayons. She even had pads of construction paper and some glitter. Putting all the stuff off to the side, Elizabeth sat down to finish her tea.

"So you bought the glitter young Frank asked for?"

"I did, Mummi. The children will be told to use but a little of it at a time. I do not want the meaning of sending a card to be lost in using the glitter."

"The children make cards to send?"

"Yes, they make cards to send to family and friends as well as their teacher. This table will be busy later on. Tomorrow is their school program. They are excited after practicing for days."

Claire hadn't thought about Christmas programs in years. Of course the program Elizabeth was talking about would be void of trees with presents underneath or fancy dresses or shiny shoes. According to Elizabeth, families would gather to hear the children sing, tell stories, and present plays. Small gifts would be exchanged marked by those hand-made Christmas cards, some more than likely decorated with a touch of glitter.

Listening to Elizabeth took Claire back to when she was in the second grade. She'd been chosen to sing a stanza of "Silent Night" in her school's Christmas program. She practiced every day in class and in her bedroom before going to sleep. Claire's grandmother made her a red velvet dress with lace around the edges of the sleeves and collar. On the morning of the program, her mother curled her hair, then pulled it back and kept it in place with a red velvet headband. Before they went out the door, Claire reminded her mother she'd be on stage when the curtain opened.

Hours later when that curtain opened, Claire could see her grandparents sitting in the front row smiling. As she stood there she continued to search for her parents. When she saw her mother sitting by the door Claire knew her father hadn't come. She knew he'd say he had a last minute meeting he couldn't miss. When it came time for her solo, Claire stood frozen in place. The words she'd practiced were no longer in her head. In seconds Claire's teacher was standing next to her holding her hand and telling her classmates in a whisper to join in. The audience loved it. They didn't know those were Claire's words everyone was singing. That night Claire threw her red velvet dress in the back of her closet. She never sang that song again.

Chapter Three

LOOKING AROUND THE CLAPBOARD HOME, CLAIRE wasn't surprised when not finding a decorated tree standing in a corner or colored lights in the windows or a plastic Santa on the table. All those things were considered distractions to the true meaning of Christmas. With greens on the mantel surrounding a small wooden stable filled with straw, and wooden figurines telling the story of Christmas, and candles lit in the windows, Claire realized the spirit of Christmas was in every nook of that home. Along with cut-out paper stars and paper angels attached to string hanging in the doorways, and the smell of the greens and the warmth of the candles, the meaning of the season was reflected in the eyes of the old woman finishing her tea and the young woman getting up to care for a baby crying in a manger with a lamb curled up by its side. Claire watched as Elizabeth knelt down by the child. Whispering sweet lullabies, she wrapped the blanket a little tighter and picked the baby up. Holding her close, Elizabeth walked into the other room. As she slipped from view, Abraham became restless in his high chair.

"Elizabeth must be changing the baby's diaper," said Catherine. "And this young man needs a few more crackers."

"I'll get some, Catherine."

"Thank you, Claire. They are in that container on the counter."

Going into the kitchen, Claire caught the scent of bayberry mingling with cinnamon and nutmeg, ginger and molasses. The sound of chickadees gathered about the bird feeders outside in the maple trees drew Claire over to the window. Standing there in the quiet of that home, she felt at ease for the first time in a long time. Before sitting back down with Catherine, Claire gave Abraham a few crackers as Elizabeth returned with the baby.

"Would you like to hold Mary while I take care of Abraham?"

"It has been forever since I've held a baby."

"It will come back to you, Claire. Come. Sit in the rocking chair."

Doing as Elizabeth suggested, Claire got herself situated. After Elizabeth placed Mary in her arms, Claire pulled the blanket away from her face and when she did, a little smile revealed dimples as precious as her traces of golden hair and thick lashes. Stretching her arms, Mary yawned while never opening her eyes as Catherine reminded Elizabeth it wouldn't be long before the children would be home.

"I told Hannah I'd have the cookies made so she can fill the tins with goodies."

"I know we must get busy. Hannah cleaned the tins before going to school," Elizabeth replied as she wiped Abraham's face and hands.

"What does Hannah do with the tins?" Claire asked.

"She carries out our tradition of filling tins with cookies and delivering them to friends and family. She will deliver the first tins once she gets home."

"You should be proud of that young woman, Elizabeth."

"John and I are very proud of Hannah. We look forward to hearing her sing in the school program tomorrow."

"I've heard her singing to the younger children. God has blessed her with a beautiful voice."

"We give thanks to God for the many gifts He has given us, Mummi."

"Amen to that, Elizabeth."

How lucky that young girl is to have the love and support of her father, Claire thought as Elizabeth took Mary from her arms and put the child down for a nap. The commotion woke the little lamb who'd been sound asleep ever since Claire walked through the front door. All Elizabeth had to do was give the lamb some attention. Minutes later, it was back to sleep by Mary's side. That's when Claire asked Elizabeth why there was a lamb in the house.

"My son Frank spends time helping the shepherds with their herd. The lamb was born late in the season. Actually it was born the same day as Mary. It took to Frank. One day he brought the lamb home while he had some lunch. The other children fell in love with the lamb and it has been here ever since. Frank cares for it. I've noticed lately how protective the lamb has become of Mary."

"I think the lamb makes a perfect pet."

"John wasn't sure. But now he looks for the lamb in the evening when the children have gone to bed. The lamb will sit beside him while he reads."

Catherine stood. "I'd better get the cookies started. Would you like to help, Claire? I have the dough chilling."

Normally when trying to figure out if she'd be able to fit something into her day that wasn't scheduled, Claire would first check her watch. But she hadn't looked at her watch since getting out of her car. She even turned her phone off when inside the barn. None of that stuff mattered as Claire considered Catherine's invitation. A few seconds later she decided to stay and make sugar cookies with an Amish woman and she was over the moon excited.

"I'd love to help, Catherine."

"Follow me."

Chapter Four

CLAIRE FELT AS IF SHE WERE following Mrs. Claus into her kitchen to make cookies for all the good little boys and girls. Catherine was quite jolly with a sparkle in her eyes. A big-framed woman, she kept those wire-rimmed glasses at the end of her nose. Putting an apron on and tying it in the back, Catherine handed one to Claire.

"It might be a little big but it will keep you covered."

Claire didn't care that it was too big. She felt like an actress getting dressed for a scene.

"You look good in an apron, young lady."

"The scent is wonderful, Catherine."

"I add a touch of fragrant oil when washing them. It is refreshing in the wintertime."

Standing in the warmth of that kitchen, Claire watched as Catherine gathered bowls and wooden spoons, flour, and utensils.

"Have you made cookies before?"

"Not recently."

Actually it had been years. Claire and her siblings would cut cookies out with their mother doing most of the work. Claire and her older sister fought over the cookie cutters while their little brother preferred eating the dough. One time when her father was away on business and her siblings were staying at their grandparents', Claire and her mother baked some cookies. When they had all the ingredients in the bowl, her mother kneaded the dough. Claire loved watching her fingers at work. It was magical.

Once Catherine began moving things around in a drawer situated under a countertop, those thoughts of making cookies with her mother drifted back to becoming a memory once again; back to another time in another kitchen.

"There's so much stuff in here. I can't even find the rolling pin."

"I have a drawer like that, Catherine. I call it my junk drawer. It holds everything that has no other place to go."

Finally, holding on to her rolling pin, Catherine shut the drawer. "I wouldn't want to lose this. It belonged to my grandmother. My grandfather made it for her before they were married."

"It looks to be in good shape."

"After all the dough it has rolled and all the little hands that have helped along the way, this rolling pin is in wonderful shape."

Turning her focus on Claire, Catherine asked if she'd like to knead the dough. "It's been out of the icebox for a good hour," she explained. "I'd say it's ready."

Noting Claire's hesitation, Catherine picked up the ball of dough and set it on a cutting board. Slicing it in half, she then kneaded the dough in the same magical manner as Claire's mother. Although Catherine's arms and hands were larger than her mother's, that Amish woman's moves were the same. Claire figured that must happen to cookie dough kneaders after kneading dough so many times.

Claire thought about that day her father wasn't home; never realizing until now her mother kneaded the cookie dough longer than usual. She'd even bothered to do a little more with her hair. Noting her mother's cardigan smelled like mothballs, Claire had asked why she'd never worn it before.

"I keep it for good," was the reply.

Claire told her mother how beautiful she looked with her hair a bit wavy.

"And the blue in your sweater matches your eyes."

"Oh, Claire, don't be so silly."

"I'm not being silly, Mom."

With her hands all dough, Claire's mother reached over the bowl and hugged her daughter. It was a very long hug.

Chapter Five

"Okay, young lady. Please bring that box over here. It is time to cut out some sugar cookies. Hannah will be looking for them."

The only box Claire could see was a wooden box sitting on a shelf of a more primitive hutch. Picking it up, Claire went over to where Catherine was flouring the counter.

"You can open it, Claire. I'm in a mess at the moment."

As Claire was about to do as Catherine asked, there was a quick knock at the door; then in came Tommy Morgan. Stopping to play with Abraham, he then walked into the kitchen.

"Catherine has you making cookies already!"

"I have a feeling Catherine is a master of cookie making."

"She is for sure, Claire. You're in good hands."

With a slight touch of his fingers, Tommy moved aside a few strands of hair off Claire's shoulders. Although slight, she felt his touch as their eyes met. It was a look Catherine didn't miss.

"You two know each other?"

"We crossed paths earlier on the front porch," Claire explained as Tommy stayed by her side, the sweet smell of pine from his fleece circling the kitchen.

"That means I do not have to introduce you. We have no time for small talk, Tommy. Claire and I are about to make cookies. We will save our story for this young woman to hear over a bowl of soup come lunch time."

"Soup sounds wonderful. Maybe John will be back by then."

"He didn't say for sure when he'd be here," spoke Elizabeth, folding laundry. "But that doesn't mean you can't enjoy a bowl of soup."

"I always enjoy whatever you prepare, Elizabeth. Would you mind if I got some coffee for my thermos? That barn gets a little chilly after a while."

"You know the coffee pot is always on, Tommy. Help yourself."

Once Tommy was out the door, Claire turned her attention back to untying a faded ribbon wrapped around the wooden box. From what Claire could tell, a latch on the front of the box had been broken. The top was worn in the corners so she took her time removing it. Claire was surprised to find a layer of velvet protecting whatever the box was holding. As she pulled the velvet back, Claire couldn't figure out what was sitting there on top of yet another layer of velvet covering the bottom of the box. Catherine didn't say a thing as she tried to keep on working but with tears in her eyes, she couldn't. Noting outlines of a star and snowflakes, a sled, a mitten, a snowman, a buggy, animals of all kinds including a kitten, Claire realized that what she was looking at were cookie cutters made out of tin. She waited for Catherine to explain.

Rubbing her hands with a towel, the family matriarch told the story of the tin cookie cutters and the man who'd made them. It turned out to be a love story. With her fingers, Catherine followed along the edges of the cookie cutters. Touching the kitten, and then going around the edge, Catherine picked it up and held it close.

"I feel my dear Paul's heart against mine. Even though I lost him so many years ago, I can still sense his touch. Whenever it snows I can smell the wet threads of the long wool coat I made him. It never bothered me when he came through the door soaking wet and took me in his arms. I only cared that he was home. I can picture him coming around the bend in the summertime, smiling and waving when seeing me standing barefoot on the porch waiting for him. My heart would quicken as Paul tied the horse and came up the steps."

"You said you lost your husband many years ago. Yet when you talk about him the love expressed in your eyes is that of a young love that never grew old."

"Paul was twenty-four when God called him home. I was five months from giving birth to our first child. When the Bishop and my father came to the door that day and I didn't answer, they walked in and found me on top of the bed Paul had made for us. I knew before they told me Paul had been taken by the Lord. I'd felt sick all morning. I was certain it wasn't the pregnancy. It was a different feeling. A cold chill filled that home despite a warm July breeze coming through the window screens. I couldn't get warm. How could I when the one who'd been my warmth was no longer on this earth? I didn't want the details. But that didn't stop my father from trying. He was a cruel man. Despite being a devoted follower of the Ordnung, his treatment of my mother was unforgiving. Paul used to tell me how he thought my father was jealous of our happiness. We are not to feel jealousy, but my father did. That man never said a kind word to my mother. He only demanded more from her. She died giving birth to their fifteenth child."

Pushing her sleeves up a little more, Catherine continued. "I do not know why I am telling you all of this. If it bothers you, please say so and we will get on with the cookies."

"It doesn't bother me. I think there was more than one reason why I came here this morning."

"I believe that to be true as well. I will hurry. I was thankful the Bishop was there. He stopped my father from going into details I did not need to hear. The Bishop expressed his sympathy after telling me my husband had drowned in a lake while fishing for our supper. I knew the lake. I'd fished that lake with Paul. He was far from the only one who'd lost his life there what with the currents and overgrowth of weeds. As the Bishop was talking all I could picture was Paul casting his line with the sun shining and a bucket of fish by his side. Paul went home doing something he enjoyed. The Lord was kind to a very kind man."

Stopping for a sip of tea, Catherine explained about the tin cookie cutters. "I later told my mother how I'd been in the kitchen that morning and heard my dear Paul whisper to me. 'Go into the pantry, Catherine.

Reach up to the highest shelf. There you will find a wooden box holding a gift for you.'

"It was this box, Claire. Paul had wrapped it in plain paper and put it away. I'm certain his plan was to present it to me after I gave birth. If Paul hadn't whispered that message to me in his passing I might not have found his gift for quite some time. I hope I'm not frightening you but that is God's truth. When Elizabeth invited me to stay here while my ankle heals I brought this box with me."

Catherine placed the tin cookie cutters in front of her one at a time as Claire asked a question.

"Is there a cookie cutter missing? The way they were sitting in the box it looks as if there is space for one more."

"I thought the same thing when I opened the box. I'm sure Paul planned on making a few more as time went on. But I did find something else."

With her fingertips, Catherine lifted up the bottom layer of velvet and pulled out a worn envelope.

"Paul left this underneath the velvet."

Catherine asked Claire to sit down with her at a small table set in front of a bay window. Once settled, she pulled a yellowed piece of lined paper from the envelope. Adjusting her glasses, Catherine read the few sentences.

> *My dearest Catherine,*
> *Through this gift, I pray the time you spend with the children*
> *God will be blessing us with will be time you will cherish forever.*
> *With love,*
> *Paul*

As young Abraham played with wooden blocks, and fresh logs in the woodstove crackled loud enough to stir the lamb, Catherine folded the note. Putting it back where she'd found it, the Amish woman pressed her apron in place before taking a minute to tell Claire more about her husband.

"Paul and I were just beginning. I am certain if the Lord had not called my love back to His side, every minute of my life with Paul would have been fulfilling. He had a way of making me feel complete just by his touch. I sense the Lord knew I would survive the loss of Paul because of the relationship we shared if only for a short time. I believe each of us has someone out there that the Lord has intended us to be with forever."

Looking at the tin cookie cutters, Claire told herself she wanted to feel love and give love. Admitting that void to herself must have shown on every inch of Claire's face because Catherine picked up on it.

Chapter Six

"I've talked too much about myself. Tell me about you, Claire. Are you married? Do you have children?"

While waiting for her reply, Catherine went back to the counter where everything was in place for making the cookies. Claire watched as she rubbed the rolling pin with more flour, then pinched off a bit of dough and checked it with her fingers.

"Is it ready?"

"Chilled dough isn't the same as dough freshly made. You have to get it to a certain consistency. It takes a little longer but without a doubt this dough is ready."

"So much to consider, isn't there?"

"It's like anything else, Claire."

"Like a marriage?"

"Like a marriage."

"My grandmother told me she'd read in her tea leaves that if I married Eric it'd be a mistake."

"Did your grandmother explain why?"

"She told me the tea leaves revealed a lack of love between us and the tea leaves were correct. But I married Eric anyway."

"You did not love him?"

"Not in the way you loved your husband. Eric told me he wanted children but wasn't sure when. After waiting over three years for him to make up his mind, he decided a child would be too much responsibility. Eric had seen his friends change once they became parents. He decided he preferred his freedom. He could go golfing or fishing without a worry. Once Eric told me he didn't want children, I began taking my photography seriously."

"Did you want children, Claire?"

"Yes, very much so."

"It must have been hard being married to a man who didn't want a child, especially after telling you he did."

"It was very hard. I felt time slipping away from me. I brought up adoption but he would have nothing to do with it."

"Were you close to your mother?"

Another zinger of a question threw Claire for a minute as she tried describing a complicated relationship.

"On one hand I loved my mother more than anyone else on earth. On the other, I resented her for never standing up to my father, for accepting the void he created. Sometimes I felt like he thought more of his job than his family."

Claire's second grade Christmas program came at her like a hurricane at the same time Catherine patted some of the dough into a ball. As the Amish woman moved the dough from one hand to the other, Claire told Catherine about that day. When she started describing the drive back home with her mother, Claire hesitated, realizing as she talked about that ride she was looking back through the heart and mind of an adult. Instead of blaming her mother, Claire could see how tired her mother seemed; how her hands were shaking, gripped to the wheel of the car.

"I remember my mother pulling off to the side of the road more than once to clear away ice on the windshield wipers, and all I cared about was my mother getting back inside the car and driving me home because I was cold. I never thought she would be cold. I never noticed how thin her gloves were yet out she went every time to clear the windshield to get me home safely."

For the first time Claire remembered her mother being dressed in a knit sweater buttoned up the front. "Thinking about her in that sweater makes me shiver. There I was inside the car in my winter coat and warm gloves and hat and my mother was out in that blizzard wearing a sweater."

Claire recalled how her mother would sing when things got rough as Catherine placed the ball of dough back on the counter. "Instead of crying or yelling, my mother would sing. I can hear her singing. She had a beautiful voice. I never thought about my mother's voice. I never cared about my mother's voice. I only thought of my needs. Whenever I had a nightmare, I'd sit up in bed and scream for her. I can still hear the door creak as she tiptoed into my room. She'd pick me up and carry me to a rocking chair by the window all the while whispering everything would be okay. The last thing I'd remember was my mother singing to me. Why didn't I ever tell my mother she had a beautiful voice? I can't tell her now. It's too late. I lost my mother and I never told her she had a beautiful voice."

As Catherine rolled the dough, Claire felt tears welling in her eyes. Stopping what she was doing, Catherine stepped over and put her arms around Claire. She didn't ask a thing. They stood huddled together in the warmth of the woodstove. After years of stuffing her feelings so far down inside that none of the professionals she paid good money to see could reach them, it took but a few minutes with this Amish woman and out those feelings came. The simplicity of that home and that woman seemed to be what Claire had been seeking.

"The key to accepting flaws and hurts of others and the pain and loss life brings is forgiveness, Claire. Forgive your father for being absent when you needed him. Forgive your mother for loving your father so deeply that she couldn't find the strength to ask him to change. That was her choice. Not yours. It was their marriage, not yours. Forgive Eric for being absent in your marriage. I dare say you were absent as well. Flaws of others can make us better by forgiving and defining ourselves and moving on. While those flaws will always be a part of us, they cannot become us unless we allow that to happen. By doing so, you hurt only yourself. Forgive, Claire. The Lord has given you gifts that are unique to only you. Forgive and life will fill you with goodness and love and the strength to endure whatever storms lie ahead. And laugh, Claire. Laugh and dance and live. Live, Claire."

With a baby in a manger cooing and a lamb sleeping and a toddler playing and a mother making wreaths as a clock ticked on the mantel, Catherine looked into Claire's eyes as she continued.

"Do not search for the light, Claire. You are the light with gifts to share and love to give."

Claire hadn't felt so in touch with herself since being that little girl playing at her grandparents' farmhouse. She remembered reading somewhere that when you're little and immersed in play, what you are attracted to is a key to what you are meant to be. Claire was always drawing pictures of people and old barns and fields. They intrigued her even then. As a photographer she remained intrigued. Claire had become what she was meant to be without knowing it. What had just taken place was not an hour session. It wasn't a session at all. It was a beginning to her liking herself without one prescription for pills being written.

"Pull your apron down in the front, Claire. I don't want you to leave here covered in cookie dough."

"Whenever I made cookies with my mother, I'd end up with some dough down the front of me."

"If you were anything like Hannah, you devoured some as well."

"I did, despite my mother telling me not to."

Pausing, Claire added, "Your words give me purpose, Catherine."

"Accept yourself. There is no need to seek approval from others."

"I feel His presence, Catherine."

"On the day Paul was called home I heard the angels in Heaven singing."

"May I ask you a question, Catherine?"

"You can ask me anything. I do not hold secrets."

"Did you remarry after losing Paul?"

"I felt no need to remarry. My love for Paul reaches beyond eternity. Our son Amos Paul has given us grandchildren. They in turn have given us great-grandchildren."

"One more question?"

"Certainly."

"Why did you choose the kitten cookie cutter?"

"Why do you ask?"

"I noticed how carefully you chose it from all the rest."

"You have a keen eye, Claire. I'd been asking Paul for a kitten. With the gift of the tin cookie cutter, Paul made sure I'd have kittens every time I made cookies."

"How thoughtful, Catherine."

"That was Paul. When I make cookies with Faith she names the kitten cookies. I'm sure Paul is laughing."

Pausing, Catherine took stock of the cookie dough and the cookie cutters while rubbing a little more flour on the rolling pin.

"We have cookies to cut out, Claire. Christmas is coming and so are those children."

Thoughts of that day when Claire and her mother were the only ones making cookies came back around. This time it was a happy memory. Claire knew her mother loved her. She knew her mother did the best she could.

Chapter Seven

"I've rerolled the dough, Claire. Now comes the most important part."

"I would think mixing the ingredients would be most important."

"When making Christmas cookies, the most important thing is cutting them out. They have to be perfect. A child has a critical eye especially when it is Christmastime."

"But Amish children don't believe in Santa Claus."

"But they do believe in the spirit surrounding Santa Claus. They do not need someone dressed in a red suit to make them feel what's in their hearts. When you are young and that belief is in your heart, that feeling never goes away. There is no let-down or questioning when reaching a certain age. That belief is as strong in my heart today as when I was a little girl."

Claire had never thought about believing in Christmas in any other way than through Santa Claus. She remembered the let-down she'd experienced when a boy in her third grade class made fun of her for still believing in Santa Claus. He made Claire feel ashamed. When she mentioned the incident at the dinner table her father said it was time Claire grew up.

The sound of Catherine gathering the tin cookie cutters on the counter pushed that memory away.

"I take my time when cutting out a cookie," Catherine explained. "I imagine little hands holding them. I imagine what they might be thinking when biting into one. There is no better time of the year than Christmas to capture their wonder of all that is around them. It's in their eyes with every paper angel they create and every cookie they pick up and enjoy. Paul remained a child at heart. He knew the memories the tin cookie cutters would bring. So, my dear Claire, pick out a cookie cutter and we will begin."

Being a knitter, Claire's first choice was the mitten.

"I am surprised. For some reason, I thought you'd choose the snowflake."

"My grandmother taught me how to knit. I still keep a project going although I don't get at it as often as I'd like."

"What are you knitting at the moment?"

"Ironically, I'm knitting mittens. There's a charity in the area that distributes Christmas packages to the less fortunate. I've been donating mittens for the last few years."

"That is the true spirit of Christmas especially if you've created what you give. Elizabeth's husband is a talented woodworker. He donates half of what he makes to charity. Although we are not a part of the English world, we are your neighbors. And neighbors take care of neighbors. John could never do it without Tommy's help."

"Is Tommy a woodworker as well?"

"No. Tommy has a creative side as well as being an electrician. He reminds me of Paul but with a sense of humor."

"Tommy seems like a nice guy. I could tell by Abraham's reaction when he walked through the door that he's a favorite with the children."

"Tommy's a favorite of mine as well. It's a long story."

"Those are the best stories, Catherine."

"And Tommy is the best."

"I'm curious."

"I think you should stay for that bowl of soup."

"I don't want to overextend my welcome."

"I know Elizabeth would insist. So consider yourself invited. John should be back soon."

"Thank you for the invitation. I feel as if I'm becoming part of the family."

"That's what happened to Tommy. And now he is a part of the family. You'll have to stay and watch the sleds being loaded. John wraps a harness decked with sleigh bells around each horse. It is quite a sight to see. It has become a family tradition for many. Every year at this time they watch for the sleds."

Holding the kitten cookie cutter, Catherine began. Placing the cookie cutter along an edge, she had that cutter in and out of the dough in seconds. There was no dough hanging off the cutter. No dough missing from the shape of the kitten. It was perfectly executed, as was the separating of the dough from the cutter and placing the kitten-shaped dough onto a sheet of parchment paper. While Claire had some experience under her belt in cookie-making, she felt nervous when placing the mitten cookie cutter on top of the dough. With Catherine's urging Claire moved the cutter closer to the edge.

"By keeping it tighter to the edge, less dough is wasted. Wasting dough is like losing a cookie. And a lost cookie is a loss of a sweet treat," Catherine explained.

Claire got into the swing of it. Every time it was her turn she'd nudge her cookie cutter as close to an edge or empty space as she could. She'd never considered cookie making as an art form until using the tin cookie cutters made so long ago. Once they'd filled the sheet of parchment paper with shapes ready to be baked, Catherine ripped off another sheet and set it aside.

"You can roll more dough into a ball while I put these cookies on a sheet and get them in the oven."

It all went like clockwork. It wasn't long before that home was filled with the aroma of cookies baking. That attracted Abraham's attention.

"Come back here, young man. I am sure Mummi will give you the first cookie. But it is time for your lunch. Once I have Abraham fed, I will get you two a cup of soup."

"I don't mean to be another that needs tending to, Elizabeth."

"You are not a bother, Claire. I can tell Mummi is enjoying your company as much as I am."

And so the bakers continued. Catherine would take the cookies off the parchment paper and place them on a cookie sheet and put them in the oven while Claire did the patting and rolling out of the dough. They worked together using the cookie cutters to cut out the shapes. When they were almost out of dough, Catherine stopped Claire as she was about to create one last mitten.

"I have to make Hannah her favorite shape. I wait until the end to gather up all the leftover dough. Once I see how much I have, I make my Hannah one big cookie snowman, bigger than all the other cookies. That is her favorite thing to do when we make cookies together."

"That is a lovely tradition, Catherine. Was it Hannah's idea?"

Claire sensed a change in Catherine's mood as she took the remaining dough into her hands. When she patted the dough it was different than before. The patting was more intense. Once Catherine had the dough rolled out to the right thickness on a cookie sheet, she reached for a knife and with a steady hand, created the outline of a snowman with a top hat and broom. There was so much detail right down to straw in the broom and design in the scarf.

"That snowman is a work of art, Catherine. I've never seen such detail in a cookie."

"It is for Hannah," she replied, taking away the excess dough with a knife.

Grabbing a hand towel, Catherine went over to the sink and as she washed her hands she told Hannah's story.

"It was a beautiful April morning when Hannah was born up those front stairs and to the right in John and Elizabeth's bedroom. I'd been asked by Elizabeth to stay with her. She did not know what to expect although she'd heard plenty about childbirth from others when we'd gather for Sunday dinners or barn raisings or the like. As Elizabeth pushed I thought of Paul and how happy he would have been that our family was extending to yet another generation. John and Elizabeth named their first born after her great-grandmothers. Catherine is her middle name. The minute I saw Hannah, I fell in love with her. Her skin was like corn silk; her eyes, like Paul's, as blue as the spring sky. Those eyes were open. She seemed curious about the world despite being minutes old.

Her sprigs of hair, a light chestnut, were the color of her father's team just steps away grazing in the pasture. When held by her mother, she yawned and fell asleep."

Elizabeth interrupted with two bowls of soup and homemade bread. "You must be talking about the day Hannah was born. She was the only one of my children who went to sleep in my arms. The others either needed to be fed or cried. Enjoy the soup."

Giving her grandmother a hug, Elizabeth went back to Abraham.

Once the last of the cookies were out of the oven, Catherine placed the big snowman on the rack and shut the door. "Let's have our soup while the cookie bakes. Tommy should be along."

Sitting back down at the table in front of the bay window, Catherine buttered a slice of warm bread. Claire watched as Catherine pulled it apart and dunked a corner of the bread in her soup.

"There's nothing as hearty as a bowl of soup in the wintertime. When Elizabeth serves a pot of it for supper, it disappears."

"My grandmother used to make what we called witch's brew. She'd make it for us on Halloween. We'd fill up on her soup; then come back later and fill up on candy. My mother eventually took over making the soup. Once in a while I'll make a pot. It lasts me a week. The key is the acini di pepe."

"Hannah would enjoy that soup. She loves pasta."

The thought of Hannah brought Catherine back to telling her story. "It was after supper on an early March evening that it happened. Elizabeth was heavy with child and had fallen asleep by the woodstove. Hannah was almost four. She was waiting for her father who was out in the barn doing chores. Before leaving the house John told Hannah he'd hurry. With enough snow still in the fields, they had plans to build a snowman. Hannah loved rolling the snowballs. Sometimes she'd roll them so big that her little hands would drop the snowballs when she tried carrying them. That never bothered her. She'd start all over again. Once a snowman was in place, she had fun digging under the snow in search of stones for its eyes. John was in charge of finding sticks for the arms.

"That particular evening Hannah grew impatient waiting for her father. With the moon and stars above, she had no problem going out the front door and down to the barn to find him. Elizabeth never heard the door open or close. John was up in the haymow never realizing his four-year-old was below when he dropped some bales down. Hannah was thrown against a plow. That knocked over some shovels and scared a few of the horses. One was new to the farm. It wasn't familiar with the other horses or the barn noises or Hannah or even John. The only thing John could figure was the horse panicked and broke out of its stall, running right over Hannah. When John looked down and saw his precious child, he thought the Lord had taken her home. But Hannah is a fighter. John wrapped her in a blanket while yelling to Elizabeth. By the time Elizabeth was on the front porch, John had Hannah in the back of a buggy. Elizabeth insisted on going. They hurried to the home of an English neighbor who rushed them to the hospital. That neighbor's wife was a nurse. She took over. A few days later a group of doctors told John and Elizabeth their dear Hannah was blind in both eyes due to head injuries and trauma. We believe in the Lord. We trust His judgement. Hannah has not allowed her loss of sight to hinder her from living. She sees through her hands and her heart and the help of her constant companion—a little dog named Bailey. We do not accept the word disability. It is God's will. Hannah's spirit remains strong."

"I'm curious about Bailey."

"Tommy showed up one day holding the dog in his arms. John hesitated at first. He wasn't convinced Hannah should depend on a dog instead of the Lord to lead her through the darkness. Tommy told John he'd found the dog on a computer. I do not know how he did that but John later told Hannah the dog used to live at a rescue shelter far away. It had no training in being the eyes for someone like Hannah. But Tommy talked John into introducing the two and they've been together ever since. Once John watched Hannah with Bailey he was fine with her having the dog. He knows his daughter. She is strong in her beliefs. Hannah named her dog Bailey because the dog loves chasing the cats around the bales of hay. While that dog has never been trained, she protects Hannah. She knows when Hannah could be in danger."

Jumping up from the table, Catherine hurried to the oven. Grabbing a potholder, she pulled the cookie sheet out.

"I thought I burned the snowman but I didn't."

"Why do you bake a snowman?"

Sitting back down at the table, Catherine explained. "On the night of the accident, Hannah never got to make a snowman. Strange as it might seem, she was more upset about not making her snowman than losing her eyesight. She later told her parents it was okay. She could see the snowman in her head. Hannah's imagination takes her places she cannot see."

"You and Elizabeth talked about how Hannah enjoys delivering the tins of cookies. How does she do that?"

"The same way she gets back and forth to school. While her siblings are near and she has Bailey by her side, Hannah's senses steer her path. She is able to define every neighbor's place by smell and sound."

"Do you put icing on the snowman cookie?"

"No. That is up to Hannah. Using her fingers she will feel the straw on the broom and designs on the scarf. More often than not, she does not add icing. I think that's because once it is covered, she has a hard time feeling it."

A quick knock at the door interrupted the conversation.

Chapter Eight

REALIZING ELIZABETH WAS UPSTAIRS WITH THE two children, Catherine went to answer the door just as Tommy was about to step through it. With his navy knit hat still close to his head Claire was able to get a good look at Tommy, brown eyes and all, as he came walking in the same moment Elizabeth came down the stairs holding the baby with Abraham behind her.

"I'm back, Elizabeth. I think I have things in order in the barn. Once John gets here we can start loading the sleds. I'm figuring it will take three sleds to get all the stuff to where it needs to go."

"John was saying the same thing last night. He made sure he had six harnesses with bells on them ready to go. I expect him any time, Tommy. Come in and get warm. I'll fix you a bowl of soup."

"Thanks, Elizabeth." Eyeing Abraham, Tommy took off his boots and went over to the little boy back building with his blocks.

"Look at you, Abraham. You're growing up too fast."

"I was thinking that earlier, Tommy. Soon he'll be making toys with his father."

"He has the hands for it, Elizabeth. By the way, I took your advice and asked him."

"You asked who what?" Catherine was curious. So was Claire but for a different reason. Since divorcing, Claire had dated a few men she'd met through online sites but decided it all was a waste of energy. But there was something about Tommy that flicked a switch. As he came into the kitchen Claire felt a bit nervous. When the two made eye contact again they smiled, then looked away.

"Sit down, Tommy. Would you like more coffee with your soup?"

"I would, Catherine. You can never have enough coffee. I heard on the news how good coffee is for your health so I should be in excellent health."

"I know they say it's not a good idea to drink a cup in the evening but sometimes when I'm working I enjoy one. So far I haven't had a problem falling asleep."

"I do the same thing, Claire," Tommy replied. "You do a lot of your work in the evening?"

"It depends on the season."

"Never thought of that and then you have to go take the photos. That must take a lot of your time."

"It does."

"Anyone help you? Any family close by?"

Excusing herself for coming between them, Elizabeth set a bowl of soup on the table along with a few slices of homemade bread on a plate with butter on the side.

"Soup is at its best when it is piping hot. Enjoy, Tommy. We appreciate your help."

Turning to Claire, Elizabeth asked if she would like another bowl.

"No thank you, the one bowl I had filled me up. That's a sign of a hearty soup."

"Hearty for sure," said Catherine, setting down Tommy's cup of coffee. "I brought one for you as well, Claire. Sit down. You two continue your conversation."

"Thanks, Catherine. Your coffee is the best I've had since moving here."

"There's nothing fancy about it, like some of those coffees you can buy at those expensive places. I do nothing but fill the top of the old percolator with scalding hot well water and use a touch of fresh cream and honey for taste."

"You should serve it at your stand this season. You'd make some good money."

"Oh my goodness, Tommy, you're always thinking."

"You have to, Catherine. Now where were we, Claire?"

"I was answering your question about family being nearby. The answer is no. I'm originally from Vermont. My husband was from here. We moved back after getting married. When we divorced, he left and I stayed."

"That's interesting. You must like it here."

"The four seasons remind me of Vermont so I feel at home. But there's something to be said about the backroads and the people in this area. Both offer endless photo opportunities. Both are rich in character."

"I get what you are saying. When I was a kid my father's company transferred him here. Coming from Florida, the winters were hard getting used to. Now I can't imagine living where the season remains the same."

Noticing the snowman cooling on the cookie sheet, Tommy remarked, "I smelled the cookies when I walked in. No matter how many times I am greeted by that smell, I can never get enough of it."

"Catherine did all the work. She even showed me the correct way to cut the cookies out."

"She taught me as well," laughed Tommy. "I see the tin cookie cutters. I'm sure you heard the story behind them."

"Yes," replied Claire. "Catherine told me her love story."

"Oh, now I am blushing."

"No reason to be blushing. You and Paul had what most of us wish we could find."

Claire took note of Tommy's remark as it mirrored her own thoughts concerning Catherine's love story. It was Catherine who spoke next.

"Finding that one person enriches your life forever. Now Tommy, I would like to go back to my earlier question. When you told Elizabeth you'd asked him, what did you mean? If you feel uncomfortable in telling me, I will understand."

"Of course it is your business, Catherine. After all the baking we've done together, I consider you to be my third grandmother."

"You like to bake?" Claire asked.

"It started when I'd go with John to do odd jobs at Catherine's. She'd most always be baking. At some point, I found myself curious. My mother never baked. My grandparents were still in Florida so here was this kind and jovial Amish woman baking cakes and pies and cookies. Her home always smelled like a bakery. I loved the feeling I'd get when walking through the door."

"Tommy was shy at first," Catherine explained. "But it wasn't long before he was asking questions. That led to his wearing an apron and mixing and stirring."

"The image of me in an apron is probably one image Claire wouldn't enjoy focusing on but it does point to the amount of time I spent with you in the kitchen."

Claire tried imagining this tall and handsome man in an apron. It was hard to do.

"Working side by side, we've had many a conversation, Tommy. That's why I was a bit surprised when the other night John told us you might be getting engaged."

Claire felt her heart racing. Tommy might be getting engaged just as her interest was perking. She had to put her brakes on. It was a hard thing to do because a man like Tommy Morgan was a rare find.

"Denise and I have talked a little about the future but that's it. I told John she's hinted at getting engaged but there is no engagement. She teaches; lives about an hour away. But I do have something exciting to tell you after our many talks about finding one's purpose."

"We had many such talks. I would tell you most people have moments in their lives when they are searching."

"I understand that now. Funny thing though, I discovered I'd already found me right in your kitchen."

"I do not understand, Tommy."

"I discovered I am meant to be a baker; not an electrician."

"Did I hear you say you were meant to be a baker?"

"You did, Catherine. And this leads me back to your question. I was hired earlier this year to do the electrical work on an old mercantile building. You know the building. It's been empty for years; sits on a main corner in the downtown."

"Don't they call that Warehouse Alley?" Claire asked. "I was commissioned by a client interested in the history of that area."

"They do, Claire. Most of those types of buildings were built with easy access to train tracks, as many who occupied space had goods to transfer. If you think about it, the depot isn't far from there and the train tracks remain in place. I stood in the alley and imagined the goings-on back then since that side of the building used to be all storefronts with everything from brooms to chewing tobacco and cigars being manufactured. I've learned this particular mercantile housed, among other businesses, a spice grinding mill, a roasting plant, and a print shop."

"That is all quite interesting. When was that mercantile built?"

"The guy who hired me said around 1914. He buys abandoned places and invests in bringing them back to life. But this time the guy extended himself too far as his wife filed for a divorce. It's still pretty messy. He was found with another woman and you know where that story goes. Anyway, there I was, in love with this old building and wanting to call it mine while afraid he'd board it back up and forget about it. But the guy and I hit it off. The bank came through and I became the owner of an historic structure at an unbelievable price in a great location. That building will once again be open for business."

"What a beautiful place with fascinating architecture. I can only imagine how beautiful it is inside."

"Now you can stop in and say hello. I plan to make the building a major player like it used to be. There's a lot going on, thanks to a gentleman whose family was originally from here. They made a fortune in the early days of the railroads and never forgot their hometown. I heard this particular gentleman was upset by the condition of our downtown when he returned for a visit a few years ago. Instead of turning his back, the guy is running a train on track owned by the State from here to a tourist attraction he recently completed up in the foothills."

"I've really been out of the loop. What's the tourist attraction?"

"It's a Santa Claus village; a place where families can take their kids to see Santa Claus with all the usual stuff except they can go by train complete with a dining car."

"That train is something that will bring people to the downtown where people like you can offer them reasons to stay."

"If this man's investment in our community can't get it back up on its feet I don't know what can. He's clever in promoting the train. He offers free train rides to any child and one night a week is for senior citizens only. They are taken to see Santa at no charge. A special menu is served as well as entertainment on the ride back."

"Why would a train take senior citizens to see Santa Claus?"

"That's what everyone asked. But it's working. Thursday night is Senior Night and that train is full to capacity."

"I can't believe I didn't know about that train or your restoration project. I've been away on one special assignment after another. Had I known, I would have taken some photographs. I've heard the trains off in the distance but never knew the story behind them."

"Nicholas Rossi likes to keep a low profile. The locals respect that."

"So thanks to his generosity, downtown is benefiting."

"That's the reason why the previous owner created spaces for shops on the ground floor. All those spaces are rented except for a few. Needless to say there's a coffee shop. In fact the woman opening that shop is tying into the history of the building, dedicating an area to telling the story of the roasting plant that was one of the original tenants. Along with the coffee shop there will be a dress shop, a card shop with plush and trinkets, a space for local artisans, and a bookstore. I'm bringing in a music store but only selling the vinyl. There are comfort foods, an ice cream shop, and a movie theater. I've talked with a magazine distributor as I want to offer a wide assortment of publications as well as newspapers. I'm not one who believes newspapers are dead."

Tommy turned his focus on Catherine.

"I've saved the best part of my story until last and it's all because of you, Catherine. I'm renovating a space for a bakery. It will be my bakery. I'll be doing most of the baking but I would be honored, Catherine, if you could find time to come in and do some baking with me.

Think about it. We can talk things over. I plan to have the building open for business by December ninth. But don't think you have to be ready to bake by then. It can be whenever you feel up to it."

"I am so proud of you, Tommy. I will think about doing some baking with you when time allows."

"Thank you, Catherine. I also lucked out getting John to do the woodworking. It was his input I was referring to when telling Elizabeth I'd asked him for the hutches and display cases. The oak chairs and tables along with the scents of cinnamon and nutmeg will pull the people in. I am as excited as a kid on Christmas morning."

"That's wonderful, Tommy," said Elizabeth. "John hasn't said much about what he has been doing. I think he wanted you to be the one to tell Mummi."

"We talked about that, Elizabeth. Now that the building is near completion with vendors moving in, I felt it was time to talk to my mentor. When you get into projects on old buildings, especially ones that have been vacant, you never know what obstacles you might encounter. We had our share, but having John working with me has moved us right along. We will meet our deadline. I wish we were already open with people out there Christmas shopping, but I think the suspense of the opening approaching will create excitement. One more thing. With your permission, Catherine, I would like to name my bakery 'The Tin Cookie Cutter.' All of this started when you showed me your cookie cutters and told me the story behind them. With every cookie we created, I became more drawn in to the process. Every step is rewarding to me. When I open the oven and pull out cookies lightly brown around the edges, the magic of that moment is what I've searched for all my life. I know it sounds strange because they're just cookies, but life can be hard. Baking the cookies and sharing them softens the edges."

Claire stood back, intrigued by this man who most might think was more the woodsman type. Over six feet tall, with broad shoulders and that slight beard, picturing him as a baker of cookies and cakes wasn't an easy thing to do until you experienced the passion in his words.

Wiping her eyes with a corner of her apron, Catherine stood looking out the window as she replied. "We are not to seek attention to ourselves. The Bishop preaches about boasting. We are to live a life of humility. I don't know, Tommy. I fear I would be going against doctrines set in stone."

Elizabeth went to her grandmother's side with Mary in her arms. "Grandpa would be happy to think a gift he made for you brings even more joy than he ever could have imagined. Your love for each other continues to touch so many."

"We are not to seek attention, Elizabeth."

"That is true, Mummi. This would not be seeking attention or boasting. This would be telling a story; a story firmly planted in love and written by the Lord Himself."

Taking hold of Mary, Catherine kept looking out the window seeking an answer. Watching birds at the feeders and deer running about the corn shocks and hugging a child of the Lord smelling of goodness and joy, Catherine realized the Lord's message of peace on earth and love of neighbor needed to be told now more than ever. While most people likely assumed her lifestyle sheltered her from glaring headlines, they were wrong. Catherine knew what was going on out there. She knew the world was in need of love stories. And her love story was one that could mend hearts and offer hope. Tommy was proof of that.

Turning around, Catherine spoke to Tommy as if he were the only one in that home. "I will do baking for your shop, Tommy, but I will not accept payment. I will offer my time up to the Lord and pray my small contributions will help comfort a tired soul or bring a smile when a smile is needed. I am touched you have chosen to name your bakery after the gift Paul created for me. It is a gift created in love and I pray 'The Tin Cookie Cutter' will bring love to those you will be serving."

"Your experience with baking and selling your products will be a big help. I'd like to tap in to all you have learned over the years."

"I will make notes, Tommy, so I do not miss a thing."

With Mary needing tending to, Catherine went looking for Elizabeth as Claire added to the conversation.

"I love your ideas, Tommy. Instead of seeing that building as an eyesore, you saw its beauty and potential."

"Buildings in that era were built to last. It remains solid from the basement to the third floor. All it needed was the electrical to be updated and new building codes to be implemented."

"What are your plans for the other two floors?"

"The second floor will offer space for meetings. I might include an area for small parties but I'm not sure I want the hassle. The third floor will be apartments. Two have been completed. I'm living in one and the other is rented by Nicholas Rossi."

"The railroad heir?"

"That's the one. He stopped by early on in the project looking to rent space for an apartment/office. When he's back in the area he divides his time between there and a family home he calls his farm outside town."

"Having Mr. Rossi as a tenant speaks volumes for what you are doing. I think all of your ideas will fit into your project. One complements the other. The location is perfect. I've been trying to get my business out of my home. When I started I thought having my life under one roof would be the ideal situation but I've changed my mind. My business needs the flow of traffic, the spontaneous purchaser. I need my home to be my home. Maybe we could discuss my renting space on the first floor."

"I have two spaces available. One is a premium location overlooking the sidewalk where you'd be exposed to traffic even when you're closed. I plan to do a lot of promotion in and out of the area. Once I finally get a website up, I want to use all the sites available to spread the word. People are drawn to old mercantile buildings that have been restored. Malls can get pretty generic despite all the gimmicks used to lure people in. And having a train nearby that takes them to see Santa Claus is icing on the cake."

"I understand what you're saying. Some malls have too much. I can't shop with so much going on. Do you have a web developer?"

"No, but that's on my list."

"I also design websites. If you're interested, I can give you some names of sites I've designed so you can check out my work."

"Perfect. I can cross off finding a web builder."

"You'd better wait to see if you like what I've done."

"A woman who cuts out cookies and bakes beside Catherine is my kind of woman. I can already tell I'll like what I see."

With Abraham playing and Mary back down for a nap, Elizabeth refilled Tommy's bowl. Slicing some bread and topping it with homemade butter, she put the bread beside the soup.

"More coffee, Tommy?"

"No thanks, Elizabeth. I believe I have reached my limit."

"Claire, please sit with me and we can talk about the mercantile."

"I'd love to, Tommy."

It wasn't long before the door opened. The children were home from school.

Chapter Nine

ONCE THEY HAD THEIR BOOTS OFF and their coats hung up, the children went over to Abraham who was excited to see his siblings. Bailey made sure to say hello with a few licks to the toddler's face.

"Come here, the three of you, and say hello. Your mother was kind enough to feed me so I'll be able to help load the sleds."

"Father told me I can drive one this year."

"That's great, Frank. We'll have a fun time."

"I can't wait, Tommy. Father said I am to stay behind him."

Drying her hands, Elizabeth joined in the conversation.

"Your father should be home soon. The lamb needs to go outside before he gets here, Frank."

"Mother, may I ask a question?"

"Of course, Hannah."

"Is someone sitting at the table with Tommy?"

"Yes, Hannah. Her name is Claire. She stopped earlier to ask about the wreaths on the front porch and we've been talking ever since. Please, children, one at a time, introduce yourselves to our neighbor and friend, Claire."

Small in frame with hair the shade of cinnamon showing from underneath her cap and cheeks still rosy from her walk home, the youngest stepped forward.

"My name is Faith and I am seven years old."

"What a precious name. I am happy to meet you, Faith."

Frank took his turn. "I am Frank. I am nine years old. I smell cookies. Did you help Mummi make them?"

"I did, Frank. We had lots of fun."

As Frank stepped back, Hannah and her dog stepped forward.

"My name is Hannah. I am thirteen years old. It is nice to meet you, Claire. This is my dog Bailey. She is my best friend."

Looking at the two in front of her made Claire wish she could photograph them. It had nothing to do with selling prints. It was all about the relationship of a small dog with fluffy white and brown and grey hair half hiding its face, and a young Amish girl with skin any model would die for and eyes so big they melted Claire's heart for so many reasons.

"It's nice to meet you, Hannah. Bailey is adorable. May I pet her?"

"You can hold her if you want to."

"I'd love to."

"I will put her in your lap."

Within seconds Claire had a dog sitting and looking at her.

"Stay, Bailey. I will be right here."

As soon as the dog heard Hannah talking to her she curled up and fell asleep.

"Besides learning how much you help around the house, Hannah, I understand you are singing in your school's Christmas program. Something tells me you have a beautiful voice."

"I love singing. My teacher told me God gave me a voice and I should share it."

"I agree with your teacher. Such a gift brings joy to others."

That simple house was bustling with excitement. Between cards that needed to be created and cookies that had to be put into tins and wooden toys that had to be loaded onto sleds, Claire was convinced she was at the North Pole. While Elizabeth took Mary upstairs, Catherine called Hannah to the kitchen.

"I love my snowman, Mummi. Thank you."

"You are welcome, my child. Claire, would you like to help Hannah fill the tins with cookies?"

"I'd love to."

With Bailey following her, Claire was back in the kitchen ready to go.

Just as Frank was heading outside with the lamb, John came through the door.

"Looks like it will be a perfect evening to be on the road with the sleds. The moon will be out. It's not snowing and the temperature is still in the twenties."

"Couldn't get any better conditions for this time of the year."

"That's what I was thinking, Tommy."

"I have things under control out there. When you're ready we'll start loading."

"I was in the barn. I could tell you've been working hard."

"I checked everything off your list."

"One thing I'm sure that wasn't on my husband's list was having something to eat before leaving," Elizabeth said, coming back down the stairs. Once she had Mary tucked back in, she greeted John with a hug.

"I didn't have to put that on a list, Elizabeth. I knew you'd have a fine meal waiting for us."

"That I do," Elizabeth replied, leading John into the kitchen where she introduced him to Claire.

"It's a pleasure meeting you, John. Elizabeth and Catherine have been more than kind after I invited myself into your home."

Once John was told the story of her coming to the front porch earlier that day, he laughed, telling Claire how many had stopped, wanting to buy Elizabeth's wreaths.

"I've told Elizabeth she might think about making more but she reminds me she has enough to do. Hannah is good with wreath-making but she is as busy as her mother."

"Maybe when the school program is over I can make the wreaths, Father. Right now, Claire and I have tins to finish filling. Then we are going to make a few deliveries."

"So you will be delivering a few tins today?"

"Yes, Father. I want to make sure I take one to Emma's first. She has been out of school helping her mother with the new baby."

"That's nice of you to think of Emma."

"She is my friend, Father."

"You are a good friend."

"Thank you, Mummi."

"While you go to Emma's, we'll load the sleds."

"It's two thirty, John. Dinner is almost ready. By the time Hannah and Claire return, I'll have the table set."

"Thank you, Elizabeth. The journey into town will go much better on a full stomach. Would you like to ride on the back of a sled with us, Hannah?"

"Bailey and I would love to, Father. May Claire come along too?"

"If Claire would enjoy riding on the back of a sled full of stuff in the cold, she is more than welcome to come along."

"Claire is a photographer," Catherine added. "And a fine one indeed. She could take photos along the way."

Claire's first instinct concerning riding on the back of one of the sleds was to say no. But this time she caught herself. Because of Catherine and her cookie cutters, and Elizabeth and her homemade soup, and Hannah and her dog, and the lamb sleeping by Mary, and Abraham playing with his blocks, and the barn full of rocking horses and wooden toys, and those wreaths on the front porch, Claire accepted Hannah's invitation to ride with her on that sled pulled by horses with bells ringing for all to hear. They'd made her feel welcomed.

"I'd love to ride along, John. Which charity do you donate to, as I am doing the same with mittens I've knitted?"

While John couldn't remember the name of the charity, he told Claire where he was making his delivery.

"That's where I was told to take my mittens. It isn't that far."

"You say it isn't far, Claire. Remember you are going by horse and sled," smiled Tommy.

Chapter Ten

With the cookie tins placed inside a quilted bag, Hannah was ready to go.

"If it's too late when you and Frank get home from helping your father, you both can make cards tomorrow evening."

"Tomorrow would be fine, Mother. Then we wouldn't be in a hurry," replied Hannah as she tried fastening Bailey's collar. It wasn't anything fancy. Her father had made it out of a leather strap. Realizing the strap was torn, Hannah took the collar off and asked her mother to keep it until her father had time to fix it.

"Here's an extra scarf and some heavier mittens, Claire."

"Thanks, Hannah. If I'd known I would be going on such adventures when I stopped earlier, I would have dressed a little warmer."

Hannah and Claire were off on their journey. A gust of wind took their breath away as they trudged through snow to reach the road. It had only been plowed a few times. Bailey walked alongside the road protecting Hannah.

"It will soon be dark. That takes some getting used to so early in the day."

As soon as Claire let that statement out into the universe, her words came echoing back, sounding cruel to her when considering Hannah's situation. The young girl felt Claire's apprehension.

"I have no problem with it being dark," she smiled. That led to the two of them laughing as they walked around a curve.

"I did not mean to offend you, Hannah."

"You didn't, Claire. I have become comfortable with the darkness. I consider myself lucky. Although I was four when I lost my eyesight I was old enough to remember what seeing means. I know what a tree looks like and a kitten and the moon and my home and the barn and this road and my school. In my eyes, my parents will never grow old. The Lord blessed me with eyesight and when He took it away He blessed me with an inner strength that I would not have if I still had my vision. Seeing objects is one thing. Seeing them through the Lord's eye is another."

"Are you afraid at times?"

"No. He chose this path for me and I have accepted it. He has given me many gifts. My ears; my sense of smell; my sense of touch are keen. My voice; my singing lifts me up to the Lord. My family surrounds me with love. They understand my need for independence. I will not be known as a cripple. I prefer to help those in need."

"Like your friend Emma?"

"Yes. The last time I visited, Emma told me she'd be in the school program tomorrow so that makes me happy. I wish you could be there too. I know my teacher would love to have you."

The two waited while Bailey went sniffing under a snow pile.

"Listen to her. She is on the trail of a little creature."

"When you take Bailey to school, does she stay beside you?"

"Yes. Bailey sleeps under my desk. At night she sleeps beside me. Tomorrow she is in the school program. Our teacher made her antlers. Bailey will be a reindeer."

"Oh how funny. But it can't be one of Santa's."

"That is right. While we are aware of Santa Claus and what he represents, we are fascinated by reindeer for their beauty and strength. There will also be a few sheep in the program and Frank is bringing the lamb."

"I remember one particular school play when real sheep were up on the stage. I was little but I can still hear everyone clapping when they came out."

"Did that scare the sheep?"

"No. They stayed still throughout most of the program."

"Did you sing, Claire?"

"I sang with my class."

"But did you ever sing a solo? I ask because I find myself afraid I will forget words or fall when I stand to sing tomorrow."

Not knowing how to answer Hannah's question, Claire kept her head down as the wind came at them again. Taking Hannah's hand, they walked a ways before Claire told the thirteen-year-old about the school Christmas program where she stood frozen in place and never sang a word of the song she'd practiced many times.

"I was supposed to sing a solo but I forgot every word. I stood on the stage looking at everyone waiting for me to sing."

"What grade were you in?"

"Second grade. I'd been excited for weeks. My grandmother made me a red velvet dress with lace around the neck. My mother fixed my hair and all I could do was stand there and stare out at faces staring back at me."

"That is what I am afraid I might do. What did you do then?"

Realizing she was putting doubt in Hannah's mind about her own ability to perform her solo, Claire felt she had to explain her situation in more detail.

"What happened to me could not happen to you. I became upset when I looked out in the audience and only saw my mother. My father didn't come. He was always away on business or at meetings but this one time when I asked him to be there, he wasn't and I was hurt. When I stood there unable to sing, the music teacher played her piano until my teacher was standing next to me. Then the entire class sang my song."

"What song was it"

"'Silent Night.' I've never sung that song again."

"That is a beautiful song."

"It's still my favorite."

"Sometimes as children we expect our parents to be perfect. We are not aware of all they do for us. While your father hurt you, I am sure he loved you."

"I could tell he did at times. There was a piano in our home, in the den where my father kept his desk in front of shelves full of books. When he wasn't away on business that's where he worked. I loved that room. It had a fireplace with brass candlesticks sitting on the mantel. That's where my brother and sister and I hung our Christmas stockings."

"Did you play the piano?"

"No. My father was the piano player. He didn't often play but when he did I'd sit next to him. I liked watching his fingers touching the keys making music happen. He played all kinds of songs. When it was time for bed my mother would have to come and take me upstairs. I never wanted to go. I wanted to stay and listen to my father at the piano."

They kept walking until a rabbit crossing their path startled them. Before Bailey could react, Hannah told her to stay.

"What made you aware of the rabbit?"

"I heard the rabbit use its back feet to whack the ground. It's a way to warn others that danger may be near." Hannah paused, turning her face to the wind before continuing. "I have never told anyone this but I pretended to be asleep when the doctor explained to my parents that I would never see again. I was only four but I remember being angry with them. The Lord should strike me down but I blamed my mother for falling asleep instead of watching me. I blamed my father for not looking before throwing those bales down. I never said anything but I was angry for a long time. I remember one night during a thunderstorm I went running to their bedroom. I was trapped in darkness and afraid of the storm I could hear all around me. In my rush, I tripped on a braided rug in the hallway and fell into a table. The next thing I remember my father was picking me up and putting me in their bed. I fell asleep lying between them listening to the storm and my mother whispering I was safe, whispering how much they loved me. Even after my mother told me they loved me, I still blamed them."

Going by a few homes decorated in Christmas lights and blown-up characters swaying in the breeze, Claire asked Hannah how she got beyond the anger.

"I prayed with the Bishop. I prayed when I was alone and I spent a lot of time with Mummi."

"Did you make cookies?"

"We made lots of cookies while we talked and prayed. The anger went away."

"When I made cookies with Catherine earlier today I learned making cookies is an art form."

"Her tin cookie cutters make it an art form. Every time I cut a cookie out, she falls in love with it."

"I would think every cookie is a part of the love between Catherine and Paul."

"Talk with Mummi while making cookies always includes stories about him. Through her stories and gentleness, that anger I felt turned into love. My becoming blind was an accident. I know my parents love me. They too were injured the night it happened. As Mummi reminds me, 'a parent's pain never goes away.'"

Bailey stopped, pointing her nose to the wind. While they waited, Claire noticed Hannah was still holding her hand. Claire found comfort in the young girl's presence. When Bailey began whining, Hannah pulled the dog beside her as the sound of wheels crunching the snow-covered road could be heard despite the wind swirling over the landscape. Even in her darkness, Hannah made the statement that the Bishop was approaching. Claire looked into the winter shadows and saw the silhouette of an approaching buggy.

"How do you know it's the Bishop?"

"I can smell his pipe tobacco."

"Are you sure it's his tobacco?"

"Yes. It smells like the wild berries that grow every summer behind the barn."

Seconds later a buggy was getting closer. Claire could see the Bishop's beard, white as cotton, moved by the wind. It was quite a scene. It took Claire's breath away. As the Bishop pulled back on the reins, his crimson cheeks and twinkling eyes had Claire remembering favorite storybooks read to her this time of year when she was little. Reality returned with the Bishop clearing his throat and smiling when realizing it was Hannah.

"Good afternoon, Bishop."

"Good afternoon, Hannah. Are you out taking Bailey for a walk?"

"I am bringing Emma a tin of cookies with my new friend. Bishop, I would like you to meet Claire. She is visiting us today."

Taking off a glove, the Bishop adjusted his pipe before extending his hand. "It is a pleasure meeting you. I am sure Hannah is wonderful company."

"It is a pleasure meeting you, Bishop. Hannah is quite enjoyable. She and her family have been generous with their time. I was lucky enough to make cookies with Catherine."

"If anyone can make cookies it is dear Catherine. It is nice of you to share some cookies with your friend, Hannah."

"I miss her."

"From what I have been told Emma should be back in school in a few weeks."

"She will still be in our Christmas program tomorrow. Will you be there, Bishop?"

"Of course I will. I always enjoy the program. The Lord has given this community many blessings but none better than our children. It was nice meeting you, Claire. And Hannah, have a nice visit with Emma. May the Lord bless you. I must be getting home."

"Thank you, Bishop. I will."

Once goodbyes were said, the Bishop placed a hand on Hannah's shoulder then continued on. Claire watched a gust of wind catch hold of that cotton beard and take it flying as the horse kept on prancing.

"The Bishop is a kind man," remarked Hannah.

"I'm glad I was able to meet him."

"When I was in the hospital, he visited every day."

"Those are things you don't forget. I'm sure Emma won't forget you bringing her cookies."

"I know she would do the same for me."

Going down an incline, Bailey was the first to hear the sound of laughter up ahead. She seemed to quicken her pace until Hannah told her to stay.

"There have to be kids skating on the creek. Emma and I skate there too sometimes. Bailey has fun chasing after us."

When the creek came into view, Claire was able to watch the Amish children at play. Just by their laughter, Hannah was able to tell who was on the ice. Each of them yelled hi to Hannah as they kept spinning around on their skates.

"I used to skate on a pond," Claire told Hannah. "It was in a field on my grandfather's farm. It was so much fun. My cousin and I would be out there for hours and we'd never get cold, even when our mittens were covered with frozen bits of ice and snow."

"Emma and I never get cold either. When Frank and I get back home, Mother fixes us a cup of snow cream. Even though it is cold, it tastes so good."

"That's with powdered milk and snow?"

"Yes. And mother adds sugar and sweet cream. She always gives me extra sugar. Mummi tells me I have a sweet tooth."

"My grandmother would make us hot chocolate. Sometimes she'd add whipped cream on top. Once in a while she'd give us some saltine crackers to dip into our hot chocolate."

"Sometimes we dip Mummi's cookies into our drink. They taste so good covered in sugar and sweet cream," said Hannah, waving goodbye to her friends out on the ice. "Emma's is around this curve."

"I am in awe of you going skating, Hannah. That takes what we say, guts."

"I understand that word but my strength comes from the Lord and the help of my family. My father takes Emma and me sliding down what people call Killer Hill. I do not like that name but again, I understand."

"We had a hill like that nearby where I grew up. I only went down it once. That was enough because I almost broke my leg when trying to avoid a tree. How do you make it to the bottom?"

"Father drilled two of those plastic sleds together. I am right beside him. We go when it is not busy. He guides us down and Emma follows in her sled. It is so much fun. I can remember what that hill looked like before losing my eyesight so as we go down, I can see in my head where we are."

It wasn't long before a farmhouse was visible. Not far from the house stood a massive barn surrounded by fields with remnants of vines still visible under the snow. As soon as they started up the path, a young girl came running out of the house with her cloak half on and boots untied.

"Hannah!"

"Emma!"

After introductions, Claire followed the girls and Bailey inside. They stayed for not quite an hour. On the way back Hannah made a few more deliveries. They were quick stops. Hannah knew she had to get back home.

Chapter Eleven

LATE AFTERNOON SHADOWS WERE STRETCHING THEIR way over the landscape when they returned to Hannah's. With the kerosene lanterns turned on in the barn and one sled sitting outside loaded and covered with tarps, Claire walked down to see what was going on while Hannah went inside to help her mother. Getting closer to the barn, Claire caught sight of Tommy, his arms full of wooden toys, directing traffic as he stood in the middle of a sled.

"You can put the rest of the rocking horses over here, guys. Be careful when you set them down. There's not much room left."

Claire guessed the young Amish boys helping Tommy were around Frank's age.

"An amazing sight, isn't it, Claire! John's going to make lots of kids happy this year."

With his hands free, Tommy jumped off the sled.

"That's quite the project. I can't believe John donates all of these items. It must take so much of his time."

"He's turned it into a mentoring project. John brings in young Amish boys interested in learning the skills he has acquired. When they get to a certain point in the process, John oversees them. He still does the intricate stuff but that's about it. John's project even attracts some youth outside their community. It's a win-win all around."

A noise caught Tommy's attention. "Must be Rudolph is acting up again. Want to see the reindeer?"

Claire's earlier suspicions turned out to be true. There were reindeer hidden in the shadows. "I'd love to see the reindeer," she replied. "Is there a reindeer named Rudolph?"

"Yes. Rudolph's my favorite reindeer so that's what I named one of them."

"I always favored Prancer."

"Why?"

"When I was little I wanted to be a dancer. I took lessons but quit when I was twelve, the same year my father died."

"Did you quit because you lost your father?"

"No. I mean I don't think so. It was such an awful year. Everything that happened is one big rotten memory. It's a long story, Tommy."

"I have some of those long stories. I was a wild kid for a while. But I grew up pretty quick when my father dropped dead one afternoon while playing golf. That was all I needed to turn it around. I worked my way through a vocational/tech school and earned my electrician's degree. My father would always say be a plumber or an electrician. To me, the choice was pretty simple."

"While some realize all along what it is they want to do with their lives, others are more complicated. Take you for example. You have your degree in a field where you'll always find work. Yet you have that creative side that needs attention."

"Exactly, Claire. I don't need to open a bakery and be the baker for the money. I need to open a bakery and be the baker because that's what's at the heart of me. I need to bring that building back around and fill it with music and people and the aromas from my ovens and the smells of coffee brewing and newsprint nearby. I can't describe my feelings when I'm baking. The entire process takes me somewhere that being an electrician never can. My father dropped dead. Right out of the blue he was gone. He was a good man. He was my best friend but he never stepped out of the box. We'd sit around the dinner table and listen to him talk about how someday when he retired, he would take my mother on a trip to Alaska. That was my father's dream. He wanted to see Alaska and he never did. My father dropped dead on a sunny Thursday afternoon while playing golf with his boss. I don't want a boss. I don't want to be building someone else's dream. I want to build mine, cookie by cookie."

"I get what you are saying, Tommy. I did my share of jobs. Then I found photography. Every day is different. And that's the way I like it."

With fewer horses in the stables, the reindeer were easier to see. Their presence, alongside frosted windowpanes giving view to spits of snow falling, made Claire stop to take it all in. Curiosity led to her asking Tommy why John raised reindeer.

"I've never heard of the Amish doing that."

"John hadn't either. Truth is it wasn't his idea. An English farmer lost most everything one night when a fire broke out in his barn. Besides chickens, he was raising the reindeer. The fire destroyed his barn and he lost the chickens. But he was able to get the reindeer out before the whole thing fell to the ground. He and John were good friends. The guy asked John if he could house the reindeer while he got back on his feet. John said yes. They had an agreement between themselves. All was fine until the English farmer was killed in a car accident. By the time that happened, John was used to having the reindeer. In fact the whole family loved the reindeer so the reindeer stayed put. It turned out to be a good decision. John rents them out this time of the year and makes some good money on the side."

"I can't believe he donates so much of his work."

"When Hannah was injured, John and Elizabeth received an out-pouring of support from the English in the area. They've never forgotten the generosity of so many. They feel it is the least they can do."

Walking into the reindeer's stable, Claire noticed the harnesses hanging on nails. Some were painted red while some were covered in a Christmas plaid material. "Did Catherine make these?"

"I heard both she and Elizabeth had a hand in sewing them. Now people order custom-made harnesses for their horses."

"I'm sure. When I saw the Christmas wreaths on the porch, I wanted to buy them all. This visit has turned out to be so much more than I could ever have imagined."

"I get that feeling every time I go into their home. I don't know if it's the aromas from the kitchen or their kindness."

"I felt that the second Elizabeth opened the door. Maybe we feel that because our world is so hectic and plugged in. At least mine is."

"Mine as well, Claire. That could be part of it. I've sat around their table before and while the food is better than any served in a five-star restaurant, it's the family part of the meal that stays with me."

"I'm looking forward to that experience."

"You must miss having family nearby."

"Sometimes, but honestly we were never that close. Since relocating here most of the connections I've made have been through my business."

"I still have my mother and brother although my mother's in a nursing home. Most days she doesn't know me."

"That must be hard on you, Tommy."

"I make myself go. My brother has written her off."

John could be heard calling for Tommy.

"I'm in with the reindeer," he replied.

Seconds later John was inside the stable. "Why am I not surprised you are with the reindeer? I wanted to let you know Elizabeth will have dinner on the table in fifteen minutes."

Turning to Claire, John repeated something Hannah said when returning from Emma's.

"I understand your grandmother would make you hot chocolate with whipped cream after you'd come in from skating on a pond. Hannah was excited to hear you used to skate outside like she does."

"I enjoyed our conversations. She even introduced me to the Bishop."

"We heard you met the Bishop."

"Hannah is remarkable. Even before the Bishop was in sight, Hannah knew he wasn't far away."

"While the Lord taketh away, He gives so much more in return. I will see you both in a few minutes."

A limb scratching its way along a windowpane frightened a few of the barn cats. Watching them scurry toward the door, Claire asked Tommy how the Amish kept such positive attitudes.

"I used to wonder that when I first started coming around. I've decided it has to do with their upbringing. Faith plays a role in every aspect of their lives. Their faith helps them accept tragedies like a four-year-old losing her eyesight."

Checking his watch, Tommy decided they'd better get going.

"We don't want to be late. Once Elizabeth has the food on the table it is time to eat."

Leading Claire out of the barn, he took her hand.

"It gets pretty slippery," he explained.

"I found that out this morning."

Holding Claire's hand a little tighter, Tommy started leading her over an icy patch, but her boot caught an edge and down they went. It took them a few seconds to realize they were flat-out side by side on the ice not far from the house. Once Tommy got his bearings, he checked to see if Claire was okay.

"You cushioned my fall. How about you?"

"I survived, unlike the last time I fell on the ice."

"What happened then, Tommy?"

"I was in the sixth or seventh grade. I was late getting ready for school. The sidewalk was covered in snow and ice and when I hurried out the door to catch the bus, I went flying. My mother thought I had a concussion but it ended up being a good bump on my head. I did miss four days of school and that was fine with me."

"You were lucky. It could have been serious."

"I'm luckier this time. I fell down with you."

One of the horses hitched to a sled shook his head, sounding off a chorus of bells.

"Look! Over the top of those trees, Claire. See those clouds. Keep looking because it's getting dark. Look at the one in the middle. It looks like Snoopy running."

"Oh, it does. I love that. I haven't looked at clouds in years."

"Reminds me of that Judy Collins song. I was in a band. The lead singer was a girl and she'd nail that song every time."

"I know the song you mean. Oh, look. Snoopy is gone."

"Gone like the band."

"What do you mean? The band broke up?"

"No. I quit."

"Why?"

"On the day my father died I was playing a gig. My mother couldn't reach me. They got him to the hospital where he asked for me up to the moment he passed away. I was never there to say goodbye. After that, every time I'd go on stage all I could think of was my father passing away and I was off playing my guitar. I should have been there, Claire. He never missed a show. He was my biggest supporter."

"It wasn't your fault, Tommy. Being with Hannah today I realized the Lord does have a plan for all of us. I'm sure your father knew you loved him. I'm sure he is at peace knowing you were doing something that makes you happy."

"You're sure?"

"I know we've just met but there's something about you, Tommy. The little boy inside you is in your heart. Your goodness and kindness show through your eyes; through the words you speak; the way you care about those around you. I can only imagine the love you shared with your father. Such a bond doesn't end when one passes. It goes forever, Tommy. Your father will love you forever. He remains your biggest supporter."

"You are certain, Claire?"

With darkness about to set in, the last bit of a sunset was fading off in the horizon. But it was enough light for Claire to look into Tommy's eyes and tell him she was certain. Unscripted moments can be unforgettable. This was such a moment. Looking into those brown eyes seeking reassurance, Claire felt the wind move around them, saw the moon coming out from passing clouds, and was certain stars were glistening like never before. Brushing snow off Tommy's forehead and shoulders, Claire took hold of his scarf and pulled him closer.

"I am certain, Tommy," Claire whispered as she kept reassuring him. "Your father will love you forever."

Wrapping her arms around Tommy, Claire brought his lips to hers. "I'm certain, Tommy. I'm certain," she kept whispering until the kiss intensified and the two were lost in an unscripted moment under those glistening stars. But moments don't last forever.

"I don't know what came over me, Tommy."

A cloud rambling by caught his attention.

"Look, Claire. Up there over the trees. Snoopy is back minus an ear."

That's all they needed. They both started laughing. They laughed so hard that giggles from inside that clapboard home could be heard behind curtains pulled open enough for little ones to peek out.

"I think we are being watched." Claire was whispering again.

"I think we'd better get inside. Who knows how long they've been there. I have a feeling the food is on the table."

As Tommy was moving away from her, Claire grabbed hold of his jacket. "Everything I said to you is the truth, Tommy."

"I know, Claire. I'll never forget this moment."

On their way up the steps Claire told herself it was just that—a moment. But her heart was telling her a different story.

Chapter Twelve

NOT ONLY WAS THE FOOD ON the table but everyone was seated. With two chairs empty, Claire chose the one next to Hannah. Tommy sat across from her next to Faith. Abraham was on Elizabeth's lap. Catherine was at one end; John was at the other with Frank beside him.

"I hope we haven't kept you waiting long. We would have been in on time but we slipped on the ice," Tommy explained, trying not to look at Claire.

"I meant to take care of that earlier. I almost slipped myself coming in," said John, folding his hands together and bowing his head. Family members did the same. In silence they prayed. Once John said "Amen," the meal got underway.

"I prepared your favorite, Tommy."

"I thought I caught the scent of broasted chicken, Elizabeth. I've never tasted anything like it."

"Thank you. Enjoy. We welcome you and Claire to our table."

As dishes began being passed around the table, Tommy caught Claire's attention long enough to share a smile. She was certain everyone noticed. With her thoughts still out on that icy patch it took Claire a few minutes to get used to the idea that she was sitting down for dinner in an Amish home. She couldn't remember the last time she'd sat down at a table for dinner; let alone an Amish table in an Amish home. Usually she was on the go, bringing take-out home and eating in front of the TV. Sometimes she'd be so tired that she didn't have the strength to take the plastic containers to the kitchen when finished. Claire left them until morning. But there were no plastic containers this evening. Elizabeth had prepared everything from scratch. Claire felt blessed to be sitting down at the oak table covered by an embroidered linen tablecloth, with this family who'd turned her quick stop into a day, and a moment, she'd never forget.

"Your tablecloth is beautiful, Elizabeth."

"Thank you, Claire. It was our wedding gift from Mummi."

"You are a woman of many talents, Catherine."

"It's all in the upbringing. Elizabeth is capable as will be Hannah and Faith."

"Knitting is my favorite thing to do," said Hannah.

"You are a very good knitter."

"Thank you, Mother."

China bowls holding mashed potatoes and green beans and Amish noodles and a vegetable dish like no other Claire had ever tasted continued to be passed from one to another, along with platters stuffed with Tommy's chicken and a gravy boat filled with piping hot homemade gravy. It had the feel of Thanksgiving and Christmas all in one. With two large pitchers of water on the table there was no need for anyone to get up and interrupt the flow of conversation, which went from tomorrow's school program, to the mission they were about to undertake, to Catherine's impending move back home.

"You don't have to leave before Christmas, Mummi."

"Oh, but my sweet Elizabeth, I do. Thanks to all of you I am strong enough to be on my own. I want to be home for Christmas."

The gathering could have gone on for hours but there was much that needed to be done. After the table was cleared Elizabeth brought out the pies and took orders for coffee.

"Hannah and Frank, would you like your coffee with pie?"

"I would, please, Mother," answered Frank.

"I would too. I can fix them, Mother." Hannah was up in seconds.

"I must explain," said Elizabeth as she sliced the pies. "Hannah and

Frank are still too young for a cup of coffee. But they are allowed a cup with small pieces of bread broken up and mixed in along with milk and sugar. In a few years, Faith will be able to enjoy that treat as well."

"It sounds delicious," replied Claire as she took her first bite of pumpkin pie.

"This has to be the best pumpkin pie I've ever tasted."

Catherine started laughing. "That's because the pumpkin was fresh. It was from my garden. That's the pumpkin I was picking when I got tangled up in the vines and fell and broke my ankle."

Laughter filled that home as a lamb watched over a baby sound asleep, and a toddler using his hands got his apple pie everywhere, even in his mouth. Once the plates were empty and the coffee had been enjoyed John led them in a silent prayer. After he stood and said "Amen," Elizabeth took Abraham into the kitchen and cleaned him up. When Elizabeth returned, she was holding Bailey's collar.

"Your father fixed the collar, Hannah. You might want to put it on Bailey before you go."

"Thank you, Father. Bailey loves her collar."

"I can tell," John replied, noting Bailey sitting still as Hannah put the collar around her neck.

"There, Bailey. You have your collar back. You look so beautiful. We will have fun tonight. You have to stay right by my side."

While the table was cleared, those going to town were bundling up.

"Put an extra pair of leggings on, Hannah. You know how you freeze when the sun goes down even in the summer. Claire, would you like a pair? They are a woven heavy knit, perfect for staying warm while sitting on a sled in the cold."

"I would love a pair, Elizabeth."

"Then go with Hannah. She will prepare you for tonight's journey."

While the two went upstairs, Frank went out the door with John and Tommy. It was going on five o'clock.

"Good night for doing a good deed, John."

"We have been blessed with a full moon and a light snowfall."

"Once you get on the road I'll head to the mercantile and jump on-board when you pass by."

"Thanks, Tommy. It shouldn't take long to get the stuff inside. It's the crowd that makes it seem like it takes forever."

"People watch for you. They've come to appreciate the quality of your work."

"It is the work of many hands."

"And those hands are under your direction, my friend."

With Bailey on one side of Hannah and Claire on the other, they walked to the barn where six horses were eager to get going. It was as if they knew what was going on. Elizabeth carrying Abraham followed behind them. Once John checked the tarps for the final time, Tommy started his truck. Then he turned his attention to Claire.

"I told John I'll jump on board when I see you going by the building." Tommy hesitated. "I want to thank you for tonight. Your words put to rest my guilt concerning my not being there when my father passed away. I'll never forget that, Claire, nor will I forget what happened after. I hope you realize I—I didn't want to stop even though we hardly know each other."

"It's not the length of time that matters, Tommy. It's the quality. What happened between us was spontaneous."

Whispering in Tommy's ear Claire added, "I didn't want to stop either."

With John getting on board his sled, Tommy said goodbye.

"Have a great time on the sled, Claire. Hannah is wonderful company."

"See you soon, Tommy."

"I'll be watching for all of you."

"Bye, Tommy!" shouted Hannah.

"Goodbye, Hannah. I hope you and Bailey have fun!"

John insisted Hannah and Claire ride behind him on the first sled. Frank would be leading the second sled, with an older lad from a neighboring farm leading the third.

Once they maneuvered their way down the path and onto the road, the rest of the way was a straight shot to town with a few curves and hills in between. John had placed several lanterns on each sled for safety's sake. Even though the road was a quiet country road, having three Amish sleds traveling together at night with it snowing could cause an impatient driver to take a risk. A neighbor of theirs had lost his life a few months back on his way home. It was at dusk. He was out on the road with no lanterns marking his buggy. The Sheriff told his widow he never had a chance. A father of eleven children was taken in the blink of an eye.

"Did you bring your camera, Claire?"

"I did, Hannah. Not because I'm hoping to get some photos but because I am used to having it with me."

"You should take photos if you find anything interesting."

"I don't want to be seen as an intruder after the kindness your family has shown me."

"We understand the intrigue our community stirs in the outside world. Photos are taken all the time."

"I will keep watch for anything interesting."

That wasn't going to be hard. While she'd tried to put her own intrigue away somewhere, Claire felt it back full force. Any photographer would have felt the same with the backdrop of those sleds and the moon and stars and horses and of course, the Amish and the light snowfall.

It didn't take long before those horses found their rhythm. The bells on their harnesses alerted bystanders that they were approaching. Vehicles pulled over to the side of the road to watch the sleds go by. Others rolled down their windows to get a better look. As they were going by the pond where the children had been skating, Claire caught sight of the Bishop.

"Hannah! The Bishop is up ahead. He is standing in the middle of the road!"

"The Bishop is waiting to bless the sleds and give thanks to the Lord for the spirit of giving."

Claire felt her juices flowing. "I will be right back, Hannah."

"Do you find the Bishop's blessing interesting?"

"Very interesting."

As John pulled back on the reins allowing the Bishop more time, Claire jumped off the sled. With a split second to decide her set-up, she ran past the Bishop. Using the moon behind the sleds as her prop, providing enough light for those sleds and horses to be seen in the muted shadows while at the same time shining on the Bishop like a dull spotlight, the photographer was in place and ready to go. With his back to Claire, the Bishop held his arms out as he stood in that road praying. Faithful around him bowed their heads as a gust of wind moved his cotton beard ever so slightly to the side, enough so Claire was able to capture it flying about like laundry on a clothesline. It didn't slow the Bishop down. His bellowing voice went soaring over the fields. Claire didn't miss a moment of the spectacle in play on that country road. The more it unfolded the more she had to pinch herself. No amount of planning could have delivered such a striking scene told in such stark simplicity. When the Bishop lowered his arms and stepped aside, John continued the journey.

Back on the sled, Claire informed Hannah that they were going by the Bishop.

"Oh, thank you, Claire," replied Hannah.

Holding on to the edge of a tarp, the young girl stood and waved.

"Hello, Hannah. You and Bailey look like you are having a good time."

"We are, Bishop. It's fun to make people happy."

"You are a true child of the Lord."

"Thank you, Bishop."

When the pond was behind them, Hannah knew her friend's farm was ahead.

"We must be getting close to Emma's, Father."

"I can see their farm up ahead and lights swaying by the roadside."

"It has to be Emma. She told me she'd be there."

Not only was Emma there to cheer them on but so was her entire family, waving lanterns and clapping their hands. As the first sled was approaching, Emma came rushing out with a basket full of cookies. John slowed the horses down long enough to grab hold of it as Hannah stood and waved, thanking her friend.

"Those are molasses cookies, Hannah. Your favorite cookies!"

"Thank you, Emma. See you tomorrow."

It was a glorious evening for a sleigh ride. John's woolen blankets were appreciated. Even Bailey was having a good time. Hannah brought along a brush she used to keep knots out of Bailey's hair.

"Bailey loves getting her hair brushed. Mummi told me she has a pretty ring of hair the color of hay around her left eye that makes her even more beautiful. I think it probably looks like sunshine."

"You are right, Hannah. It looks exactly like sunshine."

As the sleds made their way to town more and more people were lined up alongside the road cheering them on. Because their teachings prohibited face-on photos, John told those under his watch to do the best they could with cameras all around them.

"Keep your heads down if possible. If not, smile and keep on going."

Many of those with cameras were local. They respected their Amish neighbors in their belief that photographs invaded their privacy and were the cause of unaccepted pride.

"I can't believe the number of people out tonight."

"Wait until we get where we are going, Claire!"

"It reminds me of parades in the summer back home in Vermont. No matter the weather, people showed up. But this is even more amazing. They're all bundled up, waving and smiling and delighted to be a part of this despite the cold and wind."

"It is a fun night," said Hannah. "Last year there was a blizzard and still Father filled the sleds and brought them to town and still the people came."

"From what Tommy told me, your father bringing the sleds to town was a feature story in a magazine."

"My teacher told us when you take time to help your neighbor you are planting a seed of kindness. That is what my father is doing. He does it all year long."

"I can see the Sheriff's car," yelled Frank. "He is waiting for us."

Hannah explained how the Sheriff would wait for the sleds to reach the outskirts of town. Then he would turn his lights on and escort them in. Other vendors would follow behind the sleds.

"Father has tried telling the Sheriff he doesn't have to do it but the Sheriff tells him he does it for safety reasons. I think it's because the Sheriff likes to see my community and the English community joining together to help others."

"It is a feel-good story, Hannah. The Sheriff sees a lot in his position. Highlighting good over evil is a smart thing to do."

Noticing all the Christmas lights as downtown came into view, Claire added, "Frank is right. This place has gone all out."

With Bailey in her arms, Hannah described what she remembered of the downtown. "I can see City Hall lit up with strings of white lights around the trees. I can see the swings and slides at the playground all covered in snow and the stores with presents wrapped in shiny paper in the windows. I can see the plastic Santa Claus with his reindeer stretching high above the main street. When the wind blows, the reindeer look like they are flying. I remember the church steeples nearby. I remember the old post office with its wide steps and the building Tommy talks about but it was empty and dark back then. Tommy has described to me all that he has done to it. I think all it needed was some love, Claire."

"I believe you are right, Hannah. I can see it up ahead. It is beautiful, with lights in all the windows and wreaths on the doors."

"Those are Mother's wreaths. I helped her make them."

"You and your mother do beautiful work."

Taking a closer look, Claire watched as Tommy came sprinting between those gathered in front of his building. John wasn't able to slow the horses down but it didn't matter. Tommy grabbed hold of the side of the sled and pulled himself up between Claire and Hannah.

"Good evening, ladies. Such a perfect night for a sleigh ride."

"I'm impressed, Tommy. It's great exposure for your building."

"This is the first time it's being covered by a TV channel located downstate, Claire. One of my tenants told me he thinks Nicholas Rossi is responsible."

"Nicholas Rossi?"

"The guy I told you about who owns the train depot and runs that train back and forth and rents space from me on the third floor."

"He owns the depot down the street from your building?"

"I learned that about half an hour ago. The sale was finalized last week."

"That's a smart move on his part."

"He's supposed to be in town tonight but I haven't seen him."

"It makes sense your Mr. Rossi was the one who notified the TV station. Money talks, Tommy."

"It does, and I am listening."

Chapter Thirteen

THE RIDE THROUGH A DOWNTOWN COMING back to life was a glorious one. Except for a few stores still vacant, it was as Claire had described: mirroring a quaint New England village illustrated on the front of a Christmas card. Families were on every side of that main street, waving and singing Christmas carols.

"We are approaching Santa in his sleigh with his reindeer flying above the intersection, Hannah."

"Is the wind moving it?"

"Yes, it is moving. I feel like it will fly away at any moment."

"I remember the last Christmas before my accident. It was snowing so hard that I couldn't see the sleigh. I thought it really did fly away."

"No worries about that tonight, Hannah. The moon is high above us."

"Can you see City Hall?"

Standing, Claire looked ahead. "I see what you described up ahead. We will be going by it in a few minutes."

Turning back around, Claire noticed the mercantile behind them.

"Tommy. Please hold onto me. I have to take a few pictures of your building. With the stars above and the candle lights in all of the windows, along with wreaths and the oak doors and all of the surroundings, it is a magnificent sight."

"I'd love to hold on to you," Tommy whispered, jumping to his feet and putting his arm around her as the sled kept moving along the cobblestones added a few years back.

"Walking by your building is one thing. But seeing it from afar sheds light on the immensity of your project. See that cluster of stars. They look like spotlights shining down on your mercantile. I have to capture them."

"I've got you, Claire. Take as many photos as you want." Tommy pulled her even closer as John quickened the pace.

A young child running out into the street caused the Sheriff to slam on his brakes. John reacted; quickly pulling on the reins, which made Claire lose her balance and fall backwards. Tommy was forced to pull her even closer with one hand while grabbing hold of the tarp with the other.

"I have you, Claire. Don't worry. I have you."

Claire could feel Tommy's strength keeping her steady. Her cheek rubbed against his; that slight beard touched her as spectators kept singing and Claire got those feelings back from earlier in the evening.

"Are you two okay?" Hannah asked.

"Except for some strands of Claire's beautiful, long, auburn hair wrapped around my head, I'm fine."

"Thanks to Tommy's quick action, my camera survived as did I."

"We must be so close. I hear more people singing."

"The depot is within sight, Hannah. The crowd is immense. When we start to unload in the building next to it, you and Bailey stay by Claire."

"Yes, Father. Bailey and I will do as you say."

When the Sheriff put his brakes on, John was ready this time. They waited as officers pushed the crowd back so the sleds could make the turn leading to the depot area, keeping in mind there were other vendors behind them needing to unload. It was a one-way street, which would make it easier to empty the sleds and head back home. But first they had to reach their destination. Complicating the situation were those getting ready to board the train. It was Thursday night. Lots of seniors were in line. In previous years there hadn't been a train attracting passengers adding to the crowd.

Once John began the turn, people started clapping. So many were aware of the quality of his work and the number of items he'd donated over the years to help his English neighbors in need. Most knew why he did it; most looked for Hannah. That's why cheers from the crowd filled that one-way street like a wave in a football game when Hannah was in view. She'd become somewhat of a celebrity despite her parents' attempts to quell what they considered frivolity. No matter how many times they'd tell people Hannah's blindness was the Lord's will, most of them didn't seem to listen.

"Hannah is such an inspiration," they'd reply.

John and Elizabeth gave up trying to put an end to those outside their community thinking Hannah was some sort of heroine. They concentrated on bringing Hannah up with virtues they held dear. As John pulled his sled close to the curb, Claire was awestruck by the continuing outpouring of love for a young girl hugging her dog.

"While you get situated, I want to take some shots from the crowd. I'll be back in a few seconds, Tommy."

"Can I come with you, Claire?"

"I think you'd better stay on the sled, Hannah. When I get back I'll take you and Bailey into the depot and the building next door. I'll hurry."

"Take your time, Claire. I'll be right here with Hannah."

Claire took a few minutes figuring out her best angle once she was in the crowd. Making up her mind on a location, Claire turned to ready her camera as she stood alongside the third sled. Looking toward the front she caught sight of Tommy, leaning against the tarp while talking to Hannah. Under the glistening moonlight, Claire focused in on him, now holding Hannah in his lap with Bailey at their feet. Once she began, she continued snapping one photo after another as the two laughed and hugged and petted Bailey. A few shots showed them sitting quietly, content to be part of all that was going on around them. Taking a second to refocus, Claire was about to continue where she left off. But when she zeroed in on her two subjects, Claire discovered there were three. A young woman with perfect makeup and not a blond hair out of place, with French nails and wearing those stretchy jeans, boots, and a long, flattering winter coat with a stylish knit hat and holding leather gloves, was now in Tommy's lap. It was obvious they were more than just friends. When he kissed her, Claire knew it must be Denise unless he had a string of girlfriends, which she doubted. While her heart felt a heavy twinge of something, Claire kept them in focus but she couldn't snap the photo. She kept looking at her. Claire had envisioned Denise with brown hair pulled back in a ponytail, little makeup, layers of warm clothing, and absolutely no fancy manicure. Realizing John would be in need of her help, Claire took one last look at that young woman before putting her camera back in her pocket. Collecting her thoughts as she moved through the crowd, Claire figured she'd been fantasizing ever since meeting Tommy on the front steps of that clapboard home. She decided that while the fantasy was a fun diversion, it wasn't reality. The reality was, Tommy was taken, even if he didn't realize it.

"Did you get anything worthwhile?"

"I'll let you know, Tommy," Claire responded when back up in the sled and wondering where that woman had gone. "If I've captured anything worthwhile I'll email it to you."

Claire knew she hadn't been hallucinating. The strong scent of perfume was everywhere.

"Bailey and I can't wait to go with you, Claire."

"It should be very soon. I see your father headed this way."

"Now the fun begins. After we unload I'll come looking for you two."

"There's so much going on, Tommy. You'll probably never find us."

"I can spot a pretty woman a mile away, Claire."

"I'm sure you can."

Claire wanted to say more but John was back with the paperwork.

"Let's get the tarps off and start moving the stuff inside. There's a large space near the back reserved under my name. Just look for the sign."

Turning his attention to Hannah, John reminded her to stay with Claire.

"Keep hold of her hand, especially when the crowd gets to be too much."

"Don't worry, John. I will not let go of Hannah."

"Could I ask one more thing?"

77

"After all your family has done for me today, you can ask me any-thing."

"Could you carry Bailey? Maybe you and Hannah could take turns?"

"Bailey is light as a feather, Father. It will be fun."

"I agree, John. It will be fun. Don't worry about us."

As the tarps were being pulled off the sleds, Claire and Hannah started their adventure. Bailey was content in Claire's arms as they approached the depot. Holding the door for Hannah, Claire turned back around and caught Tommy giving her a wave. Claire pretended she didn't see him as a lingering whiff of that perfume came back at her.

Chapter Fourteen

"THERE'S SOMETHING ABOUT A TRAIN DEPOT that stirs one's wanderlust."

"What is wanderlust, Claire?"

"It's feeling overwhelmed with a need to travel. When I hear a train passing by I wonder who's on board and where the train is headed. Sometimes as the train gets farther away I'm wishing I were on board going wherever the train might take me."

"Father reads to me. Sometimes he reads about distant places and when he does I get that feeling you call wanderlust. But I would never leave my community."

Watching Hanna walking about the depot, Claire was convinced the young girl saw more than most of the people scurrying about. Lining the walls were merchants selling their wares. Everything from popcorn to jewelry, books, pottery, and so much more was on display. Hannah's fingers told her about the items in front of her.

"I think this would be a good-sized coffee mug for Mother."

Feeling the mug a little longer, Hannah asked what color the glazed flowers were on the front.

"One is pink and one is bright yellow."

"It is very pretty," she replied.

As they went along people would stop to say hello to Hannah and

Bailey. When they were going by a vendor selling rag dolls, Claire asked Hannah if she would like a doll.

Picking one up, Hannah felt the doll and its clothing. Turning it around, Hannah found the tag sewn into a seam.

"What does that say, Claire?"

"It states the doll was made in China."

"Father tells me China is far away. I have two rag dolls. One my mother made me before I was born. The other Mummi made me after my accident. I do not need any more rag dolls, but thank you for asking."

"You are a wise shopper, Hannah."

"There is no need to collect things. It is better to give thanks to the Lord for the blessings He has given us."

After buying Hannah some popcorn, Claire decided they'd better check in with John. As she was leading them to the door, Hannah stopped.

"What's wrong?" Claire asked.

"Do you smell that?"

"Smell what, Hannah? This place is full of smells."

"Garlic jam. The jam lady is here!"

"I don't know what you mean."

"There is a lady here who sells jams. I can smell her garlic jam. I bought Father the garlic jam last year and he loved it. She is here, Claire. I know she is."

"Would you like to buy your father some garlic jam?"

"If we can find her."

That wasn't a problem. Relying on her sense of smell, Hannah led them to the woman's booth near the back of the depot. The jam lady recognized Hannah.

"My sweet child. I remember you and your dog from last year. After we talked about growing garlic, I invited you to my farm to show you how I make the jam. Remember, I don't live far from your school."

"My father loved your jam. We stopped by your farm one day but you weren't home. I would like to buy another jar."

"So sorry I missed you. Please try again," said the jam lady, handing

Hannah a plastic bag. "I put an extra jar in there since your father enjoys it so."

"Thank you. That is very nice of you. I will ask my father if we can visit you sometime soon."

Introducing herself, Claire added, "I'll take two jars of your strawberry jam."

"Thank you. Strawberry jam is my best seller."

"I grew up watching my father put strawberry jam on his toast most every morning."

"Smart man, your father. Do you live close by?"

After Claire explained how she ended up in the area, the jam lady asked what she did.

"I'm a photographer. I'd love to visit you. Spend some time as you make your jam. I submit stories with photos to magazines and I think you would make a great feature."

"Really now? Me?"

"You have character written all over you."

"You mean lines on the face and brown spots all over my hands?"

"They show you've lived life and I dare say an interesting one."

"Well, you're right about that," the jam lady laughed. "I'll say no more for now."

Picking up one of the jam lady's business cards, Claire tried nailing a date for her visit.

"The sooner we meet the better, Lil. May I call you Lil?"

"Yes, Claire. Please do."

"I see your email address. I'll be in touch with some possible dates."

"That will work. Maybe you could bring Hannah with you?"

"Perfect suggestion, Lil. I'll ask her parents once we have the details."

"Visiting the jam lady sounds like fun, Claire. I am excited."

"So am I, Hannah," replied Claire, already thinking about angles and lighting as they made their way next door.

"We'll take our time once we get inside. I remember your father telling the boys where his space is located. We won't have a problem finding them."

With so many people still moving in bins and containers, Claire took hold of Hannah's hand, shifting Bailey to her other arm. As they went along she would tell Hannah everything that she saw.

"There's clothing hanging up and baked goods piled on tables; so many books and plastic toys and games and bags of canned goods. It's a great outpouring of neighbors helping neighbors."

Leading Hannah and Bailey around a stack of bins, Claire headed to find John and the others. When they reached that area, Tommy was talking to a reporter about his building. Claire kept going. She saw John unpacking rocking horses.

"Well, there's my girl. Are you having fun?"

"Yes, Father. So is Bailey."

"I see that. I'll take the dog for a minute, Claire. While Bailey is light as a feather, she can get to be an armful."

"She has been a good dog, John. People love her."

"Look, Father. Claire bought me popcorn."

"That was nice of you, Claire. We're done unloading. As soon as we have everything in place, we can head back home."

"I can't wait to tell Mother and Mummi about the people and the singing and the fun we had."

"Would you mind keeping Bailey for a minute, John? I want to go back for something. Would you like to come with me, Hannah?"

"Yes, I would!"

"You two go. I have helpers who can keep watch of Bailey."

Giving her dog a hug and telling her to be good, Hannah took hold of Claire's hand and off they went.

The depot was still busy. The local high school chorus was singing and Santa Claus had made his entrance so little kids were in line to see him. After Claire stopped at a few of the vendors, she led Hannah back to where the coffee mugs were on display.

"I want to buy your mother and Mummi a gift for being so kind to me today. I was thinking of the mug with a pink and a yellow flower on the front for your mother and another mug with different colored flowers for Mummi."

"While they both will tell you gifts are not necessary, I know they will love the mugs. It is very thoughtful of you, Claire."

"It is the least I can do."

After making a few more purchases, the two were back outside.

"I can imagine the stars above us, Claire. I am thankful the Lord gave me sight so I could see them twinkling when it is cold outside."

"There are zillions of them twinkling, Hannah. I am so happy you invited me along tonight."

As they approached the other building there seemed to be mass confusion of some sort. Claire pulled Hannah even closer while she tried figuring out what was going on. With Frank running from one vendor to another and Tommy looking under tables and John talking to people with his arms going in all directions, Claire had a sick feeling come over her. When John pointed to the door, he saw Claire standing there with Hannah. By the look on his face, Claire knew what had happened. As he approached them, Claire felt tears running down her cheeks. She couldn't stop them. John couldn't stop his either despite centuries of teachings concerning acceptance and the Lord's will. How much more could Hannah accept, Claire wondered? She'd lost her eyesight. Now she'd lost Bailey.

Taking his daughter's hand, John led Hannah out to the sleds. Holding her close under those twinkling stars he prayed for the Lord's strength both for Hannah and for himself. He didn't know where to begin. Before he could say anything, Hannah took over.

"I feel the same way as I did when I woke up to darkness in the hospital. What is wrong, Father? Where is Bailey? Whatever it is, I need to know. Bailey is more than just my eyes. She is my best friend. I tell Bailey everything. She protects me from the dark and when the darkness scares me, Bailey makes me feel safe. I feel empty, Father. I need to know what happened to my dog."

"The Lord has blessed you with wisdom, Hannah."

"What happened to Bailey, Father? Where is my dog? Please, Father. Tell me."

On that cold winter night John told Hannah what had happened to her dog. "I'd handed Bailey over to Frank while I moved some things around. Another vendor was attempting to move a load of crates nearby but they all came crashing down. That frightened Bailey. She jumped out of Frank's arms and disappeared into the crowd. Tommy and Frank are looking for her. They have policemen helping them as well as strangers who saw Bailey with you and Claire."

"What happens if Bailey is not found before we have to leave?"

"Tommy said he will keep looking and asking and searching. She can't be far away. She was scared. Once Bailey realizes you are not with her, she will come back looking for you."

"But what if she isn't found? Where will she go to stay warm? Who will feed her and take care of her and hold her and tickle her under her chin? Who will brush her hair and tell her stories and hug her while she falls asleep?"

"Let us pray, my dear Hannah. The Lord is watching over all His creatures."

And so they prayed as they sat in the back of a sled with horses hitched up eager to get going. When Tommy and Frank returned without Bailey, John made the decision to head home. "Your mother will be worried. Take my hand, my child. Let the Lord be our guide."

While Frank checked the horses, Tommy told John and Hannah he would search all night if he had to. " Leave your front door unlocked, John. I brought Bailey home to you once and I will do it again, Hannah."

"And I will be searching alongside Tommy," said Claire, unable to fight back the tears. "We will find your sweet Bailey."

"I know Mother will be worrying but I need to go around and call Bailey. Maybe if she hears my voice she will come out of hiding. Please, Father. I need to try. I will only take a few minutes. If I do not find her by then, we can go back home."

"I think that is a good idea, Hannah."

"Thank you, Father. I would like Claire to go with me."

"I am ready. Let's go." Taking Hannah's hand, they went back to the building where Bailey had disappeared. As Hannah went about calling Bailey in every nook and cranny, people would whisper encouragement to her. When Claire told her they'd covered every possible place Bailey could be, Hannah thanked everyone for caring about her dog.

"Bailey makes me smile even when I don't want to," she told those listening. "I will never forget your help."

The same scene played out in the depot. When it was apparent that Bailey wasn't there, Hannah asked Claire to take her back to the sleds. Again the young girl spoke to those supporting her. "The Lord gives me strength. Thank you for caring."

When Hannah walked out the door, almost everyone shed a tear.

Claire held Hannah's hand as the horses were checked one last time. That's when Frank came over to Hannah.

"I am sorry I did not hold on to Bailey. It happened so fast, Hannah."

"You are not to blame, Frank. When Bailey wants to get down, I can never stop her."

Once they were ready to go, John thanked Tommy and Claire for all they were doing.

"We do not know why at times. We only know He is our guiding light."

"Like I said before, John, we will be bringing Bailey home."

As the three sleds started down the one-way street with Hannah sitting up front next to her father, Claire took hold of Tommy. She needed support even if he was taken. None of that mattered now. They were on a mission to find a precious little dog with a ring around one eye the color of hay.

Chapter Fifteen

A CLOUD OF SADNESS DAMPENED WHAT had been a joyous celebration. But there was no time to waste. There was a dog to be found.

"What do we do first?"

"Let's start where it began, Claire. Maybe we'll find other places to check or talk to some people we missed."

With fewer people it was easier to see the more hidden areas although none held any clues. A thought that kept nagging Claire was what if someone carried Bailey off with them. She was such a gentle dog. It would be obvious to anyone that she was loved. But without a dog collar spelling out pertinent information, Bailey's chances of returning home were stacked against her.

"I bought us some coffee. We need some caffeine."

"I agree, Tommy. Thanks."

"I think we should move on to the depot. From there we'll have to play it by ear."

The station was a rush of senior citizens trying to make the last train of the evening to Santa's Village. With the stars out and the moon high above, it was the perfect setting for a train ride into the foothills in search of Santa Claus, no matter one's age.

"I can't believe the line. That Mr. Rossi of yours knew what he was doing."

"Marketing 101, Claire. Take what you have. Enhance it and they will come."

"Do we bother to ask the people in line about Bailey?"

"We ask anyone. People won't forget seeing a dog as cute as Bailey."

After speaking to stragglers hanging about the area, they turned to those waiting in line. Considering the majority were senior citizens, almost everyone had a story about a favorite pet but none had seen Bailey.

"Fifteen minutes before boarding," came over a loudspeaker.

An attendant dressed in a navy blue uniform with a badge pinned to his chest came into the station from a side door behind a roped-off area. After speaking to another attendant, he went back the way he came. Once the door shut, the line started moving. Boarding began. Time was running out. Claire found her heart racing when asking the few left in line. She felt desperate when no one offered a clue about Bailey. Taking her last swig of coffee, she waited for Tommy who was up at the window talking to the attendant, in a hurry to pull the shade and close down the ticket counter.

"Wait! Wait for us. We want to get on board that train."

Rule was if the shade was still up, tickets were still available.

Tommy stepped aside while the couple presented a credit card.

"No, wait! That's the wrong card. I'm sorry. We ran into one of your conductors carrying the most adorable dog. We were chatting with him until he noticed the time. He told us to hurry and we'd be able to get tickets. He himself rushed to get on board."

Claire hadn't heard the gentleman talking but Tommy did.

"Claire. Come on. We're going to Santa's Village. Hurry. I'll explain once we get on the train."

"I'm sorry, sir. The train is getting ready to leave."

"But you have to give us tickets. The shade is still up."

"Rules are rules, sir. This window is closed." With that statement, she pulled the shade down.

"Let me tell you about rules. A young girl lost her eyesight when she was four years old. Her dog is both her eyes and her best friend. And tonight she lost her dog and now I need to get on that train because I believe her dog is on board heading to see Santa Claus, and once it gets into that confusion that dog will be lost forever. Now back to rules—rules of life. Seems to me one rule should be that the young lady has gone through enough pain. Another rule is written in stone and that is Love Thy Neighbor. If that was your child wouldn't you try to move heaven and earth to find her dog?"

The attendant stood silent, watching the clock.

"This is my last attempt at being nice. If you don't process two tickets right now I'll jump over this counter and do it myself. That young girl is without her dog and we need to do something about that—no questions asked!"

You could have heard a pin drop as the attendant looked at Tommy, then told him her story. "I had a puppy. His name was Teddy, named after my favorite teddy bear that I lost in a house fire. One day when I was walking home from school I saw my puppy lying in the street. Someone ran over him and kept on going. So I understand about your rules, sir. I've lived your rules and rules of life can be unfair. But that won't happen here."

Pulling up the shade, the woman processed two tickets. Handing them to Tommy, she told him there was no charge.

"But you'd better run. That train is pulling out of the station."

As Claire and Tommy started through the door, the attendant yelled.

"Hey! Sir! About my puppy. He didn't die. He only broke a leg. Rule number three—don't assume the worst."

"Thanks! We won't. Sorry I came down so hard on you. Glad Teddy was okay."

"No problem! Go! Run like heck! You have a dog to find."

The two sprinted alongside the platform with steam filling the night from the vintage train slowly moving along. It was reminiscent of an old Hollywood movie where the hero runs to catch the train as his lover watches from inside, clutching hold of the windowsill with tears in her eyes. The only problem was they were both running. They both needed to take a flying leap of faith to get on the train and there were no lovers watching anywhere.

Chapter Sixteen

"ARE YOU OKAY?"

"I think so. Scraped my hand grabbing hold of the rail but I don't see any bleeding."

"How about you, Tommy?"

"Same thing. Must be a bad rail!"

Taking Claire's hand, Tommy led them through a door and into a coach car. All the seats were taken so he kept on going to the next car where he was able to find two empty seats side by side.

"What a night, Claire."

"What a day! If someone had told me I'd end up on a train going to see Santa Claus as a result of knocking at that front door I would have laughed in disbelief."

"Only goes to prove we never know what a day will bring. So now that we are on the train, we need a game plan."

"What if Bailey isn't on this train?"

"Then we go back and keep searching."

"Tickets, please."

A conductor standing in the aisle waited while Tommy took his time digging in his pocket. Tommy had hold of the tickets but pretended he didn't.

"I have them somewhere. We were so late getting tickets that I shoved them in one of my pockets and I can't remember which one."

"There are always a few late passengers."

"I bet you conductors are never late."

"Normally that's true except for today. I don't like being late for work. I never seem to catch up."

"I hear you. I'm the same way."

Tommy could tell the conductor was getting impatient so he handed over the tickets.

Once the tickets were punched, the conductor handed them back and went on to the next passenger. Tommy waited until he was further down the aisle.

"That's our guy, Claire."

"Just because he was late?"

"That and the fact he has a few of Bailey's hairs on his uniform."

"Are you sure?"

"Before bringing Bailey to Hannah, I kept her with me for a few weeks. My clothes had those hairs on them."

"So what do we do?"

"We make sure he doesn't get out of our sight once this train stops. Sit back and enjoy the ride. You're on your way to see Santa Claus."

There was something about riding along on a train that calmed Claire down. It had been a day full of emotions.

"If you feel like dozing, you can lean on me, Claire."

"I don't want to miss a thing. I love riding on a train."

"Are you hungry?"

"I can't believe it after that lovely meal Elizabeth served, but I am a little hungry. How about you?"

"Even though I had two slices of pie, I'm starving. Let's get something to eat. Just put your seat up so no one will take it."

The dining car was charming and busy. Tommy chose a small corner table for two as a waiter dressed in a starched white shirt with a pin-stripe tie and pants pulled out a chair for Claire.

"Thank you."

"My pleasure, Miss. My name is Robert. I will be your waiter on this magical evening as we make our way back to Santa's Village. May I get you something to drink?"

"I'd like a glass of Chardonnay."

"And I'd like a tall cold beer on tap, Robert."

Looking around, Tommy commented, "I can't imagine the money Rossi spent on refurbishing his train even though trains run in the family. This car alone with its glass-domed ceiling and side windows giving customers a panoramic view, with every little detail down to Robert's tie perfected, must have cost him."

The conversation was interrupted when Robert set their drinks down on the table.

"I will leave you menus."

Thanking Robert, Claire picked up the conversation.

"I think when you have money like that it's just money. There's no worry when you write a check or buy another toy or spend a bit of it on an old train. That's how he grew up. Money has always been at his fingertips. With that said, Mr. Rossi is to be commended for giving back."

"Pardon me. Did I hear my name?"

A gentleman with blue eyes and almost black hair with a bit of grey around his temples and a smile as warm as toast stood between Claire and Tommy. His leather jacket, his jeans and boots spoke of money. Claire had clients who dressed like that but none had his smile.

"Nicholas Rossi! What are you doing here?"

Tommy stood, extending his hand to the man under discussion.

"I think I told you, Tommy, how I like to take this train to Santa's Village. I'll work on business all the way up, stay on the train while it makes its stop and keep working. Then sit and enjoy the ride back. You have to remember I was brought up on trains. Sitting here is like sitting in my living room."

"I remember you telling me that when we met. This is my first time on your train. We were discussing how you nailed every detail."

Noticing Nicholas Rossi's curiosity about the woman at the table, Tommy introduced the two. Then he invited him to sit down.

"So you both noticed the details? That's good to hear. I can be quite particular. Details matter in business and in life. If I am trying to convey the experience of a vintage dining car I can't paint the walls orange or hang madras curtains. My goal when undertaking this project was to create an atmosphere that would stir the senses of anyone coming on board. Trains have never been about speed. Trains are all about romance. The world is in desperate need of romance. In most classic movies, even in some children's, trains play a role in the storyline."

"Your love for trains is obvious."

"Thank you, Claire. I became infatuated with trains the first time my father brought me along for a ride. I was seven years old. Trains create mystique. Trains can take readers and moviegoers to places only an imagination can. To create that atmosphere I felt it imperative to include a carved marble fireplace, terra cotta tiles on the floor, white walls, curved arches. It all matters. Each piece adds to the experience. The crowning glory came with the addition of a piano complete with elaborate Moroccan designs and the one hundred eight keys with matching stool."

"I get the sense every detail was thoroughly considered before becoming a part of the refurbishing since every detail adds to the mystique. It's evident the minute one steps on board."

"I appreciate your observation, Claire. I have stenciled brass lamps with matching candlesticks on order."

"Both will enhance what you already have in place."

"Excuse me, Mr. Rossi. I refreshed your drink."

"Thank you, Robert."

Picking up a tall glass of that cold beer, Nicholas Rossi explained. "I have a brewery in the Rockies. I'm watching how well this ale is received. Then I'll go from there."

"So this is your test market?"

"It is, Claire. Nothing scientific but if the waiters get feedback they pass it on, good or bad. Since people don't know the beer is connected to me, I feel any feedback is honest feedback."

"Being a part of your test market I can tell you this is one great glass of beer."

"Thanks, Tommy. I've been formulating it for quite some time."

"Hard work does pay off."

"It does, Claire. I get the feeling you're in marketing?"

"You could say that in a roundabout way. I'm a photographer. Many times I'm involved in my clients' marketing. But I also enjoy capturing the natural beauty of this area and that includes Amish homesteads. We are rich in simple beauty."

"I'm often asked why I come back here when I could be anywhere. Your description is my reason."

"I get that. I also get why you prefer people not knowing you produce the beer you serve on this train. I had a client who owned a chain of restaurants. He also raised horses. He tried very hard to keep the two separate in the public's mind so when I did photo shoots, the horses were never included. He had nothing to hide. He simply didn't want the appearance of being some rich man raising horses drowning out the fact he worked hard every day maintaining his restaurants."

"I feel the same way. In my situation, inheritance comes with both a responsibility and an ability to be humble and kind to others."

"You remind me of a young girl we know. While she lives a life of simplicity, she lives through humility and kindness to those around her."

"Would I know her? I've met so many people."

"I don't think so. Her name is Hannah. She's Amish and despite being blind, that girl generates kindness every moment of every day."

"Was she downtown earlier tonight?"

"Yes. She was riding on one of her father's sleds in the parade."

"I think I saw her waving. I was working upstairs but watched most of the goings-on."

"Claire and I were on the sled with Hannah."

"You two were on that sled? How did that happen?"

"We're friends of the family."

"That makes for a great story, Tommy. It's nice to see life coming back to the downtown. I feel having the Amish participate adds even more to that feeling of community. How does that young girl deal with being blind? It can't be easy."

"I found her a dog. While the dog was never trained to be a Seeing Eye dog there was something about her that grabbed my attention at the rescue center. She was smart and aware of her surroundings. I noticed how protective she was of the other dogs. When I introduced Hannah to the dog they bonded instantly. They were inseparable."

"Why do you talk in the past tense, Tommy?"

"In the confusion tonight, the dog was frightened and is now missing."

"Many have told me I should be a detective because I ask too many questions. But I'm curious. Why are you riding this train to Santa's Village when you could be out looking for the dog? I know it is none of my business but I repeat. I am curious."

"In a strange way it is your business, Mr. Rossi."

"Please, Claire. Call me Nick. Then tell my why a missing dog is my business."

"The missing dog's name is Bailey and Bailey is your business because Tommy and I have reason to believe one of your employees has Bailey on this train."

"Would anyone like to order? Would anyone like another drink?"

"Yes to the drinks, Robert. We'll order in a minute."

"Thank you, Mr. Rossi."

Pulling his chair closer Nick asked more questions. "There is a dog on this train? How could that be? Who has the dog and why? How did you trace the dog here?"

"You really would make a great detective," Tommy replied. Taking a drink, he answered every question. When he talked about the girl at the ticket counter Tommy made sure to speak positively about her. He had a feeling Nick would resort to some sort of disciplinary action if Tommy gave him negative feedback.

"So the girl was a big help. That's good to hear. I'll have to stop and thank her. I always tell employees that a happy customer is your best advertisement."

"That's so true. The restaurant owner I mentioned brought customer relations experts in to speak to his employees. The last I knew he hadn't received one complaint. In fact, it was the opposite. He heard from customers about issues but they'd been resolved successfully by employees."

"Smart man. Listen. Order whatever you like. Dinner is on me. I'm on my way to have a talk with my conductor. When I return, I hope to have news about Bailey."

After Robert had taken their order, Claire and Tommy sat back and enjoyed the view.

"Did you ever have a time when you felt the stars were in line?"

"I remember once when I wanted to be in a particular band. I'd played with them a few times but only when they needed a fill-in. Then just as I was thinking about hanging it up for a while, one of the band members moved away and they called me to replace him. That led to my getting my own band. Why do you ask?"

"We've talked about it before but listening to Nick Rossi I can't help but believe things are turning around for this area. It's exciting to watch it happen."

"I never doubted my gut feeling about that mercantile."

"And you've kept its history."

"The history of that place will draw people in. It's something to build on."

"I agree, Tommy. I think people are longing for a simpler time or at least a break from the world at their fingertips."

Robert arrived with their dinners.

"Everything looks delicious," Claire commented as bowls brimming over and dishes piping hot filled the table. The aromas of garlic and olive oil, heirloom tomatoes and thyme circled about as Robert left them to enjoy their meal.

With snowflakes falling, an older gentleman, dressed in a white wool tuxedo jacket with black pants and a black silk tie over a white dress shirt, pulled out the piano stool and sat down.

"Well, he isn't Humphrey Bogart but he's a close second."

"I think if Humphrey Bogart were still alive, Nick Rossi would pull strings to get him here, Tommy."

Adjusting the stool, the piano player put his fingers on some of those one hundred eight keys and filled that dining car with a medley of classic Christmas songs, songs everyone knew. That's why many sang along.

As they were finishing their dinners, Nick appeared at the door. He was holding Bailey.

Chapter Seventeen

IT WAS A SPRINT TO SEE who could reach Bailey first.

"Nick! She really was on the train!"

"Oh my! I can't believe it!" Claire was overwhelmed.

So was Bailey. As soon as she saw Tommy, her tail started going nonstop. When Tommy took her from Nick, Bailey began whining and licking a front paw.

"She seems to be favoring that paw. When she walks she hesitates. She walks with a limp. I couldn't find a bruise but it could be sprained."

"What matters is we have her back. Thanks, Nick. I'm sure Hannah's family will tend to Bailey once we get her home. Right, Bailey! You are going home!"

Despite her injury, Bailey wagged her tail and gave Tommy some licks in the face.

"You two are something," Nick laughed. "The train will soon be pulling into Santa's village. Come sit with me for a few minutes."

Even before they sat down, Robert was there. But no one was interested in a drink.

"Once the passengers are in the village could you bring me my usual in my quarters? I have some work to do tonight."

"Yes, Mr. Rossi." Nodding to Tommy and Claire, Robert went on his way.

With Bailey in his lap and Claire beside him, Tommy thanked Nick again for helping them find Bailey.

"It turns out my conductor was on his way to the train when Bailey came running by. She started to cross the street but a truck came barreling in front of her. Bailey ran back up on the sidewalk and the conductor grabbed hold of her."

"Why didn't he return Bailey?"

"He had no clue where to take her and the train was getting ready to pull out of the station. Bailey had no tags. He was afraid she'd get hit so he decided he would take Bailey with him."

"Didn't he think you or someone might ask questions?"

"He did, Claire, but he made the decision the dog's safety came first. He has a disabled son. I think he said the boy is eight years old. Anyway this boy has been asking for a dog and out of the blue, Bailey came running by. The conductor planned on telling his son how he'd found the dog and said he was going to make the appropriate calls tomorrow to see if anyone had made contact concerning a missing dog."

"So in the end, Nick, the conductor saved Bailey."

"That's the way I see it."

"I wish we could call Hannah. I can't imagine how she's feeling."

"You can use my phone, Tommy."

"I have a phone, Nick, but Hannah doesn't!"

It took a second for Nick to get what Tommy was saying.

"Oh, you're right! No electricity; no phones or computers. I can't grasp the concept."

"I was at Hannah's home all day and never missed my phone or laptop. I was unattached and loved every minute of it."

"You're stronger than I could ever be, Claire. I don't think I could survive one hour let alone a day unplugged. I've come to expect everything to be instantaneous. I have no patience for glitches in the system."

Nick changed the subject, revealing another side of him. "We have a young boy in need of a dog. As I explained, the boy is disabled. I'd like to give him the gift of unconditional love that a dog brings to the table. Could you use your sources and find me a dog like Bailey? I'd like to make that happen for the boy and for his father."

"I'll get that ball rolling tomorrow, Nick."

"Great. Thanks, Tommy. I'm planning on being around my apartment over the weekend if you need me. You also have my cell number. I don't care about the price. That young boy needs a dog."

"I understand, Nick."

"The boy will be told his dog is a gift from Santa Claus. If it happens after Christmas it will become a late gift. And speaking of Santa, we are approaching the village. Some passengers stay the night in the village lodge but I know you both are anxious to get Bailey home to Hannah. I suggest you wander about the village for forty-five minutes or so. Then get back on board. The train stays here a little over an hour before heading back to the station."

Nick had one more request.

"Claire. I would like to have dinner with you in the near future to discuss marketing strategies for this endeavor of mine. Please call me and we can make the arrangements."

"I will do that, Nick. I look forward to brainstorming with you."

After they exchanged business cards, Nick Rossi gave her a quick hug. "One more question. Have you plugged back into our world since leaving Hannah's?"

"Why do you ask?"

"I can't even imagine being disconnected for a minute. I'd be going through withdrawal."

"To tell you the truth, I hadn't even thought about plugging back in. But thanks for the reminder."

Holding on to Bailey a little tighter, Tommy followed Claire off the train.

"That was interesting. You have a date with Nicholas Rossi."

"It's not a date. It's business."

"He beat me. I was going to ask you to dinner."

"You're taken, Tommy."

"What do you mean?"

"I saw you with Denise earlier. That was Denise, right? On the sled with you?"

"Yes, that was Denise. She couldn't stay."

"That kiss you two shared looked pretty serious to me."

"It was a kiss, Claire. That's all it was—a kiss."

"So what we shared was just a kiss?"

Claire didn't mean to get into Denise or that kiss or any kiss. But when Tommy said he was going to ask her out to dinner, she couldn't stop herself.

"You're taking all of this the wrong way."

"We hardly know each other, Tommy. You and Denise are none of my business so let's concentrate on getting Bailey home to Hannah."

The line into Santa's house was long. The two stood there like parents, making sure Bailey was a good girl. What was more amazing than standing in line with a dog was the absence of children in that line to see Santa. And while they were all senior citizens, they all still had that look of wonder in their eyes. The longer the two waited, the more they forgot their petty tiff.

"Look around, Tommy. Age doesn't matter when it comes to believing in Santa Claus. Sometimes your belief is even more amazing when you are an adult."

"How so, Claire?"

"When you are an adult you know Santa is a fantasy yet you still believe. That belief is deeper. It's about family and traditions and goodwill toward others like the young boy Nick is hoping to help. The second time you believe is about believing in mankind."

"I've never thought of believing in terms you call the second time but you're right. My father was such a believer. Like Nick, he was about the details. It was never my mother who made Christmas magical. It was my father. He loved every part of Christmas. When my brother and I no longer believed in Santa Claus, my father's belief turned into the carrying on of traditions. He would link stories about his family to the china dishes put on the table Christmas day. A serving dish became a serving dish that once belonged to an aunt or a grandmother and he'd tell their stories. There's so much more my father did that stays with me today. I still have a hard time listening to 'Silent Night.' That was his favorite song and not just at Christmas time."

The line was moving a little faster as Claire found herself telling

Tommy about her second grade Christmas program. "And to this day I've yet to sing that song."

"That's understandable. Your story is heartbreaking as was your story about the purple tutu."

"Well, one good thing came from that, Tommy. I've never worn another purple tutu!"

"If you ever do, I'd like to see it."

"Don't hold your breath."

They could see Santa now. He looked pretty genuine. An elf and a photographer were standing next to him. The elf gave each visitor a candy cane. The photographer took pictures of each of the guests who sat on Santa's knee. There was lots of laughter in Santa's house.

"Bailey is being such a good dog. Do you want me to take her for a minute?"

"She's content at the moment. With that hurt paw, I don't want to upset her by moving her."

"Let me know when you need a break Tommy. You know, I've been thinking, and if this is another topic that is not my business please tell me and I'll stop. But from what you've told me about your father, it's obvious he was there for you. So what would he say if he knew you'd quit the band and the guitar because of him? If anything, it seems to me your father would want you to keep playing more than ever. Music is a language that creates memories. God gave you that gift of music. His gifts are meant to be shared. And think about this. Your father will hear you all the way to Heaven."

With Bailey in one arm, Tommy reached for Claire with the other; holding her close. "I never thought of it that way. Thank you. You're right again, Claire. My father would want me to keep on playing. My father was my biggest fan. He loved music. He too was in a band but gave it up after getting married. We'd drive my mother nuts when the dinner conversation was all about music."

"The guilt you've been carrying is unwarranted. You've been wasting your talent."

"I understand that now, thanks to you. Time to unpack my guitar!"

After they visited with Santa Claus and after Claire held Bailey while sitting on Santa's lap, they took a quick walk around the village, going through the stable and the toy factory and the shops. It was in one of those shops that Tommy bought Bailey a real collar with a leash. The last stop they made was the bakery. Claire had to pull Tommy away to get back to the train on time.

It was a quiet ride to the depot. Claire fell asleep with her head on Tommy's shoulder while Bailey fell asleep in his lap.

Chapter Eighteen

LOOKING AT HIS WATCH, TOMMY WAS surprised it was only a little after ten. Finding his keys, he opened a side door leading to the front of the mercantile where shops were sitting in a row.

"We'll save the tour for next time. The ladies' room is ahead on the left. I'll meet you back here."

"My first impression of this magnificent building is that of an old-fashioned Christmas. I'll see you in a minute, Tommy."

When Claire returned Tommy wasn't there. The sound of boxes being moved led her to an area under construction. Even though it wasn't quite finished, it was obvious this would be his bakery.

"I hadn't planned on coming in here but I remembered I'd had a late shipment of cookware to move out of the way until I decide where to put the stuff."

"So this will be your bakery?"

"Yes. Finally I get to be the baker instead of the electrician. Most of the time anyway."

"I can't wait to see it come together."

"We're almost there."

"I love what you've done so far. The stained glass in the top of the windows is outstanding."

"I was lucky to find a local artist who captured the moods of our area. Everything from the Amish to the mountains and farmland is included. As I said before, John made the display cases for the baked goods. He thought the oak would blend the best with the stained glass. The fans on the ceiling were John's idea. He said it'd give the place an old-fashioned bakery sort of feel. John surprised me when he said that. But after I thought about it, the man reads all the time."

"Are these old record albums in this box?"

"Yes. They were my father's. I've installed a sound system in here. I plan to play the oldies in the background. The soft stuff only. When I'm in here baking early in the morning or late at night is when I'll play the hard rock."

"What a collection. This is worth a lot of money, Tommy."

"I've had offers but I'll never sell a one of them. I told you before how my father loved music. Some of the albums were signed by the artists."

"While your father never had his band, I think it is fair to say he shared in so many others including yours."

"That's the truth. He saw many of them in person. He knew all their names, their hits, and the words to those hits. It was because of my father that I picked up the guitar."

"Between the music and your baked goods, this bakery is going to be one popular destination."

"I hope so, Claire."

"I'll help you all I can."

"Thanks. The closer the opening gets the more I realize I will be living in here trying to get it finished on time as well as getting the goods baked and in the cases."

"If I end up renting space I'll be on hand to assist you whenever I'm needed. I realize you have more than this bakery on your shoulders."

"I'm hoping to entice you with a space you can't refuse. I do appreciate your offer. Denise was going to take some time off to come and help but I guess that didn't work out. Anyway, let's get going. We have a young girl waiting for us."

Picking Bailey up, they headed down the main corridor as Tommy pushed the button on his remote starter.

"I'm spoiled. I like to have my truck good and warm before I get in it."

104

"And I thought you were doing that for me."

"Well, I was. I did it for the three of us. Right, my silly little dog?"

Shaking her head, Bailey snuggled back to sleep.

It wasn't long before they were on the road. The main highway was clear. The stars were still shining.

"Do you think Hannah will be sleeping?"

"Except for the two youngest, I doubt if anyone is sleeping. I told John we would bring Bailey home tonight and that is what we're doing."

Even in the dark, even when the road narrowed, Claire could make out Emma's farm and the skating rink and the turn in the road where she had met the Bishop. Once past that turn, Claire knew they didn't have far to go.

"My stomach is flipping. I'm so excited!"

"I know what you mean, Claire. It's the same feeling when you were a kid coming down the stairs on Christmas morning."

Turning into the narrow pathway that led to that clapboard home with the wreaths still on display, Tommy parked next to Claire's car. As soon as he turned the engine off, the front door opened. Hannah was peeking out. Although she couldn't see, her heart knew her dog was back home.

"Wait for me, Hannah. Do you have your boots on?"

"Yes, Father. I've had my boots on all night long."

While the rest of the family watched through the windows, John took his daughter's hand and led her down the steps as Tommy walked toward them holding Bailey. If ever a reunion earned an Oscar, this was it, even though no one was acting. Reactions were real. Tears were heartfelt and words were useless. That little dog knew. That little dog, despite a hurt paw, started squirming and crying. With her nose to the wind, taking in the smells of the fields and corn shocks and horses bedded down in hay and reindeer on alert, Bailey twisted herself up in such a knot that Tommy knelt down and let her go.

"She's running to you. Bailey is back home with a hurt paw, Hannah."

Understanding what Tommy was saying, Hannah bent down just as that furry little bundle of love jumped into her arms. Despite her injury, Bailey jumped so hard and so high that the two of them went roll-ing over in the snow. Between Hannah's laughter and tears and Bailey's barking and whining and licking her paw and then Hannah's face and hands, they stayed there in the snow, reunited under the moon, as those watching inside and out couldn't stop the tears. Despite that paw, it was a joyous reunion.

The joy continued inside that simple home after Hannah went up-stairs and changed her clothes and Bailey was dried off and resting on the old pillow by the woodstove. Mary was wide awake but content and the lamb peeking at Bailey seemed pleased that her friend was right where she usually was every evening until Hannah went upstairs to bed. Catherine warmed a small blanket and wrapped it loosely around Bai-ley's paw.

"I have water on for tea," said Elizabeth. "Would you be able to stay for a few minutes? I know it is late so if you have to get going we will understand. You have already blessed us with the return of Bailey. We thank the Lord for your friendship."

Both Tommy and Claire wanted to stay. They were anxious to tell Hannah about Bailey and the conductor who saved her.

Catherine set a plate of cookies on the table. "These are some of the cookies you helped me bake, Claire. See the edges? Perfect. I can't think of a better time to serve them than right now."

"The cookies look delicious and those edges are splendid! I agree this is the time to serve them, Catherine."

"Would you like some help, Elizabeth?"

"If you could carry this tray of cups and saucers I can bring in the rest, Claire."

It wasn't long before they were gathered around the table. Frank and Faith sat on either side of Hannah. They were excited to be a part of the celebration. Elizabeth surprised each of them with a mug full of freshly made snow cream. Once everyone had their cup of tea the way they liked it, Tommy began the story.

"We were lucky. We were in the right place at the right time; run-ning to catch the train to Santa's Village after overhearing a conversation of someone who'd seen the conductor getting on board carrying what that person described as an 'adorable dog.' It made no sense to me why a conductor would bring a dog aboard a train but from the simple description of that dog, my gut told me it was Bailey. We didn't have time to waste. The train was ready to depart. Once on board it all came together. I'd met the owner of the train before. Lucky for us he was on board. After hearing our story he spoke with the conductor and minutes later we were holding Bailey."

"Why did the conductor take Bailey?"

"The conductor didn't take Bailey. He saved her, Frank."

After explaining what he meant, Tommy jumped up. "I have to run out to my truck. Claire, if you give me your keys I'll start your car."

"I've been here so long I thought I lost them," Claire laughed after finding them in her pocket. "Thanks, Tommy."

While waiting for his return, Hannah got up and went over to Bailey.

"I am so happy you are home. I could have lost you forever. Your paw will feel better soon."

Coming back inside, Tommy overheard Hannah. Once they were both sitting at the table, Tommy handed her a bag.

"This is for you and for Bailey so you'll never lose her again."

When Hannah pulled out the leash and collar, she jumped up and showed everyone. Going over to Tommy, she gave him a hug. "Thank you, Tommy!"

Then she spoke to everyone gathered around that table in the clapboard home.

"I sat in Mother's rocking chair waiting for Bailey. When I was afraid I'd never see Bailey again I picked up lamb and rocked her, praying to the Lord to keep Bailey safe. And He did. Thank you both for finding my dog."

"It was your prayers and the prayers of all of you that brought Bailey home. Tommy and I felt you with us every step of the way."

Reaching in her coat pocket, Claire pulled out an envelope and handed it to John. When he saw the photo of Bailey sitting on Santa's knee he started laughing. Everyone did once John passed it around the table.

"I know Santa Claus isn't a part of your Christmas but I thought I'd share part of Bailey's adventure with you."

"Thank you, Claire," John replied. "While we do not include Santa Claus in our Christmas traditions it doesn't mean Bailey can't! She looks happy in Santa's lap."

Realizing the time, Tommy and Claire started saying their goodbyes.

"I made you both something tonight. Please wait."

Going into the kitchen, Hannah returned holding two small gifts wrapped in tissue paper. She put them on the table. "They are both the same."

Tommy and Claire were delighted to find their own string of paper angels. Each angel was made of white construction paper with wings covered in glitter and gold. Glittery stars were strung in between each one.

"I will treasure my string of angels forever, Hannah. Your work is beautiful. Thank you so much."

Tommy repeated Claire's sentiments, adding, "You could not have given me a more thoughtful gift, Hannah. I will keep this string of angels up all year long. But you will always be my favorite angel."

With coats zipped and goodbyes said, Tommy opened the door.

"Oh wait! Please! One more thing," said Hannah, standing between them. "Would you both be able to come to our Christmas program tomorrow afternoon? You can stop here by one o'clock; then follow my parents to the school. I think you would enjoy yourselves. The only thing is I think Bailey should stay home with her hurt paw. She won't be a reindeer in the program."

"I would love to go to your program. I think it's a good idea to keep Bailey home. I remember the Bishop saying he will be there."

"Yes, and so will Emma!"

"Count me in as well, young lady. Now get some sleep. We will see all of you tomorrow."

"Thank you, Tommy. Thank you, Claire!" The cheers continued as Tommy shut the door. Holding on to Claire's hand, they walked down the steps. Snow crunching at their every step was proof of the cold surrounding them. Billowing smoke from the chimney floated out of view as a train heading north moaned and groaned along the tracks.

"I remember thinking this morning when I turned my car off that I wouldn't be staying long. I wasn't even sure I'd get through the front door. It ends up I might as well have moved in!"

"That's because they welcomed you with their hearts and arms wide open."

"They did indeed, and so did you, Tommy."

"If only for a moment."

"Sometimes that's all we have." Lingering, as a lone owl could be heard in the woods where pine and birch bark stood covered in white, Claire kept speaking in that hushed tone she'd used earlier when they slipped on the ice. "I feel as if I'm on a movie set. That family—that beautiful family where love is in every corner of their home; where cookies are mastered and a lamb sleeps beside a…"

Tommy's cell phone interrupted yet another moment. He hesitated.

"Answer your phone, Tommy."

As the wind shifted he reached inside his coat pocket. From the tone of his voice, Claire could tell it was Denise. Tommy tried explaining to her where he was. He tried getting off the phone but wasn't successful despite telling her he'd be there shortly. Claire decided it was time to go. Heading to her car, Tommy followed, motioning he'd be off the phone in a few minutes; motioning for her to stay.

"I can't, Tommy. It's late. I can't. I just can't. See you tomorrow."

Driving down the pathway buried in snow, Claire hesitated to search for her phone. Once she had it back on she made the turn onto the snowy country road and headed home. About fifteen seconds later her phone rang. Claire almost didn't answer it. She didn't want to hear any more about Denise but curiosity got the best of her.

"Tommy?"

"No, Claire. It's Nick."

Pausing to get her thoughts together, Claire replied. "Oh, hi, Nick. I left Tommy minutes ago and thought maybe he forgot to tell me something."

"I won't keep you, Claire. I wanted to tell you how much I enjoyed your company tonight."

"It was quite the evening, Nick. Hannah was so happy to have Bailey back home. Her family was overjoyed. Thanks for making that happen."

"I'm glad it all turned out. That young girl has suffered enough."

They only spoke for a few minutes. After Nick said he'd call to confirm their dinner date, they said good night.

Once Claire was home, it didn't take long before she was changed and in bed. Her head was spinning. So much had happened since morning. With the light off, Claire pulled the blankets up around her as she imagined the soft strumming of a guitar whispering through the trees, while the moon spread its magic on a string of beautiful angels glittering in the window.

Chapter Nineteen

THE WEATHERMAN PREDICTED SNOW THROUGHOUT THE weekend as Claire poured her second cup of coffee and toasted a few slices of bread. She'd never admit it but she loved toast as much as her father did. Whenever he bothered with breakfast it was always three slices of toast heavily buttered with strawberry jam on top. While Claire didn't go overboard with the butter, she did with the jam. Then she'd slice it diagonally just like her father.

Checking her emails, Claire wondered what was going on at John and Elizabeth's. The children were most likely getting ready for their walk to school. Hannah told her they had more decorating to do so they'd be getting there earlier than usual. Claire was looking forward to attending the Christmas program. While she'd ridden by quite a few Amish schoolhouses and taken photos from afar, she'd never been inside one. And then there was Tommy. He'd be at the school. Claire wondered if he'd be coming alone.

While she was upstairs getting ready, her phone rang. "Good morning, Tommy," she replied, searching her closet for something warm to wear. When Tommy asked if she'd like him to pick her up, Claire's question if Denise would be accompanying him was answered.

"That would be great. Yes. That's the address. It's the Cape Cod at the end of the street. On the left with cranberry shutters. See you soon."

Claire went back to her closet. This time she put more thought into what she was going to wear and more time putting her make-up on. She didn't want to look like Denise with the real heavy eye stuff but she did add a little extra shadow and liner. She hadn't done that for quite some time. Instead of pulling her hair back in a ponytail she dried and styled it.

After picking up the kitchen, Claire went into her studio. It was a good feeling to be surrounded by her work. With time to spare, she began working on an order that had to be shipped out on Monday. When a knock at the door interrupted her, Claire was surprised at how much time had passed. Giving her hair a little toss with her fingers, Claire opened the door.

"Hi, Tommy. Please come in."

"What a lovely home, Claire."

"Thanks. I like it. But as I told you, I need to get my photos in a separate location."

"I can't imagine running a bakery in my home."

Noticing Tommy staring at her, Claire asked if there was something wrong.

"Just the opposite Claire. You look stunning this morning. I've had three cups of coffee and I'm still dragging."

"Well, thank you. Believe me, once you're surrounded by children you'll get some energy."

"I'm looking forward to going to the school."

"I am too. I've always wanted to get inside an Amish school but I'm more excited to be supporting the Miller children."

"I know what you mean. Before we go, I'd love to see some of your work."

"My studio is a bit of a mess. I've been getting some orders ready."

"Believe me, I understand mess."

Snow crystals blown off limbs of maple trees sparkled as they drifted by bay windows, enhancing winter photo scenes displayed against the back wall. Those scenes, along with Amish farms and Amish stands and Amish schools and old buildings and old barns and fence lines and leaves turning and gardens rich with produce, left Tommy mesmerized. Going from one to another, it was obvious her work grabbed his attention.

"It's not only the quality that is spellbinding. It's the story in each shot that comes jumping out at me."

"I've always wanted my photos to do more than hang on walls."

"I can see them in the mercantile, Claire. They'll fit in to the feel and history of that building."

"I think so too. I have one photo in particular that I'd like to show you."

Claire went searching through a bin of odds and ends of unframed photos. When she found that particular one, Claire held it up to the light so Tommy could get a better look.

"I took this during a snowstorm a few years after moving here. What caught my eye was the street light almost covered in snow yet any light escaping the snow hit your building, creating an eerie feeling as the building was empty and in need of repair at that time. With fallen bricks in the alley and a number of broken windows, it was beautiful as well in a strange sort of way. All that could be heard was the wind howling, circling the old building in disrepair. Still, there it was, standing tall and proud on that corner where it had stood for generations."

Tommy stared at the black and white photo as he spoke. "You see objects in a way others can't. While I agree this photo is haunting, I see hope as well. If this photo is for sale, I would like to buy it and put it on display in the bakery."

"I would like to give you the photo, Tommy."

"How thoughtful, Claire. Thank you."

"I'll keep it here until your opening. That will give me time to frame it."

"I will treasure it."

Realizing they should get going, Tommy took one last look at the photo. Then they were on their way.

"It's a perfect day for a Christmas program. I heard we're due a foot or two of snow later."

"I'm old-fashioned when it comes to winter," Claire replied. "I enjoy the snow. I don't mind the shoveling but when it gets way below zero, I become a hermit."

"Well, there's no chance of you being a hermit today. We are going back to school!"

The conversation made the drive a quick one. Pulling into Hannah's, Tommy noticed tracks in the snow coming from the barn.

"It looks like a buggy's already on the road."

Once inside, Elizabeth told them Frank and Hannah had been running late so John allowed them to take a buggy to school. "Frank is skilled in handling the horse and buggy. They looked happy waving goodbye with the lamb wrapped up between them. Bailey stayed home today. She is sleeping on Hannah's bed."

"Well, it was because of Hannah and that reindeer that they were late," piped up Catherine, rocking the baby.

"Reindeer?"

"Yes, Tommy. Reindeer! Most every morning that girl is out in the barn spending time with a reindeer she calls Ginger. I heard her tell John it's her favorite reindeer."

"I bet I know which reindeer it is. He's one of the bigger ones yet his eyes are gentle with long lashes. I sometimes think that reindeer is smiling at me."

"That's what Hannah told me about the reindeer's eyes, Tommy. You should see them together. The reindeer follows her around. They play in the snow. When Bailey joins in, they play even harder despite the reindeer being quite hefty."

"I'll have to ask Hannah about her reindeer," Tommy replied, giving Catherine a morning hug. "How is little Mary today?"

"This sweet baby has a cold. She must have gotten it from Faith who stayed home and is taking a nap. So I am staying with the children while Elizabeth and John go to the program. That's no place for a sick baby or a young one who doesn't like to sit still long."

"Are you sure, Mummi? You'll have your hands full."

"Mary is a good baby. You just fed her so once I put her down, she'll sleep for quite a while and then Abraham and I can have fun together.

When Faith wakes up I'll try giving her some soup. This old woman can handle the children."

"That is the truth, Catherine," laughed John, coming through the door. "Elizabeth and I will miss your help when you go back home."

"I won't be far away. Now get going. That program will be starting soon."

"Walking up from the barn I had an idea, Tommy."

"You are a man of ideas. I have a feeling this latest idea involves me."

"You are right. And it also involves Claire."

"Now I'm really curious."

"So am I," added Claire.

"I was thinking it might be fun if you two ride with us in the buggy. I have many wool blankets that will keep you warm. You'll be sitting in the back so if it snows you'll never feel it. We have warm mittens and hats and scarves. And the school is not that far away."

Claire didn't hesitate to accept John's invitation. Just as she'd always wanted to get inside an Amish school, Claire always wanted to ride in an Amish buggy.

"Count me in," added Tommy. "I don't want to miss the fun!"

While John gathered more blankets, Elizabeth went for extra mittens and scarves. They were soon on their way.

"I thought I was good at noticing surroundings when I'm in the car but sitting in this buggy I see things I've missed and I've been this way many times."

"I see what surrounds me differently every day, Claire. While I go by the same places, I am able to see the changes."

John slowed the pace as they passed old farms and barns aged by the weather. Rusted machinery left in fields was covered in snow, as were worn milk cans stacked by the side of the road. As they went along, John told stories of the places they were going by. Some farms had been in families for generations while some had been vacant for years.

"That place there," John pointed. "That place has the biggest cornfield I've ever seen. We built that third barn in the back last year."

"I've ridden by some barn raisings. I've even stopped to take photos."

"People stop all the time and most take photos, Claire."

"I keep my distance, John."

"We appreciate your understanding. A barn raising is a family event," Elizabeth explained. "The children play and we women sit and quilt once the meal has been served."

"You must enjoy those times, Elizabeth."

"There is an Amish proverb that says kindness when given away keeps coming back. That is the Lord's way, Claire."

"Those words speak truth."

"That's Emma's up ahead," John pointed. "The school is not far down the second right turn past her house. Is everyone warm?"

"I could use a cup of coffee."

"You drink too much coffee, Tommy."

"As I always tell you my friend, one can never drink enough of the stuff."

"I have a question, John. Ever since I started driving the backroads I keep finding new ones. How do you know where you're going sometimes?"

"We are taught early, Claire. Backroads can save time. And with less traffic, there's less chance of an accident happening."

"I imagine them to be like a spider's web: one thin road leading to another."

"That is true. When I was courting Elizabeth we learned most every road around."

"I didn't know you were a romantic, John."

"I'm quite the romantic, Tommy. Some of those roads get hardly any traffic."

"Oh Johnny, stop," smiled Elizabeth.

The field surrounding the school looked like a parking lot for horses and buggies. Waiting while John maneuvered his way around, Claire took a closer look at the one-room school with a bell sitting atop the roof and two outhouses sitting near a fence line. Sleds could be seen out in a field where all sizes of snowmen stood. Paper angels and hearts in the small windowpanes overshadowed the building's need to be painted. The worn clapboards seemed not to matter. Crayons, construction paper, and anticipation of Christmas had taken over.

"You three get inside. I'll be in shortly."

Elizabeth led the way. As she opened the door, a young boy dressed in a white shirt with a black bow tie and black pants with suspenders welcomed them. All the young boys were dressed the same. Realizing no photos would be allowed, Claire used her eyes as her lens, noting the chalkboards with the alphabet written in cursive on pieces of paper taped above them. In front of the chalkboards was the teacher's desk with a world globe and a glass full of pencils and pens. Rows of student desks reminded Claire of a remark Catherine had made concerning Hannah dealing with school.

"She knows the desks are arranged by grade. Hannah's fingers do the counting, keeping her aware of where she is when coming and going in the rows. Having the boys on one side and the girls on the other helps her as well. And of course she has Bailey."

Shelves full of books as well as cabinets with glass doors full of books caught Claire's attention as she heard someone calling her name.

Turning, she was happy to see Frank along with Hannah coming to greet her. She gave them a hug. They felt like family.

"We have to go get ready. Miss Fisher said the program will begin soon."

"I can't wait to hear you sing, Hannah. Don't be nervous. You will be fine."

"Thank you, Claire. Emma told me that too."

"Go get 'em, Hannah. I've heard you singing in the barn. You have a beautiful voice."

"Thanks, Tommy. I've heard you singing out there too. You are a very good singer."

Frank and Hannah joined their classmates. When the Bishop was seated, the annual Christmas program began in that simple Amish schoolhouse with paper angels and hearts decorating small windowpanes.

Chapter Twenty

A HUSH BLANKETED THAT SCHOOL WHEN all the students came together in front of those gathered. Claire wished she was able to take their photo. With not a hair out of place on any one of them and their clothes ironed and smiles genuine, seeing them with their hands to their sides would give inspiration to anyone anywhere. It wasn't the thoughts of gifts or Santa Claus that had those children smiling. Rather what had them on pins and needles was presenting a program to their families and community that they'd worked on so long and so hard.

Something Catherine had said as they cut out cookies came to mind when talking about the amount of time spent in preparing for today. "They not only learn the words to songs and poems. Teaching children to learn words or how to count is fine but teaching them what matters is even better."

The worth of what Catherine had said was evident in the eyes of the children ready to share the spirit of the season with those present. With rosy cheeks and green eyes the shade of pine boughs on display, one little girl stepped forward. Holding her head high and keeping her hands to her sides, her voice could be heard throughout that schoolhouse.

"My name is Miriam. I am in the second grade. Welcome to our annual Christmas program. We thank everyone for coming. To Bishop Yoder we thank you for your blessings and prayers. To Miss Fisher thank you for being our teacher."

After reciting a short poem, Miriam stepped back and the singing of traditional Christmas carols began. All the students joined in. As "Joy to the World" ended, Frank moved forward holding the lamb while his classmates sang "Oh Little Town of Bethlehem." The little lamb never budged.

Next came Hannah and Emma, holding hands while singing "Jingle Bells." It was obvious they loved the song. Their smiles were contagious. A few skits and more poems followed. Then there was a lull in the program.

"I see our Hannah talking to her teacher. She must be getting ready to sing her solo," Elizabeth explained.

Before Hannah sang, the Bishop stood to extend his blessings and to thank the students and Miss Fisher for all their hard work.

"As this beautiful Christmas program comes to an end, I ask you to listen to the words of this last song, which will be sung by Hannah Miller. This song represents the meaning of this most holy season. I pray that you have a blessed Christmas. And now, I introduce to you Hannah singing 'Silent Night.'"

Claire had no idea Hannah was singing that song. Tommy understood Claire's reaction. He took her hand as Hannah stepped forward holding a candle. With the wind moving about the window panes and the aromas of pine with baked goods coming from a nearby table, Hannah's voice flowed like a ribbon in the air. The power and emotion in her voice made Claire think of something Nick Rossi said about the importance of details. Hannah had nailed the details. When she came to the end of the first stanza, she was joined by Frank, his lamb, and the Wyse triplets. Then Hannah stepped forward and made an announcement.

"I would like to introduce a very special person. She stopped at our home yesterday to ask about my mother's wreaths and we became friends. My great-grandmother often tells me the real secret of happiness is not what you give or what you receive. It's what you share that matters. I would like to share this moment with my friend Claire as I invite her to join me in the singing of the last two stanzas of 'Silent Night.'"

With that, Hannah spread her arms wide open. The children holding candles began humming "Silent Night." The audience joined in.

"It's time to sing that song, Claire," spoke Tommy.

Squeezing Tommy's hand a little tighter, Claire stood and walked toward the children, their candles lighting her way. With each step she felt a little stronger. As she joined the others Miriam handed Claire a candle. Holding on to that candle, Claire addressed the audience.

"I would like to thank Hannah for sharing this moment with me. I am honored to be your guest. I wish everyone a blessed Christmas. I would like to dedicate this song to my father."

The only music playing was the cry from a young child, and the wind still whispering, and the shifting of horses getting restless outside, all blending together in this one-room schoolhouse sitting on a country road far from any metropolis. Remembering to hold her head high and look beyond the audience, Claire sang words she'd kept locked away. As snowflakes swirled past the small windowpanes, Claire didn't notice she was the only one singing. Feeling this was Claire's long-awaited moment, Hannah had stepped back. As Claire held the final note, the audience responded to her angelic voice. Overwhelmed, Claire took a minute to respond.

"Thank you. I will never be able to express how you have made me feel. May your Christmas be blessed with love and family. And to Hannah, your graciousness will never be forgotten." Embracing the young girl, Claire walked back to her seat.

"You were meant to sing that song, Claire. You had everyone spellbound including me."

"That's kind of you, Tommy. I had doubts if I'd get through it but I think the setting and the people put me at ease."

"You have a beautiful voice, Claire. The Lord meant for it to be heard."

"Thank you, Elizabeth. I will forever be grateful to Hannah for inviting me to join her."

John interrupted. "I too feel you have a beautiful voice, Claire. I only wish we had more time with you but with Catherine at home caring for the three younger ones, I feel we should be getting home. Hannah and

Frank will be leaving after refreshments. You and Tommy can ride back with them if you'd like to stay a little longer."

"I have work to do at the mercantile, but stay if you prefer, Claire. You're a star!"

"Not quite, Tommy!"

The thought of spending a little more time with Hannah seemed to be the right thing to do. Not only would it be the right thing to do, it would be fun. Besides, she'd overheard Tommy talking to Denise about making plans for the weekend. "I think I'll wait for Frank and Hannah."

After goodbyes were repeated, John opened the door and noticed it was snowing a little harder. He turned to Frank with more advice. "I want you to head home soon. It is snowing. Take your time. Make sure your lanterns are on and stay as far off the road as possible. We will be bringing the lamb home with us."

"Yes, Father. We will leave shortly."

Chapter Twenty-One

Frank went outside to check the weather. Though only nine, Frank was skilled when it came to driving a buggy. Most of his friends were as well since there were chores that had to be done whatever the time of year, no matter the weather or age of the driver.

Watching a snowfall turn into a blizzard in seconds, covering everything with a heavy wet blanket as the wind picked up, Frank knew they had to get going. He was aware it could get worse. He'd seen it happen before. Alerting Claire and Hannah to be ready to go, Frank made sure the lanterns were on and he had enough blankets to go around. After hitching up the horse and double-checking to be certain all was secure, Frank went back inside the school.

"We should be going, Hannah. The buggy is right outside the door."

Saying goodbye, Hannah fastened her cloak while Claire thanked everyone for their generosity. Taking hold of Hannah, Frank led them outside.

"It feels like the snow is really falling. Good thing we don't have far to go."

"Yes, that is a good thing, Hannah."

"Claire, you can sit in the back. You will be more protected."

"Oh no, Hannah. You sit in the back."

"I'm used to storms getting in my face. You are a guest and we are happy you are riding home with us."

Covering up in blankets, Claire settled in for the short ride back to the Miller farm. As the schoolhouse disappeared in the snow, Claire welcomed some quiet time. So much had happened in two days. It seemed like a year.

"Are you warm enough, Claire?"

"Don't worry about me, Frank. I'm warm as toast."

The two up front talked about the program as they headed to the main road. Once on that road they'd be able to get their bearings. But the weather was worsening. Frank could hardly see where he was going. Hitting a few drifts on the road, the buggy shifted to one side and then back again.

"Hold on, Hannah. We'll be okay. There's some snow on the road. Father taught me how to get through it."

"I wish I could help you, Frank."

"You are helping me by being by my side."

As the two discussed Catherine moving back home and Faith being sick and ideas of what to make their parents for Christmas, Claire listened, struck by the tenderness between them. She noticed Frank being the eyes for Hannah. Like a director on a movie set, he'd describe what he was seeing down to every little detail. This put Hannah at ease, especially out in a storm in the dark. But then, Hannah lived in darkness. The longer they talked the more Claire wished she had a real connection with her siblings. After so many years apart she wondered what their lives were like beyond what they wrote in a rare email or a card on her birthday. They never got below the surface. Everything was just fine.

When the buggy went through a few larger drifts, Claire almost got thrown from her seat. This caused Frank to turn around and check on her. As he did, Frank felt the buggy swerve. Holding on to the reins, he noticed what looked like headlights approaching. He couldn't imagine who'd be out on such a night. While Frank was able to steady the wheels, that swerve had alarmed the horse. Frank gripped the reins even tighter.

"Hold on, Hannah. Someone is coming the other way. I'm slowing the horse down while it passes."

Frank moved the buggy as far to the right as he could while keeping a tight grip on the reins. But there wasn't much room to pull over because of rocks scattered here and there. Frank didn't want to alarm anyone but they both could sense the danger.

"I am praying, Frank."

The prayers worked. Frank was certain he'd felt that pickup skim the sleeve of his coat as it roared past and disappeared into the curtain of white. While Frank put on a pretense that he hadn't been alarmed, Hannah could tell by the tone of his voice how alarmed he'd been. But she kept that to herself.

"Father would be proud of how you handled the horse and buggy, Frank. You kept us safe. You are a good driver."

"Thank you, Hannah. I see our turn up ahead. Once we pass by Emma's and the skating pond, there's the English farm. I'll be watching for the spotlight up on their silo. Father told me to always look for familiar markers to keep my bearings."

"Parents can be so wise."

"Our parents are, Claire, and so is Mummi."

Thinking for a minute, Claire replied, "My parents were wise in their own way."

Frank was attentive to what he could see of their surroundings as the snow kept pounding and the wind tried pushing them out of the way. It didn't slow them down. Frank guided the horse through the turn and onto the road home. Feeling a bit relieved, Frank settled in to the last leg of their journey. But as they went along he realized they should have passed by some familiar landmarks. Emma's farm was not that far from the turn they'd made a while back.

"We've been on the road long enough. We should have passed by Emma's unless I missed it."

"I'm sure you didn't miss it, Frank. With this storm it is taking us longer."

"Snowstorms can do that. I once got caught in a whiteout that seemed to last for miles. When I finally drove out of it I realized I'd only been in it for minutes."

"Guess you're right," Frank replied as he tried fighting off a nervousness building inside him. He didn't want to alarm anyone. It turned out his instincts were spot on. The farther down that road they went the less familiar anything seemed. From what Frank could make out, there were no landmarks anywhere. Nothing felt like the usual, not even the curves in the road. There were no houses or barns or traffic; only more and more snow piling on top of snow piles. It was as if they were alone out in the storm.

"I do not want to alarm you, Hannah, but I think I took the wrong turn. I should have waited for the second left."

"I couldn't hear you, Frank," replied Hannah almost screaming with the wind howling all around them.

Repeating what he'd said, Frank added as loud as he could, "If I'd taken the second left that would have put us on our road home. I thought this was it. When that truck almost hit us I wanted to get off that road faster than I should have."

Waiting for a strong gust of wind to go by, Hannah told Frank it wasn't a problem. "Maybe there is a place you can turn the buggy around."

"I'll keep watch, Hannah. The snow is slowing down. That will help."

"I'll keep watch as well from back here. There has to be somewhere you can turn around."

Because the snow was letting up, Frank pushed the horse to hurry along as he kept looking around. With his attention diverted, Frank wasn't keeping watch ahead of him.

"Hold on, Hannah. I know where we are. Hold on!"

"Where are we, Frank? Tell me where we are."

As he tried slowing the horse down Frank told Hannah he thought they were on an old logging road. "It's a dead end. Most of the trees were cleared away years back."

"Be careful, Frank. I've heard Father talking about this road. There are piles of rotted logs everywhere."

"I need to turn us around!"

Hannah noted fear in Frank's voice. She tried calming him down. "Take your time. I know you will get us home safely. Father always talks about your skills with a horse and buggy. He says you are as good a driver as he is."

"I'm trying to remember anything he told me that would help."

"Father always talks about safety first," Hannah yelled over the wind.

"That is true. I think I see a place up ahead."

Anxious to get back on the right road, Frank hurried the horse. He knew his father never would hurry a horse when he didn't know where he was going but Frank thought everything would be fine. He thought he had it under control. As the horse clipped along faster than he should have, more decaying logs were lying on the side of the road. When that place he'd seen in the shadows came into view, Frank felt confident all would be okay. There was just enough room for him to make the turn. Problem was he had to slow the horse down. He might have been able to do that but he never had the chance. From nowhere came a herd of deer running with the wind. The sound of their hoofs slamming through the snow alerted Hannah.

Frank yanked hard on the reins to avoid hitting the deer but they were everywhere and if there weren't deer in the way there were logs.

"Hold on, Hannah! Hold on!"

That was the only warning Frank had time to yell as the buggy went hurtling through the air. The sound of hoofs on pavement echoed about a field ladened with snow that could hide any trace of anything or anyone out on such a perilous night. It seemed like an eternity before anything but the selfish wind could be heard.

Chapter Twenty-Two

SNOW WAS COMING DOWN AGAIN, GETTING tossed around in all directions, at times blocking any light there was from the moon.

The wind blowing her hair in her face brought Hannah back to reality. Thrown from the buggy, she'd landed in a bed of snow. Because of what her father had drilled into her in case of such an emergency, Hannah stayed still, moving one leg and then the other, one arm and then the other. Slowly she lifted her head. She didn't feel dizzy. Slowly she sat up and still she wasn't dizzy. A few minutes later she was standing. Brushing snow off her bonnet and long wool cloak, she pulled up her mittens. Taking a deep breath she let out a yell.

"Frank! Claire! Where are you? Hurry! We must make a plan. Father always said make a plan to get out of a situation. Frank! Claire! Answer me now!"

Nothing but the wind replied. Putting her face into it, Hannah listened. Besides a smell she couldn't identify, Hannah heard tree branches moving. With one careful step at a time she followed that sound until reaching a clump of trees and brush. Fumbling about, Hannah found a branch that would work as a sort of cane. She'd use it as her eyes. The only problem was the branch was half frozen to other limbs and branches, some with thorns and brambles in the way. Taking one mitten off and putting it over the other one, Hannah used her cushioned hand to break through the barbs to get to the branch. Once she made it, Hannah pulled with all her might, twisting and turning the branch until finally it let loose. With the wind letting up, Hannah could hear the trickling of water. That brought back the memory of her father telling her mother how he'd followed a creek that had overflowed its banks in search of places to leave his muskrat traps. He said it wasn't far from the school. Hannah figured this was it. With the branch as her guide, Hannah followed that trickling sound. As she made her way, Hannah kept calling into the night.

"I can come to you. Please! Please answer me."

Whenever feeling the fear inside her build, Hannah would yell even louder. Then going along a few more steps, she'd stop and listen. It was in such a moment that Hannah heard a grinding noise. It triggered the time she was in the barn, standing beside her father who was fitting a wheel back on one of their buggies. The memory of hearing that wheel turn mimicked the sound getting louder as she held on to the branch so tightly that her fingers ached. When she realized she was going down a small embankment, Hannah prayed to the heavens.

"Lord, I must not fall. Please stay beside me in the darkness."

With the trickling of water getting louder, Hannah could tell she was edging closer to what she thought was the creek. The further down she went the more Hannah realized she was being sheltered from the wind. It was like being in a valley. Hannah knew the Lord made it happen. Once she reached level ground, Hannah listened. That grinding sounded as if it was right in front of her. Using the branch, Hannah began feeling all around. When touching something soft, she heard a groaning. Hannah knew it was Frank. He groaned like that when lifting bales of hay. She was on her knees in seconds.

"Frank! Can you hear me? Frank! Can you hear me?"

"Hannah?"

"Claire! Where are you?"

"I'm to your left; about twenty feet. I see Frank. The buggy's near you on its side. There is what looks like a small, nearly frozen stream of water not far from Frank. I will come to you. Is Frank alert? Are you okay?"

The moon showed up as the snowfall turned to spits of snow here and there and the wind quieted. Light from the moon didn't make a difference to Hannah but it did to the other two.

"Frank is squeezing my hand. He is alert, Claire, and I am fine."

After coughing for a few minutes Frank told Hannah his foot was stuck under the buggy.

"I'm trying to pull it out but I can't. I hope the horse is okay. He must have been scared and ran away. Father will be upset that I could not handle the buggy."

"All Father will care about is that no one was hurt. Father does not blame. He believes the Lord has a plan and we must have faith and believe in Him. If the horse ran then he must not have been injured. Father has taught the horses well. I bet the horse comes back to us, Frank. Now let me pull on your leg."

Even with Hannah's help, the leg would not budge.

"How far do you figure we are from your home?" Claire asked, sitting down next to Hannah in the snow.

"I'm not sure, Claire. We would have to go back down this road; take a left until the next crossroad. Then take another left and go by Emma's and the skating pond. In daylight it is not far. On a stormy winter night it can be very far."

"With the buggy on its side, Frank is out of the wind. You could get back under that cover with him while I walk to your farm. I see the blankets still on the seats. Wrap them around the both of you."

"That plan would not work, Claire."

"Why, Frank?"

"Because I should be the one going for help. I am to blame for the accident."

"I told you, Frank. No one is to blame. Remember last winter when you and Father were out getting more wood? You came back in the dark and went off the road and hit a tree."

"I remember. Father told me it was no one's fault we lost the horse."

"And it's no one's fault tonight, Frank. It makes sense that the one going for help is Claire."

"We could keep trying to free Frank's foot but I think it would make more sense for me to go for help."

"I agree, Claire. Father would tell us to think of more than one plan and then decide."

"Since I am not familiar with this area, what else would you two suggest?"

Standing, Hannah turned back into the wind. Taking deep breaths, she raised her arms, thanking the Lord.

"I feel your presence Lord. Amen. Thank you for guiding us home."

"What do you mean, Hannah?"

"I mean," Hannah explained, now back sitting beside Frank. "I have a plan."

Only the north wind made a sound as Hannah continued. "There was a smell in the air but I couldn't figure it out until now. That smell is garlic. It is faint but I am sure it is garlic. That means we are not far from the jam lady's farm. She told me she lived near the school."

"I remember her telling you that, Hannah."

"If you keep going down the road full of logs, I'm sure you'll see her farm. Father and I went by one evening and Father told me she had spotlights on behind the barn. If she has a cell phone, Claire, and you have Tommy's number, the jam lady can call him."

"I do have Tommy's number and I saw her cell phone. I will leave right now."

"Get your bearings. Remember the spot where we went off the road. If along the way you feel I have made a mistake, turn back and we will think of another plan."

"It has stopped snowing and the moon is above us. Let me help you two get settled before I go."

"Do not worry, Claire. I am able to take care of the two of us."

While Claire sensed urgency in Hannah's tone, she didn't say anything. She didn't have to. Claire was certain their father had drilled into them what to do in any situation.

Minutes later Claire was up the embankment and on her way to the jam lady's farm.

Chapter Twenty-Three

SINCE MOST OF THE GOOD-SIZED TREES had been cut down, the old road offered few places to escape the wind. There were no valleys to hide in. With her coat buttoned and her scarf wrapped around her neck, Claire was thankful she'd worn a warm sweater. Even though she'd chosen it because of the color, considering she was riding with Tommy, the sweater turned out to be a good choice for an unforeseen reason. So did the corduroy pants she'd selected instead of jeans. The moon proved to be a lifesaver since she was unfamiliar with any of the surroundings. The way Hannah talked, the jam lady's farm wasn't far. So with her mittens on and knit hat pulled below her eyebrows, Claire kept up the pace as she maneuvered around logs and debris and snowdrifts here and there. Once she got into a rhythm, Claire found herself singing like her mother used to do. She found it soothing. It kept her mind off the moment. That is, until going around a curve and then another. That's when Claire told herself what she thought sounded like howling was only her imagination. She'd never heard talk about coyotes being in the region. *What with the mountains nearby*, she told herself, *that's where they'd be.* Surely Hannah would have alerted her to any such danger.

A straight stretch gave Claire a chance to assess her situation. Looking down the road, she was able to see what she thought were spotlights. They were still a ways away but with each quick step they became a bit more apparent. So did the howling. Claire's heart was pounding. She told herself not to panic for panic leads to mistakes. *Anyone in my shoes would be nervous*, she told herself as that howling seemed closer. When the moon was in full view Claire was able to see a farm in the distance. If anything was in between she couldn't tell. It was a sudden strong gust of wind covering her in snow and a distinct howling out there in the darkness that ignited Claire into a full run. She'd had it with her imagination. She was convinced there were coyotes around. Claire remembered watching a PBS special on coyotes; how they'd lost their fear of people due to people invading their space. Instead of fearing people, coyotes had discovered humans were a good source of food.

Not me! Not tonight Claire told herself picking up speed; eyeing a barn with spotlights on as that howling seemed to be all around her. That's when she lost it. Screaming at the top of her lungs and sprinting to the goal post, a gunshot stopped her cold. The howling stopped. A voice came right at her.

"Whoever's out there, you're safe now. Those coyotes will quiet down. They don't like guns."

A cackling laughter came rolling over the fields as the sound of a squeaky door opened, then closed. Claire hurried to reach it before the jam lady turned out the lights.

"Lil! It's Claire. We met last night at the train depot. I was with the Amish girl. She bought your garlic jam!"

No answer. Claire tried again. This time she was more forceful. "Lil! We are in desperate need of your help. That young lady and her brother are in danger. Please. Open the door."

From around the other side of the house appeared the jam lady with her gun in hand.

"Lil!"

"Had to make sure it was you. Livin' out here alone I never know who's crawling around at night."

"Like those coyotes?"

"That was you out there?"

"Yes. I can't thank you enough for getting rid of them. They were right behind me."

"Might have seemed that way what with their crazy howling but they weren't close. When they all get going, they try to outdo each other. Come in and tell me what's going on."

"There's no time to waste."

"I never waste time, Claire. Life's too short."

Lil waited for Claire to step inside. Then she shut the door.

"How did you know this was my farm?" she asked, putting her gun in a cabinet, then locking it.

"Hannah could smell the garlic."

"I haven't made garlic jam in a while. I suppose moisture caused by snow on the fields where I grow the stuff could have caused the odor of the garlic to be released. I didn't smell it when I was outside but I'm sure someone in Hannah's shoes wouldn't miss it. Her senses must be on high alert. So, tell me what's going on."

In one deep breath Claire filled Lil in on what had happened. The urgency in her tone did not escape the jam lady's attention.

"I've witnessed how the Amish teach their children what to do in all types of circumstances. Those kids are survivors."

"I agree, Lil. Hannah sees more than I do. Would you mind if I used your phone?"

"It's plugged in over on the counter. Feel free to call as many people as you feel necessary. Would you like a quick cup of tea? The water's hot."

"One call will do it, Lil. No time for tea. Next time."

"Make your call. I'll grab some extra blankets, first-aid kit, water, some dry mittens and flashlights."

As Claire was dialing Tommy's number she heard Lil yelling. "Oh no. I forgot. My truck is at the garage."

"I hope I can reach my friend!"

"I'll hitch up the horse and sleigh. It only takes me minutes."

Trying Tommy a few times with no luck, Claire left a message. She explained in detail what had happened. After telling him everyone was okay, she made a point to say they'd need help getting Frank up the embankment. Claire repeated the location.

"My friend Lil is taking me back there by horse and sleigh. I'll explain when I see you. Please hurry, Tommy."

"I'll get some warm stuff on. Then we're off to the barn."

The jam lady was ready in seconds. Grabbing what she'd gathered, they rushed out the back door. Lil had the barn door pushed aside before Claire caught up with her.

"Let me help."

"Grab those reins Claire. I'll do the rest."

One thing the jam lady didn't have to do was coax the draft horse out of its stall.

"Such a mighty horse, Lil."

"This chestnut brown is a favorite. We've been on quite a few adventures together. Tonight will add to the list."

It wasn't long before Lil had everything ready to go.

"Climb aboard, Claire. Blankets are in the back."

"This is the perfect sleigh for tonight."

"If Frank is unable to walk, this sleigh will give him the room he'll need."

Leading the horse down a drifted path, Lil pulled back on the reins.

"No traffic tonight. There's never any traffic and that's the way I like it. We should be there in minutes, Claire."

With a flick of her wrists, the horse took the lead. Despite being hefty, he moved around logs left to rot without a problem. When Claire felt they were getting close to where they needed to be, Lil slowed the horse down.

"Be thankful it has stopped storming, Claire."

"I am, Lil. I'm also thankful the moon is out so I can pinpoint where we flew off the road. In the darkness, this area all looks the same."

"Watch for any sign of tracks from the wheels of the buggy or areas that seem disrupted. Keep looking. Something will trigger a memory."

"Can we go back a little ways?"

Without saying a word, Lil had them heading back until Claire put her hands up.

"This is it! Stop! I remember those rocks; feeling grateful we didn't hit them. Frank and Hannah are down that embankment."

Securing the horse far enough off the road, Lil grabbed the supplies she'd brought with her.

"Here's a flashlight, Claire. I have one too. Lead the way."

"I'm certain this is it."

"Take your time. We're no good to anyone if we fall."

Heeding Lil's advice, Claire slowed down. She knew they didn't have far to go. She could hear the creek, though the water sounded more forceful, as if it was flowing a little faster. Claire hurried, throwing that advice to the wind that was picking up.

"Hannah! Frank! I'm back with the jam lady."

Only the frightening howling answered. Claire told herself to ignore the pack, remembering Lil explaining they were only trying to outdo each other.

"Hannah! Frank! Answer me," she yelled, once down on level ground, using her flashlight to do the searching. When it brought the buggy into view, Claire took off. Lil was right behind her. They both reached the buggy at the same time. Seeing it half in the water horrified Claire. A zillion scenarios went through her head. And when she looked inside the buggy and found it empty, then scanned the area with the flashlight and saw no trace of the children, Claire felt sick to her stomach.

"They're gone! Something horrible has happened. When I left, the buggy was not in the water. It was far from the edge of the water. Frank's leg was trapped underneath. Could they...could they have drowned? Where are they! Maybe the coyotes were nearby. I should never have left them."

"Claire!"

"What? What?"

"Look behind you."

Standing there wrapped in blankets was Hannah. Her cloak was dirty, her hair was a mess, but she was smiling.

"Why didn't you answer me? Where is Frank? What happened?"

Frustrated by fear, Claire took Hannah in her arms.

"Over here, Claire," yelled Lil. "I found the boy. He is sleeping. He is sheltered by a rock wall."

"Sleeping?"

"Frank fell asleep after I pulled him away from the buggy."

"Hannah. Please tell me what happened."

Taking hold of the young girl's hand, Claire led them to where Lil was waiting. As they walked, Hannah told Claire she had to do something quickly.

"I heard the ice breaking; then the creek water coming faster. I knew I had to free Frank's foot because he was in danger."

"You brave girl. What did you do?"

"I remembered Father telling us to find something sturdy like a fence post or big tree limb and shove it under the buggy as far as it would go. Then push it down with all our strength to get the buggy to rise up enough for the one trapped to escape. So that's what I did."

"But how?"

"The Lord was with me. He led me to a pile of rubble and in that pile I found old fence posts. I felt the nails. They felt like what my father uses. I dragged the biggest one I could find to the buggy and the Lord did the rest. When I raised the buggy I told Frank to roll out from underneath it as fast as he could. And that's what Frank did. He almost knocked me over."

"How did you find the rock wall?"

"When I was searching for something to use I found some rocks piled on one another. I kept feeling the rocks. I followed them. There were more and more of them. I knew it was a rock wall. When I became tangled in low branches falling to the ground and covering most of the rocks, I thought there might be space enough between the rocks and branches to provide us shelter. Father told us many times to use what the Lord provides, so I did. I got down on my hands and knees and crawled my way in and found space enough for both of us. It was out of the wind, away from any snow that might fall. I ran back, grabbed some blankets, and made a bed in that space. Frank's foot is injured but I got him to his feet and held on to him all the way to that shelter. Once I had him under there, I crawled in and we both fell asleep."

"You are one brave young lady, Hannah."

"I agree."

"And so do I. You are a true child of the Lord."

"Father?"

Turning around, Hannah repeated, "Father!"

"Yes. I am here, Hannah. Tommy and I heard your story. You saved your brother, Hannah. I am proud of you, my child."

As father and daughter had their moment, Tommy took Claire into his arms. Magically, the moon showed up again.

"Where did you come from, Tommy?"

"You called me, Claire."

"I know that but how did you find us? How long were you walking behind Hannah and me?"

"Long enough to hear about the ordeal she and Frank went though. What a smart girl; saving her brother and bedding down beside a sheltered rock wall. She is amazing."

"She is that for sure."

"And so are you. You gave great directions. When we saw the horse and sleigh, John was out of the truck before I even stopped."

"It's good for the children that you thought to bring John."

With the moon behind them, Tommy whispered, "You scared me tonight, Claire. I was afraid for you."

"I didn't mean to sound afraid over the phone."

"You didn't. It was me."

"Father," Frank yelled as he made his way with Lil almost carrying him.

"Son! My boy." John took Frank into his arms. "My boy! The Lord kept you safe. I will forever be thankful."

Claire introduced Lil. "This is the jam lady, as Hannah explains."

"So you are the one who makes that delicious garlic jam."

"I am that person, John. I'm glad you enjoy it."

Claire explained how much of a help that jam lady was to her. "She even thought to bring flashlights and water, extra blankets and a first aid kit. Even dry mittens."

"I've learned after living out here alone to be prepared for anything."

"I wouldn't have thought about dry mittens."

"I tell you, Tommy. If your hands get cold, the rest of you gets cold. I found that out the hard way."

"I too have learned that to be true the hard way," John added.

"I checked Frank's foot. From what I could tell, his ankle isn't broken."

"You continue to amaze me, Lil."

"Nothing amazing about me, Claire. I took a first aid course."

"Thank you for tending to Frank. I think it is time to get the children home. They must be cold and tired."

"I agree, John. I'm wondering what would be the best way to get Frank back there."

Lil spoke up. "We can lift him into the back of my sleigh. There's plenty of room and plenty of blankets."

Everyone including Frank liked the idea.

"But how do we get Frank up the hill?" Claire asked.

"I'll carry him."

And that's exactly what Tommy did as Frank talked to his father all the way up the incline about the accident.

"I am sorry, Father. I was careless. And the horse took off."

"No, the horse did not take off. Look! He is here beside Lil's horse. We will talk tomorrow, son. Right now, we are going home. Your mother and grandmother are waiting. The Lord has blessed us once again. Praise to the Almighty Lord."

With blankets keeping him warm, Frank was comfortable in the sleigh; John would be sitting beside him. Hannah was up front next to the jam lady who was happy to be helping her neighbors on a cold winter's night.

"I can smell the garlic again."

"Your smelling the garlic made the difference tonight, Hannah. Here's a pair of dry mittens for you and pass this pair to Frank. There are blankets at your feet. Pull them up around you. If you'd like some water, there are bottles under the seat."

"Thank you," Hannah replied. "I kept telling myself I was not cold but now that we are going home, I'm freezing."

"You feel it because you've let your guard down. You did what you had to do regardless of the circumstances."

"I did what I had to do with the Lord's help," Hannah replied, pulling the blankets up around her.

"Claire told me about your dog Bailey. I'm so happy she was found."

"I can't wait to see her."

"You will be home shortly, Hannah."

After checking the other horse for injuries, John decided he was fit to run along with them as they headed home. He tied the horse to the back of the sleigh. It was like a parade with Tommy driving his truck and Claire sitting beside him.

"Mind if I turn the radio on?"

"Not at all, Tommy."

"Music calms me down."

"Even rock?"

"Even heavy metal. Any music. It's an escape for me."

"From what?"

Going from one station to the next, Tommy answered. "From commitments, if I'm honest with myself. Did you ever get yourself into situations that you wished would take care of themselves instead of being a drag on you?"

"That's how I felt when I knew my marriage was over but there we were—still married."

"I'll tell you one thing. I'm not good at commitments. My head is off doing business or my mind is spinning about a recipe and that leaves no room for commitments. They come in last every time."

"Are you talking about Denise?"

Choosing the Oldies station, Tommy started singing along. Claire waited. "That was a favorite of my father's. He met the guy in Philadelphia. I have the album he signed."

Claire didn't say a word. They kept going for a few minutes until Tommy turned the radio down.

"Yes. I was talking about Denise but it could have been about any girl I ever dated. When they'd get serious I'd slowly disappear."

"What about you and Denise being engaged?"

"The idea sounded okay. I hardly see her and I like that. Mummi tells me I should settle down."

"I'm sure Mummi doesn't mean with just anyone. While I've never met Denise and I've only known you for two days, I have a feeling she doesn't get you, Tommy."

"That never mattered to me. It gave me space to finally be who I am."

"But if you make a commitment, wouldn't it be better if the one you are committing to understands you and accepts who you are and encourages you, maybe even works beside you?"

"I never thought so. I just wanted to be left alone to do as I pleased."

"That's what my husband told me."

"But I don't mean it in a selfish way. It's hard to explain, especially now."

"Do you mean with your building and your bakery opening soon?"

"I think that's it. I'm on overload and I find Denise getting more demanding of me to take her places, buy her things, and spend whatever time I have with her. I don't roll that way. I get smothered. I get lost."

"Talk with her."

"Most times it's easier to go along with it."

"I know what you mean, Tommy."

"I know you do, Claire."

"How?"

"You're just like me and I don't know what to do."

"About?"

"About—about. Oh I don't know."

Claire didn't push him. Instead she turned the radio up.

"You like this song?"

"I love it, Tommy. I'd sit by my father and listen to him play it on the piano. It was a favorite of his."

" Imagine that! 'Crazy' was my father's favorite song. He'd play it over and over when he was in the garage tinkering. He must have had about every album of hers. It's funny how a song can take you right back to a place and time. It was never about the words with him. It was always about the steel guitars."

"Sing to me, Tommy."

"Right here in my truck? You want me to sing Patsy Cline's song?"

"Yes. Sing to me. I'm feelin' crazy!"

"I think we both are, Claire. I don't know what I was trying to say. I'm not good at that stuff; talking about feelings and things."

"Oh, but I think you could be good at that stuff. As my mother used to say, some people wear their heart on their sleeve. You are one of those people. You need to understand that all commitments are not the same. The right commitment can make you complete. Now please—sing to me."

And so as that truck followed along in the parade under dazzling stars that came out of the darkness, Tommy sang along with Patsy.

"I'm crazy for trying. And crazy for lying. And I'm crazy for loving you."

Claire moved closer to Tommy. With her fingers dancing about the nape of his neck, she whispered as they drove down the road leading to the Miller farm. "Keep singing, Tommy. Along with your guitar and love of baking, you have many gifts to share."

Moving her lips over his ear, Claire pulled away as that simple house with candles in the windows and smoke coming out of the chimney came into view.

Chapter Twenty-Four

ONCE COATS AND BOOTS AND HATS and mittens were warming by the fire and Frank was settled in a hickory rocker, covered in blankets with his foot up on a stool, and a horse was bedded down for the night, Mummi went to the kitchen to prepare hot chocolate for those sitting at the table waiting for the story of what had taken place to be told. Lil joined Mummi. The new friends had a lot in common.

"Wonderful kitchen, Catherine. My life is in my kitchen what with the jams I make and the breads I bake. Then there are the pickles and relishes."

Catherine explained it wasn't her kitchen. "But when I am home I too spend much of my time in the kitchen. I have tasted your garlic jam. It is delicious."

"Thank you. It was a favorite of my father's so I make it in his memory."

"I do that when I bake cookies."

"In memory of your father?"

"No. In memory of my husband."

With that said, Catherine went to the hutch for the box with the tin cookie cutters.

"When John and Elizabeth invited me to stay with them while my ankle heals, I brought this box with me."

Opening it up, Catherine explained about its contents.

"Such a beautiful love story," spoke Lil. "I've never been married but I have been in love."

"There's no greater force. I feel Paul with me every day."

"I wasn't so lucky. I guess you could say I got left at the altar although we never made it that far along in the relationship. He led me to believe that would happen but after four years I said see you around! By then, he'd taken what he wanted from me, which was money and a place to stay."

"I'm so sorry, Lil."

"No need to be. Because of him, I sold my place and moved to where I am now. I love it there. Love my gardens and my horses. I am happy. Truly happy with my life. I learned not to depend on others for my happiness."

"While a hard lesson, from that you grew into the strong woman you are today."

"Yes. That's true. That scoundrel wouldn't believe what a blessing in disguise his leaving turned out to be."

"Could you please put these cups on that wooden tray, Lil, while I whip some heavy cream and put some cookies on a plate?"

The two women made a good pair. While Catherine added vanilla and cinnamon to the heavy cream, Lil arranged the cups on the tray and found spoons and napkins. Once cookies were arranged on the plate, they presented the tray to those waiting at the table. Taking a cup to Frank, Elizabeth moved a small table by the rocker and set it down with a few cookies on a napkin. After checking Mary, Elizabeth whispered to Frank.

"I am so glad you are safe, my son. If you'd like more hot chocolate, let us know."

"Thank you, Mother. I am happy to be back home."

Kissing him on the top of his head, Elizabeth joined the others.

"Mother. Is Bailey still on my bed?"

"Yes she is, Hannah. I've taken her out a few times and when she gets back inside, she stands at the bottom of the stairs. I took that to mean she wanted to go back up on your bed. I looked in on her just before you came. She was sound asleep."

"Thank you, Mother. I will let her sleep a little longer."

"Your children were amazing, Elizabeth. Hannah knew what she had to do and Frank did not hesitate despite his ankle."

"John has taught them what to do if they are in danger."

"I hope the ordeal wasn't too difficult for you, Claire," Catherine said, stirring her hot chocolate.

"With Hannah and Frank, I was in good company. And Lil made all the difference, putting my mind at ease about thinking coyotes were surrounding me. Then hitching a horse to a sleigh in minutes and remembering to bring needed supplies. It couldn't have been scripted any better than it turned out."

"As I told Hannah earlier, she is the one who made the difference, picking up the scent of the garlic in the field, which led to Claire coming to my door."

"All God's plan," said John, excusing himself as Hannah explained about the fence post and rock wall. Frank added how his sister pulled him out as she held on to the post.

"You worked together. That is why we are here as a family once again, thankful for the love we share and the blessings from above."

"Amen to that, Elizabeth," said John, coming down the stairs with Bailey in his arms. She was wide awake and shaking her tail.

Hearing her whine, Hannah was up from the table in seconds. Hugging Bailey, Hannah told her how much she missed her. "I'm glad you weren't with me. You might have been hurt, Bailey."

Sitting in a chair beside Frank, the two kept petting Bailey. That led to the lamb bleating and Mary waking up.

"I didn't mean to wake Mary, Mother."

"She is due a feeding, Hannah."

It wasn't long before Elizabeth was rocking Mary back to sleep.

"More hot chocolate, anyone?"

"I'd love a little more, Tommy."

"My pleasure," he smiled, picking up Claire's cup as Lil asked for more.

"It's that whipped cream of yours, Catherine. Makes it so creamy and warm on a cold night."

When Tommy returned, the cups were brimming with hot chocolate. Lil's had extra whipped cream.

"Thank you, Tommy. You are satisfying my sweet tooth."

"If Faith wasn't sick, I'd wake her up. She loves Mummi's whipped cream."

"How is Faith, Mother?" Hannah asked.

"She had a little broth earlier. I'm hoping a good night's sleep will help."

Setting Claire's hot chocolate on the table, Tommy took hold of her hands.

"Checking to see if you've thawed out."

"The hot chocolate helped. It's funny, Tommy. I was thinking how I panicked after the accident. Not because someone might be hurt but because I didn't have my cell phone. I'm glad I didn't. I never would have met Lil. Who knows how it all would have turned out."

"I remember the time I ran out of gas and didn't have my phone. I walked a ways before finding a home. When I knocked on the door, I was surprised when an old friend of my father's answered. I hadn't seen him in years. He told me all sorts of stories about my father that I'd never heard on our way back to my car with a can full of gas."

"That's a beautiful story in itself, Tommy."

Catherine stood yawning. "Excuse me but I am tired. I thank the Lord my dear young ones are home. With that I will say good night. Tomorrow will be a busy day with my move back home."

"If you need help, we can use my truck."

"Thank you but I don't have that much, Tommy. Come visit when you can and we will talk about your bakery."

Getting up from the table, Tommy gave his dear friend a hug. "I will stop by. Have a good sleep, Catherine."

After embracing Frank and Hannah one more time and saying good night to Claire, Catherine turned to Lil. "It was a pleasure meeting you. Stop by anytime."

"I enjoyed our time together. I will be around to continue our conversation."

Catherine started up the stairs as the clock on the mantel kept ticking away and a baby yawned in her sleep. Halfway up those stairs, Catherine stopped to clear her throat.

"Do you have a cold, Mummi?"

"Nothing to worry about, Elizabeth. Good night, my child."

The talk around the table continued a little longer until John turned his attention to Hannah and Frank. "I think you both should get to bed. I'll help you up the stairs, Frank. It has been a long day and tomorrow we have to help Mummi after I find you a walking stick."

"I am so happy to be home, Father. For a few minutes when the water started rising I thought I'd never see you or Mother again."

"Do not doubt the Lord's presence, my son."

"Never, Father. Good night, everyone. Thank you for helping me."

Hugging his mother, Frank asked if she would take the lamb outside for him.

"Of course I will. And when we come back in the house, I will bring your lamb upstairs to sleep with you. I have a feeling she will comfort you tonight."

"I have that same feeling, Mother!"

Saying good night, Hannah told her parents a thought she had when trying to get Frank out of the buggy. "I remembered the last time I saw your faces. You were up in the haymow, Father, with your sleeves pushed back and your work gloves on. And you, Mother. I remember thinking as you slept how beautiful you looked. With your bonnet off, your hair was falling around the pillow. Even though I was only four, I remember thinking your face was like an angel. The Lord has given me parents I cherish and today I feared I'd never feel your touch or hear you call my name again. Good night."

With Frank holding on to John, and Bailey by Hannah's side, they went upstairs to bed.

It wasn't long before Tommy and Claire said their good nights and followed Lil out the door and down to the barn while she hitched the horse to the sleigh.

"If I can help, let me know."

"Thanks, Tommy, but I could do this in my sleep. Of course it helps that John gave me this lantern. What a time we've had!"

"I can't thank you enough for everything. You kept me focused, Lil."

"Glad I was able to help. Stop by anytime."

"I'll be in touch after Christmas. We'll pick a day when I can spend some time with you, do the interview and shoot some photos."

"Sounds like fun, Claire."

"Good thing you have that lantern; makes it safer once you get on the road."

"I'm travelling the back fields, Tommy. I know where every fence, tree, and farm is out there."

"I'm sure you do. Just watch out for a certain embankment."

"Oh that's a good one, Claire," chuckled Lil as the horse picked up speed and headed home.

There wasn't much talking on the way back to Claire's; not even any discussion about the music on the radio.

When Tommy pulled into the driveway, Claire thanked him for the ride. "I'll say good night right here. I have some photos I need to frame."

"You could ask me in and I could help you."

"I'm afraid I wouldn't be great company with all that took place today."

"I didn't mean to go on like I did. I've never been one to get into feelings. I guess it's easier for me to be aloof; the nice guy who shies away from commitments."

"I wouldn't say you shy away from all commitments. Look what you're doing downtown. That is a huge commitment. And don't forget your bakery. Don't sell yourself short."

"You know what I'm saying, Claire."

"Yes, I know what you mean. Speaking of commitments, aren't you expecting Denise later?"

"She called and said she won't be coming until later on tomorrow."

"I'd like to stop by early in the morning to check that space you have available before I visit Catherine."

"Great. I'll be there. If I can get away I'll go with you to Catherine's."

Reaching over, Tommy pulled Claire closer. "I was worried about you tonight."

Kissing her on the cheek, he went to kiss her on the lips but Claire opened the door and got out. "See you tomorrow, Tommy."

Before going to bed, Claire checked her messages. There was one from Nick asking her out to dinner on Monday. Claire was too tired to reply. She'd tell him yes in the morning. Another message was from her sister.

"You must call me as soon as you hear this!"

The message wasn't like her sister's usual messages, full of fluff and talk of money and where she'd been and where she and her husband were going next. Claire wrote herself a note to call Ellen in the morning. She couldn't handle talking to her right then.

Thoughts of the last few days lingered as Claire tried falling asleep. So much had occurred since going up the front steps of that simple clapboard home. In a way it was crazy, just as Patsy Cline described.

Chapter Twenty-Five

WITH HER COFFEE AND TOAST BESIDE her, Claire sat at the kitchen table and checked her emails. She could tell Christmas was getting closer. Orders were increasing by the day. For a moment Claire thought about the day before and the photo opportunities that passed her by. But that thought didn't last. Claire realized yesterday was not about the pocketbook. It was all about matters of the human spirit.

Deciding it was too early to call her sister, Claire replied to Nick's message. Then taking a little quiet time, she enjoyed her coffee while watching snow buntings gather at the feeders hanging in the maple trees. With that special order needing to be mailed on Monday, she didn't sit for long. After getting ready for the day, Claire was in the studio when the phone rang. It was Ellen.

"Yes, I received your message late last night. I was going to call this morning."

Claire could tell her sister was upset. "No. I'm not ready for Christmas. You know me, Ellen. I'm a late bloomer in so many ways. I suppose you have everything wrapped and ready to go."

When her sister replied with a no, Claire knew something was going on. That's when Ellen explained her husband had lost his job.

"I understand. It is definitely a tough time for newspapers. But Bill has made some great connections there. Any leads?"

Learning the paper had to cut back wasn't surprising. This wasn't the first time Ellen's husband had lost a job in that industry.

"Something will come up. Yes, I know it's hard but you'll get through it."

Hearing they hadn't saved a thing over the years answered Claire's curiosity about how they paid for the lifestyle they lived. Her sister went on to say she might be looking for a job. Claire wondered what kind of a job. She hadn't worked since getting married. Then Ellen told Claire she'd be unable to buy her a Christmas gift.

"No problem, Ellen. I've often thought how silly it is that we exchange gifts when we never make an attempt to see each other and we only live two hours apart. You've been through this before and bounced back. What? Okay. Talk to you later."

Her sister's sudden need to get off the phone wasn't surprising. Claire was mindful of how Ellen manipulated people. She was certain the only reason Ellen called was to relish the moment, expecting to hear disappointment in Claire's voice when hearing she wouldn't be receiving a gift from her this year. When Ellen didn't hear any such thing, she wiped her hands clean of the situation and hung up the phone.

Claire knew it made no difference to Ellen that Bill had lost his position at the paper nor how hard he'd worked to get there. She didn't care about him. She didn't care about Claire. Ellen only cared about the money. That husband of hers had been whiplashed long enough to realize he'd better find something soon to pay for the toys and bobbles because Claire was certain her sister would never lower herself to go looking for a job.

While gathering photos, it dawned on Claire she was in a much better place than Ellen, who judged people by appearances. While status was everything to Ellen, it never meant a thing to Claire, although she did wonder about Nicholas Rossi. It wasn't because of his fortune but rather his love of trains and commitment to his family's hometown. Nick Rossi had character that money couldn't buy. The same could be said about Catherine and her family. Imagining Ellen inside that clapboard house only made Claire laugh. She'd be back out that door and down the cement steps in seconds with her nose in the air. Ellen never would have cared about the Christmas wreaths with red bows or the barn full of wooden toys.

Reaching for packing tape, Claire remembered Catherine telling her to be in the present.

"You can't change the past. You can't predict what's ahead, so enjoy the moment," the Amish woman said more than once when they were cutting out cookies.

Birds squabbling at the feeders pulled Claire back to the window. Watching the older ones shove the younger ones out of the way reminded her of the times Ellen had shoved her aside. Those days were over.

After she processed a few more orders, Claire went looking for Christmas decorations she'd put away after divorcing Eric. Every Christmas since then the box remained out of sight. But being around Hannah and Frank, listening to them talk about their Christmas traditions, sparked Claire's interest in the contents of the box. She couldn't remember what was inside. As Hannah talked about the simple manger her father had made for the family and how they'd gather one night before Christmas, after having her mother's homemade soup and bread, to decorate and make more strings of hearts and angels and put the manger in place, Claire felt a longing to open that box and see what treasures and memories it held.

Although the box had been stuffed away, Claire knew where it was hiding. There was a closet in a spare bedroom where Eric kept his golf clubs and clothes he never wore. After Eric moved out, Claire used the closet for stuff she didn't want but couldn't throw away. Way in the back of the top shelf sat that box of Christmas stuff. When she opened the closet door the smell of Eric hit her. Standing on a chair she grabbed the box, jumped down, and shut the door. She didn't need to dwell today. Her dwelling days were behind her.

Walking down the hallway, Claire hesitated in front of a door that had been closed since Eric declared he didn't want children. It would have been the nursery. This morning Claire opened the door and went inside the room with pale yellow paint on the walls and snow-white Swiss pin-dotted curtains hanging in the windows and Winnie the Pooh sitting on top of a dresser. Putting the box down, Claire picked up a teddy bear sitting next to Pooh. It had been Claire's when growing up. It still felt warm when she hugged it. Taking a closer look at the bear, Claire decided all the hugs she'd given the bear was why it looked so loved. Keeping hold of it while pushing the box with her foot to a rocking chair by a window, Claire sat down. With the bear in her lap, she pulled the box open. After getting through the crumpled newspapers, Claire felt her heart beat a little faster. There in front of her were hand-drawn Christmas cards and old letters to Santa her mother had kept, along with decorations made in school, and ornaments made out of bread dough, and snowmen made with Styrofoam balls, and lopsided reindeer with pipe cleaner antlers, and so much more. One worn, oblong box grabbed Claire's attention. Setting it on her lap next to the bear, Claire opened it and as she did memories came flying out. It was a simple decoration, always sitting on her grandmother's kitchen table over the holidays. Then it was passed on to her mother, who gave it to Claire with instructions.

"I know your sister would throw this out. You appreciate little things, Claire; especially little things with special meanings. Every time you put this out remember how much I love you."

Tears fell on a tired teddy bear as Claire pulled out a decoration wrapped in memories. The four small brass angels that would twirl around when small white candles were lit underneath them were still in good shape. Claire remembered thinking it was magic when an adult would light the candles. The more heat those candles produced, the faster those angels would go around and around, hitting the chimes just so, creating a most heavenly sound. Of all the decorations, this was her favorite. As she put all the parts of that decoration back in the box, a card with a snowman colored pink caught her eye. She remembered it. Ellen had created it for her one Christmas when Claire was sick with a cold. She was so sick she couldn't get out of bed. When Claire woke up the next day, the pink snowman card was on her pillow.

Opening the card, Ellen's handwritten note in red crayon was still visible.

"Merry Christmas Claire. I missed you. Santa left you presents.

*There's lots of snow outside. I will build you a snowman. I love you.
Ellen."*

Looking out the window Claire noticed children playing in the
snow. She remembered the times she and Ellen would spend hours outside making snowmen and sliding down the hill. She wondered how the
bond they treasured disappeared. They used to be inseparable. Touching the pink snowman with her fingers, Claire decided she would send
the card to Ellen. She felt it might be a good thing to do. Somewhere
along the way those little girls had lost each other. Despite years of growing apart, Claire felt there had to be something left they could salvage.
Watching the children outside the window laugh when the snowman's
head came crashing down and a carrot went flying, Claire sat in the chair
and let the tears fall. It was a good cry. The tears were healing tears. After
the children went back inside a house with a wreath on the door and
lights in the windows, Claire felt a peace come over her. Healing comes
in many forms, even by holding a beloved bear from long ago.

Except for the card and brass angels, Claire put everything else back
in the box. She'd deal with the rest later. Right now she had to get going.
After one last hug, Claire sat her bear next to Winnie the Pooh, then
walked out of the room with pale yellow walls and shut the door.

Before leaving the house, Claire set the brass angels with the four
candles on the kitchen table right where they belonged.

Chapter Twenty-Six

AN EARLY MORNING SNOWFALL HAD THE plows on the road, which was a good thing, considering it was the first Saturday in December and people would be out shopping. Parking on a side street, Claire looked over at the mercantile decked out for the season, recalling a conversation she and Tommy had when riding in the back of John's buggy.

"We'll be ready to open on the ninth," he'd told her. "The invitations have been mailed for the private showing the night before. Consider this your personal invitation, Claire. It's going to be a classy evening. I'll have to break down and wear a tie."

Tommy went on to say he'd been meeting with merchants renting space in the building along with others interested in bringing the downtown back around. "We're implementing some great ideas, complementing the history of both the building and the downtown. I've hired a caterer with experience in handling events such as private showings. Entertainment is lined up with good soft music in the background. You're welcome to attend our meeting next Monday evening. I'd appreciate any input you might have plus you'll be able to meet the merchants."

Crossing the street as the clock on the town hall struck nine, Claire noted Tommy's truck parked in the back of the building. She reminded herself to tell him she wouldn't be able to make that Monday night meeting. The thought of Nick Rossi made her wonder where he was taking her to dinner. His message said he wanted to talk marketing. That was fine with Claire. She had plenty of ideas. She imagined he did as well. With a key Tommy had given her, Claire opened a side door to a mercantile back in business.

The place was busy with shop owners on a deadline. Trying to get her bearings since she'd only been in the place at night and they were in a hurry, Claire went searching for the space she hoped to rent. She kept an eye out for Tommy until the aroma of coffee diverted her attention. Claire remembered Tommy talking about the coffee shop and how the owner was devoting a wall to tell the story of a roasting plant that had been one of the original tenants. Nostalgia was most always a draw. It seemed to be this morning. People were already standing in front of that wall discussing the photos. With her coffee in hand Claire continued on.

The smell of something baking was her first clue where she'd find Tommy. Once inside the bakery her second clue was the clanging of pots and pans through a doorway behind a counter. Claire kept going. At first she didn't see him standing between shelves that held more pots and pans and cookie sheets and mixers. It's when a few of those items fell to the floor that Claire caught sight of him.

"Good morning. I heard the sky falling around you so I am here to make certain you are okay."

"I'm not sure about that but I'm glad you're here."

Stepping away from the shelves, Tommy grabbed a towel to dry a pan and spatula.

"I think this is the first time throughout this entire project that I am feeling overwhelmed."

"Why? What's wrong?"

"Nothing but a bunch of annoyances all going on at once. Crunch time is here and that means no time for errors."

"When that happens to me I take a step back. It doesn't have to be for long. Can I get you a cup of coffee?"

"That's one of the annoyances. I had a cup but I dropped it in a bowl of flour."

"I'll be right back. You need some coffee. By the way, you look handsome in your apron. It looks like one of Catherine's."

"You have a sharp eye, Claire. That must be why you're a photographer."

Claire wasn't long. When she returned, Tommy was taking pies out of the oven. The sight of a tall and handsome man wearing an apron and baking pies warmed Claire's heart. He'd taken the risk. Despite annoyances, that risk was taking shape.

"When I see these apple pies coming out with the crusts just so, I calm down."

"Are you already selling items?"

"I'm testing the ovens. Every oven has its quirks. There won't be room for quirks once I'm open. Right now I sell what I'm baking to the merchants. What doesn't sell I take to a food bank down the street. Let's sit for a minute. Then I'll show you your space."

"My space?"

"Yes. Have I got a deal for you."

"I've heard that line before, Tommy."

"Not from me."

It turned out Tommy did have a deal. Sitting in a corner of The Tin Cookie Cutter, Tommy spelled out his idea as snowflakes flew by windows overlooking a side street showing increasing traffic

"I was thinking. If you could build me a website and maintain it I could knock off half your rent. What do you think?"

"I need to take a look at it but I'm thinking you might have a new tenant."

"That's the best news I've heard today."

"It's early."

"It feels like midnight."

"Were you in here working late?"

"I was, and this morning Denise let me have it."

"I thought she wasn't coming until later today."

"She surprised me."

"So what did you mean when you said she let you have it?"

"She has no use for this project of mine and expects my full attention. I couldn't do that even if I wasn't involved up to my neck with this old building."

"Denise should be supporting what you are doing."

"That's not going to happen. Right now she's out getting her nails done."

While waiting for Tommy, Claire stepped outside the bakery in time to see a giant tree being pulled inside the building. The men doing the pulling stopped in the middle of the welcoming area as Tommy joined her.

"I have to go talk to those guys before we end up with a fallen pine tree and me getting sued. Come with me, Claire. We can learn how to secure a twelve-foot balsam in an open space inside a mercantile building."

The men handling the tree appreciated Tommy's questions. Once they explained how they did what they did, Tommy was satisfied the tree would be secure.

"I've hired professional tree decorators to come in and decorate the tree," Tommy explained, on his way with Claire to that potential space. "I never knew there were people who did that until I needed them."

The area Tommy was offering at half price was prime property, what with exposure to outside foot and vehicle traffic. Claire visualized a table in the back for matting prints and a countertop near the entranceway.

"I love it, Tommy. I can see it."

"If you can see it that means you can feel it, Claire. When I first stepped inside this building it was a disaster yet I was able to see the potential. So it's a deal?"

"Yes, we have a deal."

"Maybe after the meeting Monday night we could talk about the website."

Claire hesitated before telling Tommy she'd had something come up. As soon as she told him, Nick Rossi came walking by.

"There you are, Tommy. I was upstairs when I saw a tree being hauled into the building. I had to come down and see what was going on. As long as I'm here I've been meaning to ask what you'd think about adding some old photos of the depot somewhere on a wall for people to see."

When Claire turned around, Nick reacted.

"I didn't realize that was you."

"Good morning, Nick. Yes, it's me renting this space for my photography. Maybe we could add a few of your old photos in here."

"I like that idea. We can talk about it over dinner on Monday. Tommy, think about what I said. I'll be around most of the day. See you Monday, Claire. I'll call for directions."

Once Nick was out of sight, Tommy laughed. "So you're standing me up for Nick Rossi. I don't blame you."

"It's nothing like that. He left me a message, asking if we could go out to dinner to further discuss marketing ideas. It's not that I didn't want to attend your meeting. I'd be happy to go to the next one. By then I should have some designs for your website that I can share."

"Okay. I forgive you. Be sure to order a good dessert. Desserts are the best part of a meal."

"I'll let you know what I choose. I'm on my way to Catherine's. I'm sure she's home by now."

"I thought about going but there's too much here that needs to be done and too many who will be looking for me to answer questions."

"That's what happens when you are owner and baker."

"I welcome it despite my complaining earlier. Please tell Catherine I will stop by."

"Certainly. She seemed tired last night. But then, I'm sure she was worried about Frank and Hannah although she kept most of that to herself."

"She's one strong woman, like you, Claire."

"Like who? Who's a strong woman, Tommy?"

It was Denise, back with her French nails out. Taking a good look at her, Claire decided she was pretty with a hard side. The makeup was too much. Her streaked hair was too much as was her short skirt in the middle of winter. When she grabbed hold of Tommy's arm, Claire felt as if she was declaring him as her property. After Tommy introduced them, Claire tried to figure out a polite way to say good-bye. Denise made it easy.

"Tommy honey. I'm starving. Can we go get something to eat right now?"

Feeling bad for Tommy, Claire helped him out. "Why don't you two spend some time together? I have to get going. It was nice meeting you, Denise. Tommy, I'll give Catherine your message."

As she was walking away, Claire could hear Denise asking about Catherine.

It turned out Claire's visit with Catherine was a short one. While she was in her home, she was far from alone. Claire told her she'd return early in the coming week.

"Get some rest. You look tired, Catherine."

"I'll be fine now. I'm back where I belong."

Chapter Twenty-Seven

CLAIRE FELT AS IF SHE HADN'T been home in ages. With so much catching up to do, Sunday flew by. While making herself a late supper, Nicholas Rossi called to confirm a time. After giving him directions, Claire asked how she should dress.

"I don't want to be over-dressed or under-dressed," she explained.

"I would suggest in between, Claire. I have something special planned."

After they spoke Claire couldn't help but wonder what Nick Rossi had in the making. All she could think of was the scene in *Pretty Woman* when Edward and Vivian flew off to the opera in San Francisco. Claire decided that could be exciting. She'd never been to the opera. Her mother would sometimes mention the opera but they never went. Claire wished her mother was still alive. She'd take her on a train to New York during the holidays. They'd stay at the Plaza and go to the opera. That was the last thought Claire had before falling asleep a little before midnight. But she didn't stay asleep. After tossing and turning she decided to call Tommy. She knew Denise wouldn't be there. Something was telling her Tommy would be awake. With so much to do, Claire could see him still working in his bakery. He answered on the second ring. After convincing him nothing was wrong, Tommy told her he was glad she'd called.

"Denise told me she'd be here for both events next week. I couldn't tell her not to come."

"No, you couldn't, Tommy."

"You sound like Catherine."

"That's a compliment."

"Did she get back home?"

"Yes. I only stayed a minute. She had a lot of company. I told her she looked tired and to get some rest."

"I thought she looked tired the other day. I hope she didn't rush getting back home. I'll have to tell her not to worry about helping me."

"If you get in a pinch I can help in the bakery."

They talked for a good half hour. Tommy laughed when Claire told him her thoughts about *Pretty Woman* after Nick said he had something special planned.

"All I could imagine was flying off to the opera with him."

"Nick does have that presence about him like Edward in the movie."

They both kept laughing until Tommy kidded Claire she should get her beauty sleep for her dinner date.

Turning out the light, Claire pulled the blankets up around her. Their laughter had her smiling as she watched stars glistening about the moon. She couldn't remember the last time she'd had a good laugh. It felt good. It put her right to sleep.

As she did almost every morning when first getting up, Claire looked outside to check the weather. She wasn't checking the conditions as much as she was looking for conditions conducive to photo opportunities. Early morning was the best. When looking out the window this particular Monday morning, nothing was glistening or hidden underneath frost or fog. It wasn't snowing. Except for the birds in the feeders it was quiet outside. For that, Claire was thankful. She had a lot of running around to do before four p.m. Her first stop was the post office. It took longer than expected. After the grocery and dry cleaners, Claire found herself sitting in a nail salon. This was not a usual stop but a necessary one. When she left, Claire started laughing again. Her nails looked just like Denise's.

The day rushed by. Once back home Claire spent time trying to decide what to wear. Figuring out what was between over- and under-dressed wasn't easy. Realizing she still had to take a shower and put her makeup on, Claire chose a pair of designer jeans she liked but hardly ever wore. A long black velvet jacket with a shawl collar and black leather ankle boots were pulled out from the closet to go with the jeans. Claire decided she'd pick out a scarf when she chose her earrings.

A hot shower was relaxing. Claire hadn't been out on a dinner date where the date came and picked her up in a long time. She felt like she was back in high school despite the fact her only date had been to the prom and it was a disaster. Claire decided tonight would not be a disaster. With her hair styled, makeup on along with those designer clothes plus a silk scarf and pearl earrings, Claire was downstairs in plenty of time. Nicholas Rossi was at the door at precisely four p.m.

"I'm ready, Nick. Please come in while I shut the lights out in my studio. I'll only be a minute."

"You look stunning, Claire. I'd love to see your studio."

"Thanks, Nick. The studio is a little messy. I've been filling orders."

Nick was in awe of Claire's talent evident in every photo on display. "You have the eye, Claire. You're able to discern a photo in places and things most would never notice."

"You're being kind. My problem is there's no more room for displaying photos. It looks like a jumbled mess. That's why I'm moving all of this to Tommy's. Besides having more space, the exposure will be invaluable."

"I'm looking forward to our discussion later on. I need help on that end of things."

"I enjoy creative conversations."

"Do you enjoy such conversations with a glass of wine?"

"I do. A little wine spurs the imagination."

"Well then, let's get going. Be sure to bring your camera."

"I always have it with me. Can you tell me where we're headed?"

"I prefer an element of surprise."

"Then I'm ready to go."

Chapter Twenty-Eight

Claire became even more curious when Nick stopped at the train station. She thought maybe he had some business to take care of but when he parked the car and went around and opened her door, Claire knew something was up.

Unlike the last time she'd been in the station, there were no long lines or people running in and out. There was a lone gentleman dressed in a white suit coat and black dress pants. It became obvious he was there to greet them.

"Good evening, Mr. Rossi. This way please."

All along the way employees acknowledged Nicholas Rossi. He and Claire were the only ones walking on the platform next to a train that had steam coming out of its smokestack. More employees were there to welcome them aboard. Claire remained speechless as they were led through one empty car after another. And even though they were empty, every car was decorated with twinkling lights and wreaths in the windows. When they reached the dining car, Claire was spellbound by Christmas trees of all sizes decorated with twinkling lights and wreaths hanging and candles lit. A gentleman wearing a double-breasted black tuxedo with wide lapels and grosgrain accents in both the jacket and matching trousers was playing the piano.

"Mr. Rossi. Your table is ready."

Following the gentleman to an intimate table out of the way, they were seated as another gentleman filled their water glasses and wished them a beautiful evening.

"The usual, Mr. Rossi?"

"Yes, Robert. Thank You."

When they were alone, Nick apologized for not asking Claire's preference in wine. "I am so used to ordering that red label that I failed to ask what you might enjoy."

"I'm sure I'll enjoy your selection, Nick."

"Tonight is a special occasion calling for fine red wine."

"I must tell you I am stunned by your surprise. The decorating is done to perfection."

"I felt an abundance of trees was necessary to make this old dining car feel even more intimate. We are just getting started, Claire."

"Are we going to visit Santa?"

"No. Tonight we are forging a new run for this train."

Nick was interrupted by Robert. Once he popped the cork, Robert poured a touch of wine into a long-stemmed crystal glass for Nick's approval. Moving the glass around in his hand and then sniffing the wine, Nick was satisfied.

"Perfect."

After filling two glasses, Robert placed the bottle of wine on the table.

"I'll let you know when we are ready for dinner. Thank you, Robert."

Raising his glass, Nick toasted his guest. "To Claire, whose presence adds grace and beauty to this train steeped in history. Welcome aboard."

Sipping her wine, Claire realized this man taking hold of her hand and kissing it was a gentleman. She was certain he'd been taught the rules of etiquette at a young age and was expected to live by them. Growing up he undoubtedly met the rich and famous because his family was just as rich and just as famous, rooted in the gilded age where their fortune was built alongside the likes of the Vanderbilts and Carnegies. Watching Nick center the candlestick sitting on the table offered a small window into his obsession with details.

"That looks better, Nick."

She could tell he didn't understand the comment.

"The candlestick. You centered it."

"Not a big deal but it bothered me. Excuse me for one minute, Claire. I must speak to the pianist."

Proper was a perfect description of Nick Rossi. To Claire, proper meant they had their life together. Up to now, that wouldn't have described Claire but she felt her life was turning a corner. She knew she couldn't measure herself against Nick. He had a head start. Wealth shaped him the minute he was born. Watching him speak to the pianist, Claire decided his quirks added to his attractiveness. Put the money aside and there was still something there. It wasn't Nick's wealth that stood out. It was his sense of self. Remembering Nick's concern for Hannah and the conductor's young son convinced Claire his priorities were in order. Of course those blue eyes were one detail she couldn't miss. With a chestnut brown corduroy jacket, jeans, and boots, Nicholas Rossi was the total package. Claire wondered if he'd ever been married. She guessed he was in his mid-forties. But these days and with his fortune, who could tell. When Nick returned to the table, he was all smiles.

"I like seeing you sitting at my table, Claire. It's usually me with my computer and a pile of newspapers."

"Thank you for asking me."

"I've taken the liberty of creating our menu. I wanted us to have time to enjoy our dinner before getting on with our evening."

Giving Robert a nod to begin serving, Nick explained. "This new run we are forging tonight is another phase of my overall plan. The track was already in place except for the last one hundred or so miles. I made a deal with the State to get that last one hundred miles of track in place. In addition we worked out an agreement allowing me to construct a station at the end of the run. By doing so, this run will increase the number of tourists coming to the area."

"That's good for all of us."

"It is a win-win for sure. I was sick when I returned a few years ago and found the community in such dire conditions. That has happened to many rural areas but it doesn't have to be like that. People have to dig in and get creative. I am willing to back ideas if I feel they'll benefit the whole. I'm working on bringing in high speed internet throughout this region. We can't grow without it. Nostalgia is wonderful but it can only go so far. Good ideas properly supported create jobs and jobs create growth. I'm all in favor of ingenuity."

"Forging a railroad track up a mountain tops anything I could ever imagine."

"There is another reason I wanted that track laid. My forefathers loved these mountains. They bought hundreds of acres before the area became as prestigious as it is today."

"Meaning they got the land for a steal?"

"Yes. And on that land they constructed a lodge which has been passed down through generations. I am now the guardian of the property. The problem with the lodge has been its location. It's hard to get to when the weather is inclement. Now with the station built, a good part of the journey can be by train. While I'm happy to give people another reason to come spend time and money in our community, I am pleased the family lodge will be more accessible for those coming to visit. Don't get me wrong. They too will be spending lots of money when they're here."

While the pianist in the white wool jacket played his piano softly in the background, Robert and staff served a dinner right out of a gourmet magazine. The presentation alone would have made one spectacular photo shoot but Claire didn't say a thing. She had a feeling Nick would agree. After they enjoyed Amaretto served in engraved glasses, he asked Claire if she'd like to dance.

"I'd love to, Nick."

"My father insisted I take lessons, telling me a gentleman always asks a lady to dance."

"I took lessons with my brother. He kept stepping on my feet."

As the piano player filled that dining car with beautiful music and as the tree lights twinkled and candles flickered, Claire felt like Cinderella in Nick's arms.

"I love your perfume."

"It's Toujours Moi. I think every woman in my family wore it. I'm not much of a shopper so when I saw it on the shelf I grabbed it."

"A woman who doesn't like to shop is unique. You intrigue me, Claire."

"Your dance lessons paid off, Nick. You are a fine dancer."

"Get ready for my famous dip."

Seconds later Claire felt herself falling backwards into his arms as he led her around the dance floor. Closing her eyes Claire imagined herself skating on a pond under the stars. Pulling her back up, Nick embraced Claire in both arms. Slowing the pace, he gently kissed her forehead over and over again as the snow fell outside a train going up a mountain. With the music fading to one last note, Nick whispered in her ear.

"Thank you for the dance, Claire. I hope I did not exceed my bounds. Between the wine, your perfume and beauty, I was caught up in the moment."

"I enjoyed every minute of our dance, Nick."

Again this powerful man, who could buy and build whatever he wanted, revealed his proper side. Turns out Nick had one more surprise.

"It's time to get on with our evening."

"You mean you have more up your sleeve?"

"Would you like dessert?"

"I love dessert. Anything sweet is my downfall."

"Good. Then here we go."

On the way back to the table, Robert appeared with their coats and boots.

"Bundle up, Claire. We are going for a ride."

"But we're already on a ride."

Without saying a word, Nick took Claire's hand and led her back through the train as it was slowing down. With bells clanging and brakes screeching, an employee standing at the door made an announcement.

"Hear ye. Hear ye. We are about to make our maiden arrival at Reindeer Station."

Before the train came to a stop, that employee jumped onto the platform. Making sure everything was in place, he gave Nick an all clear sign. Being the only passengers, Nick and Claire were off without a hassle.

"Thanks, Herman. It's invigorating to finally arrive at Reindeer Station. See you in a few hours."

"We'll be waiting for you, Mr. Rossi. Enjoy your time in the mountains."

Chapter Twenty-Nine

"Welcome, Mr. Rossi. From latest reports the weather will remain clear for your visit."

"Perfect. That's rare for December," Nick replied as he introduced Claire to the station manager.

"Your vehicle is ready."

"Thanks, Bill. We'll be right with you. I want to give Claire a quick tour."

It was apparent to Claire that the décor combined a feel of the mountains with Nick's taste for the gilded age of the railways.

"Your blend of the surroundings with a history of the railroads will make for great conversation while waiting for a train. I love the old benches."

"They are originals. I salvaged them from an abandoned depot in Baltimore. Those glassed-in cases on the wall announcing arrival and departure times came from there as well."

"Your attention to details again proves they matter, Nick."

After a few more minutes of looking around, they were out the door. Within seconds Claire found herself inside a vehicle built for winter travel.

"Are you warm enough?"

"Yes. And again I am curious as to where we are going."

"Let me surprise you, Claire. I love seeing your eyes light up with excitement."

Claire couldn't begin to imagine what Nick had up his sleeve as the vehicle went deeper into the woods. Suddenly Nick put his arm out in front of her as he slammed on the brakes. "I've never seen so many deer crossing a road at one time. There's proof why I named the station after the abundance of reindeer up here."

"They're beautiful animals."

Continuing on their way, Nick talked more about the reindeer. "There are family stories of how some of the reindeer became regulars at the lodge. About twenty-some years ago a stable was built to house horses and once in a while reindeer have been found sleeping there as well. They are left alone to come and go. It's fascinating to see them mingling with the horses."

"How heartwarming it must be to watch such mighty creatures sharing space."

"If we have time, before or after dessert, we can check out the stable."

"What are you saying?"

"I am telling you we are on our way to enjoy a most delectable dessert known as Bûche de Noël at the lodge."

"At your family's lodge?"

"Yes. I hire people to keep watch on the place. They've gone in, turned the lights on and the heat up and built a fire in the fireplace. Some Bailey's Irish Cream coffee will be ready along with my favorite French Christmas cake shaped like a yule log. All details have been completed."

"You are the perfect planner, Nick."

"Wait until you taste the dessert."

Listening to the delight in Nick's voice as he talked about the French dessert, Claire imagined him in a stately den surrounded by shelves of books, with a mahogany desk to one side, and a comfortable chair where he'd sit in a casual yet classic tweed jacket on the other. His pipe would be sitting on a table next to him.

"It's a flourless chocolate cake," he explained. "I found a cake without flour interesting. It's rolled in homemade chocolate whipped cream. To get a snow effect, confectioners sugar is used."

"I can't wait to taste it."

"The lodge is up ahead. I'm sure the Bûche de Noël is ready to be sliced."

The narrow road in was getting wider. A few lights shining down from poles allowed Claire a full view of Nick's family lodge as they made their approach.

"Your lodge could serve as a cover for a destination promotion."

"It takes constant maintenance."

"From what I can see it doesn't look as if one thing is out of place."

"That's what I pay for, Claire."

Once Nick turned the vehicle off, someone opened his door.

"Good evening, Mr. Rossi."

"Good evening, Eddie. Are we in good shape?"

"Yes. I've timed the coffee to be served in half an hour."

"Perfect."

After making the introductions, Nick and Claire walked down a stone path to the stable.

"We'll enter nice and slow in case there are a few reindeer staying the night."

They were in luck. In the far stall there were two reindeer. While they couldn't be seen from the doorway, their antlers gave them away.

"You could try taking some photos. I don't think you'd bother them."

"I don't want to scare them away. I'd rather watch the reindeer mingle with the horses."

Claire was granted her wish as some of the horses came over to Nick. It was obvious they knew him and were expecting some treats. They weren't disappointed. Getting a bag from a shelf in the other room, Nick fed one after another. Being curious, the reindeer made their way over to see what was going on. When they discovered food was involved they stayed put. After a few miniature ponies joined the group, a dappled horse came from nowhere. Instead of lining up by Nick, the horse went over to Claire and nudged her forehead along Claire's arm.

"She likes you, Claire. The little filly is always hungry. Want to feed her some treats?"

"I'd love to."

There was something about the dappled horse that perked Claire's interest. Something was stirring her memory. When the horse shook her long grey mane, Claire recalled a dappled horse named Molly. The horse loved to eat apples. It lived on a farm with other animals not far from where she grew up. Her father was friends with the farmer and the few times he visited the farm, Claire went along. Her siblings never wanted to go. They didn't like the smells. Nick interrupted her train of thought.

"I'm out of treats everyone! I think it's our turn for dessert, Claire."

The lodge was more breathtaking than she'd imagined. A traditional stone fireplace reaching to the ceiling was the focal point. The popping of burning logs reminded Claire of that simple clapboard house on that snowy back road.

"The mantel was hewn from a log not far from here," Nick explained. "Whoever chose it knew what they were doing as it picks up the hues in the stone."

"I can see that. It must be even more evident in the light of day."

Overstuffed sofas with matching chairs were nearby along with antique rockers and oak hutches. A grandfather clock ticking away in a corner caught Claire's attention. Nick explained one of his relatives had been a clockmaker.

"The intricate engraving on the wood is marvelous."

"From family diaries I read he had offers from people around the world wanting to buy the clock. When he wouldn't sell it he had people wanting him to duplicate it. But he refused. So this is a one-of-a-kind Rossi original."

Knowing the weather was clear but could change at any moment, Nick hurried the tour. When he showed Claire the den, she had to laugh.

"I imagined such a room lined with books and a desk like the one sitting there with a comfortable chair on the other side. I could see you in the chair reading with a pipe nearby."

"I do spend endless hours in this room. I get lost in a book. But I've never smoked a pipe although many in my family did. The books on that particular wall behind the chair are centered on the early days of the railroads."

"I would think the Rossi name is on many of those pages."

"That is true, Claire. Now, I think we've waited long enough for our Bûche de Noël."

While Claire sat on one of those overstuffed sofas in front of the fireplace, Nick went into the kitchen. Seconds later he returned carrying a serving tray hewn from wood.

As he placed the cake and the dishes and cups full of piping hot coffee down on the table in front of them, Nick explained he'd made the tray.

"I went through a period of working with wood. While I enjoyed it, I'd get impatient with the process. This tray was my one and only finished project."

"If you ever get bored you could make a line of trays. If you put them on the internet they'd sell like crazy with the name Rossi attached."

"I'll keep that in mind if I ever get bored. For the moment, I'd prefer to discuss in detail some of your thoughts and ideas on marketing both the area and my train runs. That is if you don't mind talking business over dessert. When we're through, figure out how much I owe you for your expertise."

"Talking about marketing never gets old, Nick. There's no charge. I love the process of turning an idea into a reality especially while enjoying dessert."

So while the flourless chocolate cake rolled in a delectable chocolate whipped cream was enjoyed along with Irish coffee, ideas filled that room with its traditional stone fireplace and antiques rooted in a family's history. Somehow the conversation came back around to the horses.

"Do you like to ride, Claire?"

"I discovered I enjoyed riding when I was hired by a client to take photos promoting his expanding insurance company. I talked a man into allowing us to come onto his property and shoot photos of his horses."

"Was it the same man who owned the restaurants?"

"No. Remember, he tried to keep that behind the scenes. Anyway, the campaign was about strength and trust. It worked. The insurance broker had great response from our image campaign featuring the horses and I went back and took riding lessons."

"Have you ever ridden in the winter?"

"Yes. The first time I forgot sunscreen. The next time my feet got cold. From then on I had no problems. I loved it. You must enjoy riding this time of the year. You have the perfect backdrop."

"I do. Maybe we could go riding sometime before Christmas."

"I'd love to, Nick."

They could have kept talking for hours but Eddie interrupted.

"I have your car warming, Mr. Rossi."

"I can't believe it's time to go. I have enjoyed our conversation, Claire. I look forward to our implementing much of what we've discussed."

"I am anxious to get the ball rolling, even though a Bûche de Noël will not be part of the plans."

"So you enjoyed your dessert?"

"I enjoyed every minute of the evening."

Claire was not just being polite. Nick Rossi was quite charming despite coming from a world she'd never known. And that was fine. Catherine had talked about how our own unique experiences make us the unique adults that we become.

Claire kept that in mind when Nick responded to her telling him she'd had a lovely evening. "I am not good at relationships. While most people think money can buy anything, I can tell you it can't buy happiness. It can buy things. In some ways, money can buy you people. Money can take you places. Money can make you cynical and self-centered. That was my father. Money kept him away from home when I was growing up. What I would have given back then for a home with a backyard and a dog and a father who spent time with me. That probably sounds silly considering the mansion that was my childhood home but it was cold. Money can't buy you the warmth that matters."

Nick finished his coffee. "I don't know where all of that came from when I was simply making a point that I do not fare well in relationships. I am looked upon as this rich man with toys and homes and railroads and women at my fingertips. It's hard to get past that with most women.

But you are different, Claire. The money part of me doesn't seem to faze you."

"I grew up poor, Nick. I am finally coming to realize I grew up surrounded by love. Even though it was chaotic at times, my parents did their best and I know they loved me."

"Think you could ever love me?"

"I don't even know you, Nick."

"My father had an older gentleman friend who told the story of when he got married. He was home on a three-week leave from Vietnam. It was Christmastime. When out one night he met a girl who liked to ski. He'd made plans to go skiing for a few days so he asked her if she'd like to go along. When it was time for him to go back to Germany and on to Vietnam they'd married. And you know something, their marriage remained strong after knowing each other less than a month. That friend told my father he knew she was the one the minute he looked into her eyes and introduced himself."

"That's an amazing story, Nick."

"My point is a relationship isn't measured in time. It is measured in love. I believe you feel that inkling about someone the minute you meet them. You can't buy true love. But you can take hold of it."

Claire understood what Nick was saying but she didn't reply. She let his story sink in.

Chapter Thirty

THE MOON FOLLOWED NICK AND CLAIRE all the way back to Reindeer Station. Once on board the train they settled in for the ride home.
While they'd been at the lodge, the dining car had been converted into
more of a lounge. That included yet another overstuffed sofa to sit on
and get lost in as Robert served tea in china cups that caught Claire's
eye.

"I am an admirer of fine teacups, Nick. I've never seen one so simple
yet elegant with its pink flowers and gold leaves."

"They've been in the family for as long as I can remember. That particular cup you are holding dates back to 1887. I thought they'd add a
nice touch to our time together."

"They add the perfect touch."

With the piano player playing one beautiful song after another and
the lights on so many Christmas trees twinkling, the journey home was
enchanting. They were back at the station a little after eleven o'clock.
Nick had his vehicle running in no time.

"Look at those stars, Claire. It's a perfect evening to go driving
through downtown all decked out for the holidays."

"I enjoy seeing the downtown dazzling. The tree in front of City
Hall reminds me of Rockefeller Plaza. It's only lacking a skating rink."

"Good idea. An outdoor public skating rink would bring even more people downtown. It would add to the feel of community. I'll bring that up at the next council meeting."

The ride was short-lived. Going toward Tommy's mercantile, Claire happened to look down the alley behind the building.

"Oh no! Look, Nick! There's a fire. I have to find Tommy!"

"Wait! I'll call 911."

Claire couldn't wait. Her heart was pounding. Her head was spinning as she rushed toward the fire.

"Claire! Stop! The fire trucks are on their way."

But Claire couldn't stop. How could she stop? She was certain Tommy was inside. "Tommy! Tommy! Wake up! Please, Tommy! Your building is on fire!"

As she was about to try another door closer to the flames, Nick grabbed her arm.

"Stay with me, Claire. I hear the sirens. It looks like there's more smoke than fire."

Claire stayed quiet as she watched fire trucks enter the alley from the other end. The flashing lights and sirens brought out the spectators. Within seconds the hoses were employed. With so much smoke Claire didn't see Tommy rushing out a door. But Nick saw him. Holding her close he pointed toward the building.

"Look, Claire. It's Tommy. He's safe. He's talking to a fireman."

Seeing Claire and Nick, Tommy walked up to them after being told everything at that point seemed to be okay.

"Tommy! I was so worried when I saw the flames."

"The fireman told me it looks like it started in one of the trash bins full of limbs from the tree we put up inside. Someone walking by could have ignited it."

"So there was no damage done?"

"I was told not much if any at all. Not even smoke damage. All I could think about when I heard the sirens was the fire in 1953 that destroyed most of the downtown. This place survived it but if you go downstairs you can see where a few of the timbers were singed."

They lingered until a fireman wanted to ask Tommy some questions.

"We'll leave you alone, Tommy. I'm glad everything seems to be under control."

"Thanks, Nick. Your space upstairs is safe and secure."

Giving Tommy a hug, Claire told him how happy she was that he was safe.

"I'll see you tomorrow. I'm anxious to move into my new location."

"Something tells me we're going to be busy these next few days, Claire."

Halfway up the alley Tommy shouted her name. "I meant to tell you John stopped by earlier. He told me Catherine isn't doing that well at home."

"What's wrong?"

"The cough she had turned into bronchitis. John said Catherine's not herself. She gets disgruntled because she can't do what she used to do."

"I'll make a point to go see her in the morning. Good night, Tommy."

It was snowing a little, making those downtown decorations sparkle all the more as Nick continued their drive down the main street.

"Tommy was lucky. I can't imagine losing that place after all his hard work."

"Besides the work, Tommy was making his dream come true," Claire explained.

"How so?"

"By opening a bakery."

"Opening a bakery has been his dream?"

"No. Being a baker has been his dream."

"I didn't know that. I knew there would be a bakery in the building but I didn't know Tommy would be the baker. Only proves you can't judge people by what you see. Would you mind if I asked a personal question?"

"Not at all, Nick. I've taken the liberty of asking you a few tonight."

"What is your relationship with Tommy?"

"I haven't known him that long but it feels like forever."

"You two seem happy when you're together."

"Tommy is in a relationship."

Pulling up in front of Claire's, Nick asked if she'd be at the private opening on Sunday evening.

"I wouldn't miss it."

"I plan to be there as well. I'm travelling the rest of this week. Due back late Saturday."

Moving closer, Nick put his arms around Claire. "You are a very special woman. I thoroughly enjoyed your company this evening."

Kissing her gently as snowflakes fell, he whispered, "I do have other surprises up my sleeve."

"I'm sure you do, Nick."

Pulling away, Claire said good night. "Thanks for a wonderful evening. You made me feel like a princess."

It was still snowing when Claire went to bed. Lying there, her thoughts went from a man who considered cutting out cookies to be an art form to a man who owned trains and things and had people opening doors for him and serving desserts to him on fine china. They were so different yet both were intriguing. Claire couldn't figure out how her life had become more complicated than usual. Neither of them was anything like Eric, which was a good thing. Pulling her blankets up around her, Claire watched the snowflakes flitting by her window. Closing her eyes she could still feel the rocking back and forth of the train chugging along through the darkness of the mountain. That rocking lulled Claire to sleep.

Chapter Thirty-One

Up early with the coffee going and her shower taken, Claire was in her studio figuring out how she was going to pack up the prints and transport them to Tommy's. Even though it wasn't far she still had the same considerations to address. Remembering a gentleman she'd hired to haul a light table to her studio, Claire messaged him about moving everything to her new location. She made sure he understood the move needed to happen immediately. Meantime Claire filled her car with what she could. Tommy had the shelves in and the internet ready to go. Claire loved the windows. She couldn't wait to build her displays. She knew where she'd put everything, including a small table and chairs where her customers could sit and go either through albums of photos or check them out online.

Running upstairs, Claire grabbed that box of old decorations, thinking there might be something in it she could use. On her way back down, Claire remembered the card she was going to send her sister. Sitting at her desk, Claire wrote Ellen a short note. She ended by telling her she'd come to the conclusion their parents did the best they could.

"That's all any of us can do," she wrote. "Life is a learning experience. Bottom line, I know Mom and Dad loved us."

Telling her sister she missed her, and this time she meant it, Claire addressed an envelope. Putting a stamp on it, she was ready to go. After stopping at the post office, Claire was on her way to see Catherine.

Once she turned onto that narrow country road, a part of her felt as if she were going home. Claire couldn't stay long. From what Tommy said, Claire felt Catherine would prefer she stay only a few minutes anyway. Slowing down as she approached the bend in the road, Claire tried imagining Catherine as that young woman standing barefoot on the porch now within view, waiting for the love of her life to come home. Most women would have given up when losing such a love at such a young age. But Catherine not only survived, she became the family matriarch beloved by those in and out of her community. Now she was tired and Claire was worried. She'd planned on bringing Catherine something that might cheer her up but decided Catherine didn't need a trinket bought at a store. Making the turn into the drifted path leading to Catherine's was when she realized what Catherine needed was a sign from Paul not to give up.

Seeing a horse and buggy in front of a large red barn behind the house, Claire got out of her car and made her way to the barn. If Catherine was sleeping, she didn't want to disturb her. As she moved slowly through the deep snow, a few birds perched on a windowsill near the top of another barn caught her eye. While that barn was old, it possessed a character all its own. The weathered boards and weeds and burrs were almost buried in drifts near the front, where the door with an interesting use of woods and patterns made Claire want to run for her camera. But she didn't. Instead she looked beyond those birds to the cupola at the very top. There she caught sight of a weathervane. There was something haunting about it sitting up there, somewhat worn yet still doing its job.

"Can I help you?"

Adjusting her eyes, Claire turned around as an Amish man was walking toward her. Noting his frame and strong jawline, Claire felt as if she'd already met this man through his mother's praising of him.

"You must be Amos Paul. Your mother told me about you. I'm Claire. I met your mother at John and Elizabeth's."

"Yes, I am Amos Paul. It is a pleasure to meet you. My mother told me about the time you shared together. I could tell she enjoyed herself."

"My intention when stopping there last week was to only spend a few minutes. By the time I left several hours later your mother had taught me the art of making cookies."

"Welcoming our neighbors into our homes follows the Lord's teachings. According to my mother the dearest things in life are mostly at hand. She treats each cookie as though it is the only cookie."

"I realized that once we got into the cutting of the cookie dough. I loved her story about the cookie cutters."

"Those cookie cutters remain dear to my mother. I wasn't surprised when she took them with her to Elizabeth's."

"I'm sure you weren't. Some things, like those cookie cutters, are irreplaceable."

"So what brings you out here so early in the morning?"

"I heard your mother isn't feeling well. I wanted to know if there is anything I can do for her."

"That is thoughtful of you, Claire. We can walk up to the house. She is awake."

"If you have the time I would appreciate that, Amos."

"When I stopped in earlier she was saying her morning prayers."

"So you live nearby?"

"I live past John and Elizabeth's. The red barn behind us is my barn. I am a tinsmith and carpenter."

"You're a tinsmith like your father."

"Yes. I was going to build the barn on my property but Mother asked if I'd build it next to my father's barn. That's where he worked with the tin. I decided it was the least I could do to honor my parents. Although I never knew my father, he has always been in my life because of my mother. I feel as if I know everything about him."

"Talking with her the other day I sensed the love she has for your father is as strong today as it was when they were young."

"That is true. I hope to surprise Mother this coming summer by doing some work on the old barn. I am sure you are aware of how we Amish can build a barn in a day. Well, we can preserve them as well."

"That would be wonderful."

"I wouldn't take anything away from it. I'd only redo what is needed and refurbish the weathervane."

"That caught my eye. I've never seen a more intricate weathervane."

"My father made it for my mother as a wedding gift. It's made of copper. To my father the weathervane represented storms they might go through over the years but he stressed their strength would see them through."

"Such a beautiful gift with a beautiful message, Amos. Are those sleighs in the barn?"

"Yes, those are sleighs. There are three of them. My father built them. Often my parents would hitch up a horse and go off in a sleigh. My mother used to do the same with me. She's a good driver."

"Does your mother still have horses?"

"Yes. There are horses in the barn. The stalls are in good shape. When Mother is up to it she feeds them. Lately I've been taking care of them."

Hearing the back door of the farmhouse open, Claire looked up to see Catherine standing there without a shawl or coat.

"Get back inside, Mother. You shouldn't be out like that."

"I saw my dear friend through the window."

"We will come inside if you are up for an early visitor."

"I am up for seeing Claire."

The minute they came through the back door, Catherine embraced her friend.

"The Lord knew what I needed when he brought me you."

"I will only be here for a few minutes. It is important that you stay rested."

"You sound like everyone else."

"That's because you are loved, Catherine."

"Please, Claire. Sit with me."

Pulling a chair out for his mother and then Claire, Amos said he'd be right outside if they needed him.

"Amos is good to me. His father would be proud of him."

"I became aware in the short time I spent with Amos that you've made Paul a part of his life. It's as if he grew up having both of his parents' guidance and support. You must be happy he is following in his father's footsteps."

"There is a proverb I wrote down when Amos was a baby. I still keep it in my Bible on my nightstand. Over the years when I needed guidance in matters concerning raising Amos, I would go up to my room and shut the door. Sitting on my bed I would open the Bible and read those few words. They brought me back to reason every time."

"May I ask what those words are?"

"Though it sounds simple, the proverb is quite powerful: *Always treat children in the direction you wish them to grow, not as they are now.* I would read those words as a reminder that a decision I was making concerning rearing Amos at that moment would influence him in years to come."

"How wise of you, Catherine. Those words are as you described, simple yet powerful."

"Amos has grown into a fine tinsmith. I would tell him stories of how hard his father worked at his craft and now he is doing the same."

Stopping to catch her breath, Catherine asked Claire if she'd like a cup of coffee.

"No coffee this morning. I didn't come to be waited on. I came to see how you are doing."

"I haven't been myself since I broke my ankle. And now I can't seem to shake this cold or whatever they call it. I pray to the Lord; asking Him for strength. I have so much that I need to do."

"You must put yourself first. I'm sure you've never done that before."

"My duty is to my family."

"If you don't take care of yourself you will be of no use to them."

"I think you and Amos had a talk down by the barn."

"If we did it was out of concern for you."

"I understand what you are saying."

Turning toward a kitchen window with muslin curtains pulled back, Catherine looked out at the old barn. She asked Claire if she'd noticed it.

"The front door caught my eye. And when I looked beyond some birds sitting on a windowsill, I noticed the weathervane. I'd never seen such a weathervane. That's what brought my attention to the barn itself as Amos came along."

"Though the barn is in need of repair, I am able to look out the window when doing dishes and imagine Paul in there working."

"The barn is rich in character. I've never seen such detail on a weathervane. When Amos told me his father made it I wasn't surprised, from what you shared with me of his talent."

"That weathervane is the first thing I see in the morning and the last thing I see in the evening." Catherine hesitated; remarking how "the way the wind is blowing, the snow looks like dust drifting over open fields, reminding me of sleigh rides from long ago."

Looking back at Claire, Catherine continued, speaking of her frustration almost in a whisper. "Being old is a reward from the Lord. His plan is for you to gain wisdom as you age and in return for longevity, the Lord expects you to mentor those following. Because Paul was taken at a young age, I made it my duty to mentor for him as well. How else would the younger ones know of his kindness; his love of tin and his barn and the fields he walked? There were the nights we'd bundle up and go off in a horse and sleigh as the snow kept falling. How else would little ones know of the tin cookie cutters and the love that made them? I do understand what you're telling me and how those around me worry, but I know no other way. As my health slows me down, I feel my spirit going down as well. I worry. Who will be the mentor? Who will make Hannah the snowman cookie? Who will embrace her as only an elder can? I do not worry so for the other little ones. They see the world. Hannah's path is dark despite the brightness in her heart. I need Paul. I need him to tell me I will be the one making Hannah's snowmen until a point in time when I understand it is time to let go; a time to believe that all I have given to those I love will continue on without me."

"My mother passed away worrying who would be our mentor. Who would be the one to keep the family together? Filling the shoes of a mentor is not easy to do. In our case, we fell apart but I find myself missing my brother and sister. Every family has their difficulties but underneath those difficulties is a bond only those involved would understand. I've come to appreciate my parents and the roles my siblings and I played in the family as the years have gone by. I'm letting go of the pettiness. I'll be reaching out to my siblings. I will be the mentor. Please, Catherine, don't stop living. Don't waste precious moments worrying about something only the Lord knows the answer. You still have so much to contribute. Rest. Let those you've mentored give you strength. I dare say Hannah is the strongest of those children, thanks in part to you being by her side, going beyond a mentor; being her great-grandmother with arms wide open. Your wisdom is needed as are your sugar cookies baked to perfection."

"You are a thoughtful young woman," Catherine replied. "I'll tell you a secret, Claire. It's never been about the cookies. It's been all about time spent listening and sharing."

"I realized that after our afternoon at Elizabeth's."

"You have a spark in your eyes, Claire."

"That's because of our time together. Now, I repeat, you need to rest."

"I will rest after I pack up some cookies for you. Hannah and I baked them."

As Catherine arranged cookies on a plate, Claire commented on her surroundings. "Your home is lovely, Catherine."

"It was all Paul's doing."

"While Paul did amazing work down to every detail, it's the love you've added that makes the difference. Your presence is in every corner of this home. Your quilts and crocheting, your sewing, your knitting, your baking and your warmth turned this house into a home." Claire paused. "And I see some beautiful crayon drawings in the windows."

"Oh yes. Those children love to color."

"You said Hannah was here making cookies with you. How is she getting along?"

"She and Bailey are doing fine. She visits most every day."

"Please tell her I said hello."

"And could you please tell my dear Tommy that when he's making Christmas cookies the most important thing is cutting them out."

Catherine had more to say but she ran out of breath.

"You were his teacher, Catherine. He remembers your every word."

"My Tommy is dear to me."

"I know he is. He feels the same about you."

"Tommy has a heart full of kindness, Claire. That's important in a man if you know what I mean."

"I felt that the minute I met him."

"I keep praying he finds the right woman," Catherine added with a smile.

"Tommy seems quite serious about Denise."

"I only have to look into Tommy's eyes and know what's in his heart. Eyes speak the truth, Claire."

Catherine paused, looking at Claire, who didn't add to the conversation. That's when a cat came strolling into the kitchen from a front room.

"Catherine. You have a cat. You didn't tell me that when we were making cookies."

"Yes, I do have a cat. Hannah named her Nutmeg. That young girl seems to have a fondness for spices. Nutmeg showed up at my back door one day when I was feeling sorry for myself. I believe that was the Lord's work with help from Paul. She's good company. Most nights she sleeps at the end of my bed."

"She's beautiful, Catherine."

"Animals have a way of making one's world feel good. But getting back to Tommy, please tell him I will be at his bakery as soon as I am able. Let him know that once I get my strength back I will be doing some baking for his Tin Cookie Cutter. And please remind him how wasting dough is like losing a cookie."

"I will give Tommy all of your messages. I must go now. I'm moving my studio into his building today and you need to get off of your feet and rest."

"I keep my rocking chair in the front room facing the barn. I sit there and rock with Nutmeg and look at the weathervane Paul made and the fields he worked."

"That sounds to me better than any pill a doctor could prescribe."

"I consider it medicine for my heart."

"I meant to ask about the buggy that was overturned the other night. Was John able to fix it?"

"Yes. John had Frank help him in hopes the young boy would re-member when out driving in those conditions that a buggy and a horse are to be treated with respect."

"I'm sure Frank learned his lesson."

"John is an excellent teacher of many things including life lessons."

After a long embrace, Claire, holding on to a plate of sugar cook-ies, was out the back door and down the steps covered in snow. Amos walked with Claire to her car. After questioning how she found his mother, Amos asked Claire not to say a word to Catherine about his plans to work on the old barn.

"I would never spoil your surprise, Amos. Your mother talked about the barn. It's obvious how much that barn means to her."

Once inside her car with the engine going, Claire rolled down her window and asked Amos to keep her informed as to how Catherine was doing. "I'll be spending most of my time at Tommy's building but I will get here when I can."

"I've stopped in a few times with John. I look forward to seeing Tommy's place finished."

"Grand opening is six days away. Thanks again, Amos. I'm so happy we met."

Claire headed back toward town. While she was excited to get started on the next chapter in her life, Claire felt drawn back to that old barn with its copper weathervane. She didn't know why.

Chapter Thirty-Two

THAT NEXT CHAPTER STARTED OUT TO be a busy one. The days leading up to Sunday's big gala were hectic. By Thursday morning Claire was settled in her space and ready to go. It was Tommy who needed the help. Claire was there for him Thursday evening.

"I am all yours right up to the opening," she explained when walking into the bakery and finding Tommy lying underneath a counter in a storage room.

"Perfect timing, Claire. Could you get me the box wrench out of my toolbox? It's a long, skinny-looking wrench."

"You're asking the right girl. I know my wrenches."

"In that case, grab the socket wrench while you tell me if you and Nick went flying off to the opera."

"Oh, Tommy. You'll never believe where we went."

When Claire got to the part about Nick's family lodge she remembered the Bûche de Noël. "It was a flourless cake shaped like a log and rolled in chocolate whipped cream and sprinkled with confectioners sugar. My sweet tooth was in heaven."

"I've seen recipes for that cake. I might make a few. See how they sell. So it sounds as if Nick laid out the red carpet for you."

"He's down to earth as much as he can be; a bit set in his ways but

I guess money can do that. It wasn't a date. It was more of a getting to know each other so we can work more effectively on his marketing."

"So what's next for you two marketing gurus?"

"We're supposed to be going horseback riding in the snow."

"He'll probably take you to what he calls his farm. It's actually a ranch with all the trimmings. It's out on Rt. 73, not too far from here."

"That's better than taking a train up to his lodge. Don't get me wrong, it was a beautiful evening. But when we go horseback riding, I'll have to have someone cover for me since we'll be open for business."

"You're going to do great there. The way you have your photos displayed enhances their appeal. Do you already have someone who can come in when you have other things that need your attention?"

"Like go horseback riding in the snow?"

"Exactly."

"Yes, I do have someone. She's been helping me out for a while when I'm in a pinch. Do you have someone who can help you out with all the baking you'll be doing?"

"I have a recent grad from an area culinary school ready to pitch in. She'll be helping with the prep work. She's due here tomorrow."

Taking a look around, Claire commented. "It looks like a bakery, Tommy. I'm so excited for you."

"It's getting there. I get energized watching it all come together. Did you see the magazines and newspapers? That guy has done a tremendous job setting up his space. And I could get lost in the bookstore. That place is about complete. They're waiting on more shelving. When we open they're offering some great specials. The movie theater is amazing. That will be a huge draw. One night a week they're showing classics."

Back on his feet, Tommy checked his work. "Chalk another to-do off the list."

"Where would you like me to start?"

"You could organize all that stuff I have in boxes over there."

"I've never seen so much flour."

"I got a deal on it. Same with the sugar."

"Want the stuff in any certain order?"

"No. Just keep all the vanilla together and so on."

"I can do that."

"I'll be out front working on getting prices up on the display boards."

"When do you start making cookies?"

"Late tomorrow afternoon. I have to get in touch with the TV station. They called earlier. They're interested in filming the first batch of cookies coming out of the oven. And then there's the gala. Hiring that guy to do the catering takes a load off my shoulders. He'll even deal with beverages and anything else that's needed including the cleanup."

"That's great he'll take care of it all."

"I meant to ask. How did you find Catherine?"

Claire didn't go into too much detail. She kept it upbeat. "I met her son Amos. He's keeping an eye on her."

"I can't wait until she's strong enough to stop in and tell me what she thinks. So that means I better get back to work."

The bakery was soon shaping up with shelves getting stocked and prices put in place and display case windows cleaned. Round tables with marble centers were accented by single candles set in tin candle holders made by Amos. Wrought iron chairs were placed around the tables while the two doing all the work were pushed along by good old rock 'n roll. Tommy kept those classic albums playing one right after another. Close to midnight, after arranging his cookbooks and hanging what the saleswoman called Folk Lace curtains in the windows below the stained glass, Tommy went looking for Claire.

"I think we've crossed off every little thing that needed to be done except for one."

"What is that?"

"Come with me."

Moving behind the counter where apothecary jars sat on top, Tommy went in search of something below it.

"I know I put the box down here. Just give me a minute."

"I love these old jars."

"I'm filling them with cookies. Catherine gave me the idea when she told me how she leaves samples of her cookies out for customers to try. The idea is to get potential customers to taste the cookies in hopes they'll buy them."

Hesitating, Tommy went down on his knees and pulled out an over-sized box. Once he had it on a table, Tommy told Claire to shut her eyes.

"Okay," he said seconds later. "You can open them."

"Oh, Tommy," was all Claire could say when looking at him holding a sign declaring this bakery would from that point on be known as The Tin Cookie Cutter. "You've worked so hard for this moment. The sign represents what your bakery is all about."

"I think so too, Claire. I'm thinking I'll hang it behind the counter. There's already a sign outside the door."

"Behind the counter makes sense. Let me help you."

It wasn't long before they had the sign secured.

"It's full speed ahead, Tommy. Congratulations!" Claire felt such happiness for this man given nothing but a spark that told him he was meant to be a baker. All of his hard work led to this moment in a bakery named The Tin Cookie Cutter. Tommy's brown eyes were dancing with excitement. In fact, dancing is just what he did.

Taking hold of Claire's hand he walked over to the record player where he made a selection, then led her to the middle of the room.

"Wait right here."

Hurrying over to the light switch, Tommy dimmed the overheads. Back by Claire's side he took her in his arms just as Patsy Cline sang her song again. Pulling Claire even closer, Tommy led them around the tables, moving slowly or hardly at all. The moon seemed to know when it was needed, sneaking through the curtains adding magic to the moment. They didn't say a word. There was no need. With his hint of a beard and the scent of Ivory soap and spices, Claire was lost in his arms as her fingers played ever so slightly with the nape of his neck. Around they went in that bakery full of promise, built upon hope and prayers. When Patsy was on her last stanza, Tommy put both arms around Claire and whispered those words in her ear.

"I'm crazy for trying. I'm crazy for crying. And I'm crazy for…" That's as far as Tommy got. His phone was ringing.

"Yes. Hi, Denise. Excuse me for a second."

Shielding the phone, Tommy whispered, "I got carried away, Claire."

"We got carried away, Tommy," Claire answered in a whisper. "I can't wait to see that first batch of cookies come out of the oven. I'll take pictures to show Catherine."

"You mean that, don't you?"

"Mean what, Tommy?"

"I thought I was the only odd one getting excited over baking cookies."

"I think Catherine has something to do with our enthusiasm."

Giving Tommy a quick hug, Claire said good night.

On the way home she never turned the radio on. Patsy Cline was still singing in her heart.

Chapter Thirty-Three

WHEN THE PHONE RANG CLAIRE WAS curled up in her bed half asleep. At first she thought it was an oven timer in Tommy's bakery going off. That thought fit into a dream she'd been having involving the cookies that would soon be baked. Realizing it was her cell phone, Claire sat up and got her thoughts together before answering. She noticed it was only seven a.m. At first Claire thought the worst. Early phone calls do that.

"Oh, good morning, Nick. I'm fine. Just half asleep."

Having to sound perky was hard but Claire did it. Nick was calling to discuss a date for going horseback riding. Tommy was right. Nick would be taking Claire to what he called his farm. He had holiday events coming up at art galleries in New York and Washington so he was getting his December calendar in order. Claire explained she'd check her calendar and they could discuss it Sunday evening.

They didn't talk long. Nick was meeting some Board members of a railroad association for breakfast.

"I'll see you Sunday night at the gala," were his last words.

Those words reminded Claire she needed to go shopping for something to wear. And she needed to get her nails done again. Both had to be accomplished before getting to Tommy's. She was out the door by nine.

Claire knew where she'd go for a dress. Although she'd never been inside, she'd driven by the boutique a few times. It was small, her type of place to go shopping. It turned out Claire's instinct was spot on. She fell in love with a scarlet red velvet dress the minute she zipped it up. The dress was a perfect fit.

"With your auburn hair, you look stunning in red," the shop owner told Claire when she stepped out of the dressing room in bare feet wearing the off-the-shoulder dress with bell sleeves and above-the-knee cut.

"I've never worn such a dress," Claire replied as she thought of the other red velvet dress she'd worn and ended up tossing to the back of a closet. There was something liberating wearing red velvet again. After the owner helped her pick out some heels, Claire was on her way. The owner tried talking her into buying a sterling silver jeweled necklace but she wasn't interested. She planned on wearing her grandmother's pearls.

Once her nails were done, Claire headed to her shop. She'd thought about getting her hair styled but decided against it. A few times she'd made the mistake of getting her hair styled for a special occasion only to get home and wash it out. Claire preferred her hair to flow freely instead of being sprayed in place.

The mercantile was humming. Shop owners were busy with last minute stuff. Decorators were back adding to where they'd left off. Claire noted tables dressed in holiday linens with crystal platters and wine glasses, silver candlesticks, and centerpieces made from pine trees accented with silver-laced ribbons and silver beads. Claire figured all of it belonged to the caterers. She noted a man in a suit standing guard. Decorated trees were everywhere as were wreaths. Claire thought Elizabeth's were the most stunning. Simplicity stands out when surrounded by wreaths covered in shiny beads and trinkets made in China.

After stopping to talk to some of the shop owners, Claire bought herself a coffee and went to her space. She didn't think she had much left to do until turning on her computer and finding lots of orders. She'd get her helper Gayle on them. After building more displays and playing with the windows, Claire paid some bills. When Gayle arrived Claire was ready to go to the bakery. It was getting to be that time.

"There's no need to stay after five," Claire explained to the older woman with an obvious creative flair. "Just turn the knob from the inside and the door will lock. We're not open for business until Monday but you might get some shop owners wandering in to take a look."

The Tin Cookie Cutter was busy. Claire could hear the music in the background. Looking over at the tables she could see herself in Tommy's arms swirling around them. A man with a clipboard and a pencil behind one ear shattered all such thoughts when asking Claire her position in the bakery.

"I am a friend. I'm here to help Tommy."

"Oh, excuse me. I'm from the TV station. We're getting input from shop owners. Then we'll be back to film the first batch of cookies. This is an exciting event for downtown."

"Very exciting. I'm a photographer and a shop owner."

"Would you mind answering some questions? Then I'll get some shots from inside your place. Is it open?"

"Yes. I have a woman watching it while I'm here."

"I checked your window displays earlier. You have an ability to capture the character of your subject and make it look easy."

"Thank you. My name is Claire. It's nice meeting you."

"I am Ari Zaken. It is nice meeting you as well. While I take photos, they are nothing like yours."

"I found out early on that there are all types of photography. The trick is to find what interests you. It took me a while. Once I started riding backroads I knew I'd found my interest."

"Mind if I ask you a few quick questions?"

"As long as they are quick, Ari. I don't want to keep the baker waiting."

Ari was quick. Claire was on her way into the kitchen before four. She couldn't find Tommy so she introduced herself to the young lady she assumed was hired for helping with prep work.

"It's nice to meet you, Claire. I'm Susan George. Tommy will be right back. There was a problem with some shelving at the bookstore."

"Is there anything you need me to do? I came to help Tommy with cookies."

"That would be Tommy's call. He shouldn't be much longer."

Looking around at baked goods made that morning, Claire was surprised to find a Bûche de Noël sitting amongst them with the confectioners sugar sprinkled around and on top of it, ready to be placed in one of John's oak display cases. Claire had an idea. Hurrying to find Ari she talked him into going back to the bakery to take a picture of the flourless cake.

"You could use this in your feature. It certainly speaks Christmas."

"Great idea, Claire."

After giving Ari the details, he took some photos and was on his way.

"So how much do I owe you for the marketing?"

Turning around, Claire was surprised to find Tommy smiling at her.

"It's included in your website design."

"That's clever, promoting The Tin Cookie Cutter along with the history of this building."

"When you think about it, Tommy, the two go together. They make for a captivating holiday story and it's free advertising."

"I knew it was a smart move when I hired you."

Moving a little closer, Tommy added, "Plus you're a pretty good dancer."

"I followed your lead around the tables."

They were interrupted by Susan.

"Did you two meet?"

"We did. I don't mean to interrupt but I have a question about a recipe."

Following Susan into the kitchen, Tommy went over the recipe with her while Claire organized the spices. It turned out they never began mixing the ingredients until after 8:30 what with everyone after Tommy for help or advice. By that time Susan had left along with the caterers and shop owners. Claire told Ari she'd take the photos of the first batch of cookies coming out of the oven and email them to him.

"Here we are again, Tommy. It's late and we're just getting started."

"At least now we won't get interrupted. Put this apron on and we'll get busy."

With rock'n roll in the background, the mixing of ingredients began.

"How do you know how much dough to mix?"

"That depends on how many cookies I want to make. It involves math and that was my worst subject in school."

"Mine too. It still gives me a headache."

As flour and sugar were sifted together, Claire told Tommy about Nick's call.

"You were right. He referred to the place where we'll be horseback riding as his farm."

"When are you going?"

"He wasn't sure. Nick has many commitments but he's coming back for the gala."

"I have one commitment and we are standing in it. I'm not surprised he'll be here Sunday. Nick Rossi has a vested interest in this place succeeding. Now it's time for the eggs and vanilla."

Once all the ingredients had been added to Tommy's brand new professional mixer, he pushed a button and the magic began. Scooping some of the dough into a huge bowl Tommy brought it over to a counter where they both reached in for a fistful. Slowly they patted the dough into round balls.

"Here's your rolling pin, Claire."

With Tommy on one side of a counter and Claire on the other, they slowly rolled out their dough.

"Catherine always told me to take my time at this stage. She likened rolling out of the dough to laying down a carpet. Once a carpet is in place, then everything else comes together."

"I found her wisdom remarkable, Tommy."

"My dear Catherine is a woman of many gifts. Let's see if we can cut the cookies out with no dough hanging off the cutters and no dough left inside them."

"I never gave any real thought to what I was doing when I cut out cookies before meeting Catherine. But now I'm sure I'll be conscious of every step."

"So let's get started."

Placing a plastic container full of cookie cutters between them, Tommy and Claire were ready to go. "They aren't made of tin but they'll do for now."

199

"Maybe Amos would make you some. He could use the ones his father made for his mother as a guide."

"That's a great idea. What good is a bakery named The Tin Cookie Cutter if there are no tin cookie cutters being used?"

"I bet Amos could make those for you in no time. I have an idea, Tommy. Why couldn't Amos make tin cookie cutters and you could sell them? Package them together around some primitive artwork and I'm sure they'd be a popular item."

"Great idea, Claire. But instead of primitive artwork I'd prefer to license some of your photos in the packaging."

"Possibilities are endless, Tommy."

With great care Tommy and Claire placed their cookie cutters as close to the edge of the dough as possible. Once a cookie cutter was in place, it was in and out of the dough in a flash. Any remaining dough was gathered back up into a ball and rolled out again and cut into shapes. The entire process took quite a while but the end result was worth it, when the dough reindeer and cats and dogs and horses and sleds and snowflakes and stars and mittens and snowmen and Christmas trees were on baking sheets ready to go into the oven.

"We did it, Claire. We didn't waste any dough."

"I want to take your picture putting the cookies in the oven."

Tommy carefully placed the cookie sheets on a rack as Claire took photos. When he shut the door, Tommy set the timer and the two bakers started cleaning off the counter.

"Do you have a dishwasher or are you doing dishes by hand?"

"The dishwasher is over there under the counter."

"Fancy, Tommy."

"Cleanliness is a priority. That dishwasher is guaranteed to get off any bits of dough from bowls or cookie sheets."

"So much to consider, isn't there?"

"It's all been worth it, Claire. Think about it. We are in a bakery named The Tin Cookie Cutter in honor of an Amish woman who considers baking cookies to be an art form and has us believing that as well. And, the bakery is set inside an old building left to decay for years until it was treated with the respect it had earned, and given the tender loving care it needed to bring it back to the status it deserved. So while there were endless hoops to jump through to get here, the journey has been worth it. The Tin Cookie Cutter is about to become real. Smell the dough cooking and the cinnamon and nutmeg blending together. There's magic taking place inside that oven."

As they stood in front of the oven, reveling in the aromas swirling about, Tommy added, "I feel like I'm in a hospital standing in front of the nursery window waiting to see my babies."

"That's a lot of babies, Tommy."

"You know what I mean. I know you do."

"Yes. I understand what this first batch of cookies represents."

When the timer went off, Claire went for her camera. As Tommy opened the oven door and pulled out cookie sheets filled with reindeer, cats, dogs, horses, sleds, snowflakes, stars, mittens, snowmen, and Christmas trees, Claire took frame after frame of the moment Tommy's dream of a bakery became a reality.

"Their edges are that golden brown."

"Oh, Tommy. They are beautiful. Each one is perfect."

Claire snapped more photos of the cookies as they sat cooling on the countertop.

"I am bursting with excitement!" Taking hold of Claire, Tommy led her around and around the kitchen as they laughed and cheered and let their emotions run free.

"I am so happy to be sharing this with you, Claire. You get me."

"What does that mean?"

A cold voice shattered the moment. It was Denise standing in the doorway. "What did you mean by that silly statement?"

"We were celebrating the first batch of cookies coming out of the oven. It was a moment I'd been waiting to happen for what seemed forever."

"Oh, Tommy. Please! They are just cookies!"

With that remark, Denise walked out of the bakery.

"I should be going."

"Please, Claire. Take a cookie with you."

"I'd love a cookie. Thanks, Tommy. See you Sunday night."

Back home, Claire covered the reindeer cookie up in plastic wrap to protect it. She decided to turn the cookie into a tree ornament for Tommy. It would be a Christmas gift. Sometimes when Claire and her siblings were little they'd find some of the cookies they'd made with their mother hanging as decorations on the tree Christmas morning. For a few years they were certain Santa Claus made that happen.

Claire couldn't get to sleep. All she could think of was Tommy being with someone who didn't respect him. Aromas of spices and his after-shave lingered into the wee hours of the morning.

Chapter Thirty-Four

SATURDAY BROUGHT AN EARLY SNOW SQUALL but by the time Claire got going the sun was out. She wasn't moving too fast despite orders that needed to be processed. She'd decided before leaving home that she wasn't staying late. The emotions from that quick encounter with Denise the night before were still lingering.

Downtown was bustling with shoppers. While working on orders, Claire noticed many slowing down in front of her windows. Some stood there pointing at photos on display. Watching that taking place convinced Claire she'd made the right move. She also convinced herself to keep her distance from Tommy. It'd be hard to do but watching him being treated with such indifference both angered her and broke her heart. He'd become dear to her more than she liked to admit.

Because she brought her lunch, Claire never stepped out of her shop until going on four. She was about to exit the main door when she caught sight of Denise instructing the caterer in what else he should include in his menu for the gala. By the time Claire put her head down to avoid being seen, Denise spotted her.

"Claire! Wait!"

She didn't want to but she did, keeping her hand on the doorknob.

"I thought that was you, Claire."

"I've been working in my shop most of the day. I'm on my way home."

"Tommy told me you take pictures. I looked in through your windows. Do you take anything else besides old barns and Amish people?"

"Not really."

"No summer pictures, maybe flowers, weddings perhaps? I love weddings. I'm looking forward to planning my own soon. Do you know anything about the caterer over there? I'm thinking of asking him for his card."

"Check with Tommy. He's the one who hired him."

"Tommy has his head in his cookbooks. That's a good thing since a kitchen isn't my favorite place to be."

"What's he baking today?"

"Well, you and I know it won't be cookies. Before he got out of bed this morning we were talking. He mentioned eclairs and more cupcakes and some other things I'd never heard of before."

"It sounds like he's had another busy day."

"I gave him a few hours in that place of his. We're going out with friends."

"Have a good time, Denise."

"Will you be here tomorrow night?"

"Of course I will be."

Claire wanted to add she'd be wearing a red velvet dress but was afraid Denise would run out and buy her own.

Once back home Claire changed into some comfortable clothes and curled up on the sofa. She never bothered to eat. She never noticed the moon turning the snow into sparkling crystals. Most nights, if she'd seen the moon doing such a thing, she'd grab her camera and get outside no matter the time or temperature. But instead she stayed curled up, thinking about Denise digging her nails into Tommy and Tommy, being caught up in opening his bakery, going along with whatever she said. A knock at the door around nine startled her, scaring her enough to tiptoe to a side window where she looked out and saw John. He was shivering in the cold.

After fumbling with the lock, Claire pulled the door open as she turned the porch light on. "John! What's wrong? Come in. You're freezing."

"I am sorry to awake you, Claire. But Elizabeth and Amos sent me."

Claire couldn't ask why. Her heart was tripping over itself. Instead she led John inside and shut the door. Claire didn't breathe awaiting his explanation of why he stopped.

"It's Catherine."

Claire wanted to open the door back up and run into the wind but she didn't.

"Please, John. Please sit down."

"I can't stay."

"Tell me about Catherine."

Sitting on the edge of the sofa, John explained Catherine was in the hospital.

"Amos went over to feed the horses and bed them down for the night. Catherine leaves a lantern in the kitchen window so he knows she's gone to bed. But there were no lanterns on anywhere in the house. When Amos went inside he found his mother on the floor in the front room. He felt a pulse but couldn't get her to respond. Covering her up, Amos ran down the road to the Perkins farm. Thank the Lord someone was home. Catherine was at the hospital in no time."

"What did they find out?"

"Catherine has pneumonia. At her age, the doctor told Amos and Elizabeth it isn't good. She is weak and confused but she asked for you and Tommy."

"How did you know Amos was at the hospital with Catherine?"

"Mr. Perkins came and told us and took us to the hospital. He is waiting outside."

"How did you know where I live?"

"You told Hannah when you were riding with her on the back of the sleds."

Claire remembered the conversation. Hannah thought Claire lived nearby so she asked where, thinking she and Bailey could walk to her place once in a while.

"Let me try to reach Tommy. I know he had plans tonight. Then I will follow you to the hospital."

When Tommy didn't answer, Claire left him a message asking him to give her a call, telling him it didn't matter what time. Then Claire and John were out the door.

"Your neighbor is such a help tonight."

"Greatness is not trying to be somebody but trying to help somebody. Mr. Perkins understands what being a neighbor means."

The hospital wasn't far from downtown. When they pulled into the parking lot Claire said a prayer for Catherine, asking the Lord to give her the strength and the will to return home. After introducing Claire to his neighbor, John explained, "Mr. Perkins is staying here until we feel Catherine is out of danger."

"You are very kind, Mr. Perkins."

"Please. Call me Bill. My wife and I have become good friends with Catherine and her family. She is a wonderful person, always bringing us cookies."

John led Claire up to the second floor. As soon as he opened the door, Amos and Elizabeth were on their feet.

"Thank you for coming, Claire."

"Of course I would be here, Amos. How is she doing?"

"She is being given fluids."

"The doctor said she is dehydrated. Her temperature is below normal and her heart rate is low. I do not understand what all that means but I do understand the power of prayer," Elizabeth added.

"Who is staying with the children?" Claire asked.

"Frank and Hannah are with the younger ones."

When John questioned a nurse taking Catherine's pulse if he could speak to her, the nurse said yes but only for a minute.

With Claire by his side, John told Catherine Claire was with him. Catherine didn't speak but a few minutes later she lifted her hand.

"I am here, Catherine," Claire whispered, taking her hand. "I have a call in to Tommy. I know he would tell you how much you are loved. Everyone is praying for you. Everyone wants you to take care of yourself. Remember our talk the other morning. You need to get some rest and do what the doctors tell you."

Catherine let go of Claire's hand to motion for her to come closer. When Claire did, Catherine mumbled something that Claire could not understand. Moving even closer, Claire asked her to say it again. This time Catherine spoke so Claire could hear what she had to say.

"I need my rosary beads and my cookie cutters. Ask Tommy to bring them to me when he can. I don't want the others to worry. I must rest, my dear, dear Claire."

Seconds later Catherine was asleep. The nurse said that was the best medicine for her.

Speaking to the family, Claire suggested they go home for the night. "I don't see the need for you to stay but that is not up to me. I can leave my phone number with the nurse. I'll get Mr. Perkins's number and I'll call him if I have to. Then he can bring you back. It makes no sense for you to be sitting here all night. Catherine is getting the rest she needs. She is in good hands. You need to stay rested yourselves."

"I think Claire is right," said John. "We can get here fast if we are called."

Amos and Elizabeth agreed.

After giving the nurse her phone number, Claire repeated what she'd said before.

"I can be here in minutes. Please call me if Catherine asks for me or if she takes a turn for the worse."

As they were going out the door the nurse told them Catherine's temperature was the same.

Once in the parking lot they talked some more.

"The Lord is with Mummi."

"Yes, Elizabeth. Mother is in good hands. Thank you for your help, Claire."

"You are welcome, Amos. My place is open for anyone to stay at any point if need be."

"We will remember your generosity," John replied.

After letting Mr. Perkins know their plan, Claire asked him for his number. "If I hear anything during the night I will call you."

It was close to midnight when Claire turned out the lights. She kept her phone on her nightstand in case Tommy returned her call. He never did until three a.m.

"I knew something was wrong, Claire. I could hear it in your voice."

After telling him about Catherine's situation, Claire conveyed Catherine's request for her rosary beads and cookie cutters. Tommy asked Claire if she'd meet him at Catherine's around nine.

"I'll be there. I think I should call Mr. Perkins and ask that he let the family know when we'll be at Catherine's."

"Good idea, Claire."

"I know you have a lot going on with the gala tonight. I can take care of this if you like. Catherine would understand."

"Thanks, Claire. I appreciate the thought but if it wasn't for Catherine there'd be no reason for a gala tonight."

"Tommy, I'm worried about Catherine. I've tried to think of something to say or do or bring to her that would turn her around but so far I've come up with nothing. I am praying. I know the power in prayer so maybe I am doing all I can."

"Being around Catherine and the family, I've witnessed the power of prayer. If the Lord feels she needs you to say or do or bring her something that would help turn her around He will show you what that is."

"You're right, Tommy. See you soon."

Claire didn't ask why he hadn't called her back sooner. It was none of her business. She fell right to sleep.

Chapter Thirty-Five

BECAUSE OF THE GALA HOURS AWAY, it felt more like a Saturday than a Sunday. But with Catherine in the hospital priorities had changed. Instead of having a leisurely second cup of coffee, Claire was in and out of the shower and dressed by seven. After taking her red velvet dress out of the closet and her shoes out of the box, Claire called the hospital. She was told Catherine was asleep after a restless night. She was due another breathing treatment. The doctor had already been in. He ordered more blood tests. After hanging up the phone, Claire called Bill Perkins.

"I was sitting here reading the paper hoping you'd call."

After filling him in on Catherine's condition, she asked if he'd be able to pick up Amos as well as John and Elizabeth and have them at Catherine's house by nine. She explained why.

"I'll gas up and have everyone there on time. Is there anything else I can do?"

"Not at this time, Bill, but if something changes I'll give you a call. See you soon."

"Wait, Claire. Did you get a sense of how Catherine's doing other than her temperature and breathing treatments?"

"Not really, Bill. I sensed caution. Maybe that's because I'm not family."

"What does your gut tell you?"

"I can't go there. It frightens me."

Claire saved calling Tommy for last. Before the fifth ring, he was on the other end.

"Morning, Claire. I was in the shower trying to get my head on if you know what I mean."

Hearing Denise in the background, Claire kept the call short.

"You're busy, Tommy. I'll be at Catherine's a little before nine."

The plows were out after a heavy snowfall most of the night. Claire took her time. She'd learned in such weather the narrow country road could be tricky to negotiate especially with oncoming traffic. Despite the conditions Claire was the first to arrive. With none of the snow cleared away, she was cautious when parking. Once she made her way onto the porch, Claire found a shovel and started clearing off the steps. As she was working on a pathway through the snow, Tommy pulled in with his truck. It had a plow. Claire kept shoveling around the house while Tommy moved snow aside all the way down to the barn. It wasn't long before he had the job done.

"That should be good for now," Tommy said, joining Claire on the porch. "You must be freezing."

"If you must know, I have my long johns on."

"You might need them tonight as well."

Pulling out a key, Tommy opened the door. As they went inside, the others arrived. Claire was happy to see Hannah and Bailey.

"I'll stoke the fire. I was here filling the woodstove when I got back from the hospital."

"It's not too bad in here, Amos."

"My mother is a stickler for warmth. Once we get her home I'll be sure to keep her good and warm. I have the shed stacked with wood."

"The nurse told me she was restless during the night, Amos."

"I don't think she's been sleeping much here either."

"Mummi can always come back and stay with us, Father."

"Thank you, Elizabeth. Although she'd never say so, I think she found it hard being alone after living at your place with the children coming in and out."

"Don't forget Bailey!"

"I would never forget Bailey, Hannah. It looks like she wants to go outside."

"She can go out, Amos," said John. "Bailey won't stay outside long and besides, Hannah knows her way around this place."

"I do. It's just like our home, Father."

While Claire and Hannah caught up, the others gathered what Catherine requested.

"I think Mummi would like her favorite sweater."

"Take a look around, Elizabeth. Is there anything else you see that Catherine might want or need?"

"Maybe this small blanket, Tommy. She covers her knees with it when she is sitting in her chair."

"That chair has rocked many little ones over the years and heard many a tale. Sometimes I'd wake up during the night and listen to my mother rocking in the chair. Often times, she'd fall asleep."

"She'd do the same when staying with us, Father. She loved sleeping in the rocking chair by the lamb and Mary."

Silence filled that home until Claire remembered the tin cookie cutters.

"We can't forget the tin cookie cutters. Do you know where they are kept, Hannah?"

"Yes. They are in here." Going to a corner hutch, Hannah opened the middle drawer and took out the wooden box holding Catherine's treasured cookie cutters.

It was Tommy who was the first to hear Bailey barking. "Sounds like Bailey might have something cornered out there."

"Could be a rabbit," said Amos. "Can you see where she is?"

"That's not her rabbit bark," Hannah explained. "She's found something but she can't get at it."

"I think she's inside my father's old barn."

Elizabeth stayed at the house while the others including Hannah went out the back door.

Amos went ahead. "She's in the old barn all right. Her paw prints lead right inside."

"Is it safe for all of us to go in here, Amos?"

"Yes, Tommy. It is sturdier than it looks."

Weaving his way around the old sleighs, Amos led everyone toward his father's work bench. It was in fair shape considering it hadn't been used since Paul passed away. His tools were still sitting there, looking as if he'd be back any minute. There were piles of yellowed, dirty scraps of paper filled with designs and notes in his handwriting.

"If your father's bench could only talk, Amos. Can you imagine the stories?"

"I can. From what my mother has told me those stories would be something to hear."

Bailey continued barking. She'd wiggled her way behind the work bench. With her nose sniffing around, Bailey kept barking as she seemed to be trying to reach something caught under a board.

"I know Bailey. She won't stop until she gets what she is after."

"Don't worry Hannah. I'll get back in behind there and see if I can move that board enough for Bailey to get to whatever it is that has caught her attention."

Everyone watched as Tommy made his way behind the bench. Grabbing hold of the board, he pulled as hard as he could but it wouldn't budge.

"It's nailed down in a few places. Do you have a crowbar, Amos?"

"I do. Or rather my father did. I'll get it."

Amos was back in no time. It wasn't long before Tommy had that board out of Bailey's way. That's all the dog needed. She barked and pawed through years of grime and pebbles and bits of straw until finally the bark turned to a whine.

"Bailey has hold of whatever she was after," said Hannah as she called for Bailey to come drop it.

With her tail wagging as fast as the wind, Bailey hurried to Hannah's side.

"Drop it, Bailey."

Bailey obeyed. Whatever she'd found wasn't very big. Grabbing a cloth, Amos cleaned it the best he could. "Looks like it's made of tin," he announced.

A gasp from behind echoed through that old place.

"What's wrong, Claire?" Tommy asked. "You look like you've seen a ghost."

It took Claire a minute before she could get her thoughts together. Walking over to Amos she took the small object in her hands and held it ever so tenderly.

"Tommy! Remember I told you how I was worried about Catherine; how I wished I could think of something to bring to her. This is it!"

"I remember but what does that old piece of tin have to do with Catherine?"

"This is not just an old piece of tin."

Holding it up for all to see, Claire explained. "I have a feeling this is a missing cookie cutter. When I made cookies with Catherine I noticed an empty space for another cookie cutter in the wooden box. Catherine thought Paul's plan was to make a few more tin cookie cutters as time went on."

Taking the cloth Amos used, Claire cleaned the object off even more.

"This tin cookie cutter is in the shape of a heart! Oh, but that's not all."

Putting the old tin heart up to the light, Claire tried to make out what appeared to be words engraved along one side of the cookie cutter. Not able to decipher them, she hurried outside in the daylight. With a slight wind still moving snow around, Claire read two words engraved so long ago. *"For Keeps."*

"Such a beautiful gift, Amos," said Claire when back inside the barn and telling everyone gathered about the words. "I'll clean the heart the best I can before putting it in the wooden box beside the other cookie cutters. This gift from your father may be the medicine your mother needs."

Fifteen minutes later they were all on their way to the hospital. Bailey stayed in the truck with Bill Perkins while the others brought Catherine a miracle.

Chapter Thirty-Six

THE PARKING LOT WASN'T BUSY. BEING a Sunday most visitors waited until the afternoon unless it was an emergency. Everyone arriving with the thought of those tin cookie cutters on their minds considered this an emergency. They were on the second floor in no time. When they reached Catherine's room the door was shut. Claire led everyone to the nurse's station where she spoke with a nurse.

"Her door's shut so we didn't intrude. Is Catherine okay?"

"Catherine had another coughing spell. She's a bit dizzy. She didn't eat anything for breakfast. Her blood pressure is a little elevated. If you'd like to have a seat in the waiting room up on the left I'll let you know when she is resting."

"It sounds as if there's no better time for this surprise than now," said Tommy as they walked into the waiting room.

"If anything can give her strength it's the tin heart."

Everyone found a seat except for Amos who stood looking out a window. When Claire went over, she found him with tears in his eyes.

"I realize this is an emotional moment for you, Amos. You must feel your father's presence stronger than ever."

"I do. When I think of how many years that tin heart had been lying under that board and how many times I walked by it, I feel he made this moment happen when it needed to happen. It is a sign of love from my father to my mother when she needs it the most."

As Amos finished talking, a nurse was at the door. "The doctor is back. He would like to speak with Catherine's son."

"I am Amos. I am Catherine's son and this is her family. I know she would want all of us to hear what he has to say."

"I understand. Would you come this way, please?"

The nurse led them further down the hall. "Please. Have a seat in here. Dr. Northrup will be in momentarily."

A big table with several chairs sat in the middle of a room with no windows. A whiteboard was on the wall. In one corner there were shelves holding books and folders and a few plants in need of water. Attempting to get their minds off Catherine for a minute, Claire asked Elizabeth who was with the other children.

"One of my sisters. Not knowing how long we'd be, John and I decided Frank would need some help watching Faith and Abraham while caring for Mary with his bruised ankle."

"Frank gets a little nervous with Mary," John added as the door opened and in stepped the doctor. He was short and bald. His white jacket seemed long on him. One pocket was loaded down with pens. The doctor didn't smile. He was all business, sitting at the head of the table going through notes on a clipboard. When he lifted his head and looked around the table, he asked for Catherine's closest blood relative.

"I am her son—Amos."

"I will direct what I have to say to you. Your mother is in serious condition meaning her vital signs are not within normal limits. If I don't see improvement by this afternoon I may have to consider moving her to intensive care."

"I do not understand. I was told pneumonia is treatable."

"It depends on the patient. You mother is elderly. She is weak. I suspect she has been for a while. At the moment she has slipped into a deep sleep. She's not responding to the nurses."

Overwhelmed by what was thrown at him like darts on a board, Amos tried to get the doctor to slow down and explain in more detail.

"I do not understand all that you said. Do I have a say about my mother going to that intensive care? I want to bring her home."

"I am a doctor. I speak in medical terms. I will send a nurse in to explain. As far as taking your mother home, that is up to you. My medical opinion is she would most likely die. She is a tired old woman."

With that the doctor got up. "Excuse me. I have other patients to see. Wait here. The nurse will be right in."

Elizabeth embraced her father. "I too am confused. The doctor spoke so fast."

Tommy got up and went over and sat by Amos. "I remember when my mother had a stroke. Every time her doctor came in the room I tried making sense of what he said. I'd write things down to go research later."

"There is an Amish proverb my mother would recite whenever there was a problem. '*If the river had no rocks, it would not have a song.*' Those words explain how she overcame such sorrow. We are taught to endure illness with faith and patience. But we are also taught to let our lives speak. It was because of my mother that I felt I knew my father. She'd speak of my father's life as if he'd never been called Home. We need to speak to her about the life of a woman who shed light to those she embraced. And we need to do it now before the doctor sends her to that place he called intensive care."

As Amos was finishing, the nurse came in. "I understand you have questions."

"I wouldn't call them questions," he replied. "They are requests. I will need a candle and my mother's curtains drawn."

"What am I to tell the doctor?"

"You tell him we are treating Mother with love."

Once the nurse walked out the door, Elizabeth again embraced her father. "I do not understand, Father, but I have faith in the Lord and faith in you."

"Thank you, Elizabeth."

"How can we help?" Claire asked.

"I would like you and Tommy to come with us to Mother's room. I know you have a busy evening. I do not expect this to take long."

Picking up the wooden box, Amos led the way.

Chapter Thirty-Seven

THE CURTAINS WERE DRAWN. A NURSE explained they were searching for a candle.

"Thank you. I asked for a candle because my mother always has one lit in the window for my father. I want to make her feel comfortable. Please everyone, sit down."

Taking hold of Claire's hand, Tommy pulled two chairs together as he whispered. "I think we are about to witness a miracle."

"Well, it is Christmastime and it is Catherine," Claire replied.

"Funny isn't it? While Catherine doesn't think of Christmas as we do, she gives of herself every single day."

"She loves you like a son, Tommy. She told me every time you walked into her home, you brought sunshine with you."

"That is so like Catherine to say something like that. How lucky I've been to have her in my life."

Once a candle was secure in one of the windows, Amos went to his mother's side holding the wooden box. Placing it on her bed stand, Amos spoke to his mother as if they were having a conversation.

"Mother. I was thinking about your wedding anniversary coming in a few days. You have to get better so we can celebrate with the special dinner you always prepare. And as we sit and enjoy your fine cooking you can tell me again about the day you married Father. I love how you've always described the snow falling down as you said your vows and how still the house became when the minister finished the ceremony and Father shook his hand over and over because he was so happy. You talk about everyone being so happy. You must have looked beautiful in purple as Father must have been so handsome in the black suit you made him. I love the part in your story of how Father had arranged for a few of his brothers to have a horse and sleigh ready in the barn. When he thought the time was right, you two snuck away to be alone while the celebrating continued. He even made sure there were blankets in the sleigh. He was a thoughtful man, Mother. So thoughtful that he has sent a gift to you for your anniversary."

As Amos turned to the wooden box, he didn't notice the doctor coming into the room or Tommy wiping tears from his eyes. He didn't notice nurses crying or his daughter being held close by her husband or the snow falling as it did so many years ago on a December day when a young Amish couple pledged their love for all of eternity.

"Mother," Amos whispered. "I am placing Father's gift in your hands. He made it for you at his work bench in the barn with the weathervane. It has taken many years for this gift to find its way to you. Open your eyes, Mother. Father is wishing you a Happy Anniversary. Open your eyes, Mother. Your beloved wooden box with the tin cookie cutters is beside you."

Motioning for John to bring Hannah to him, Amos paused as the young girl took her place by his side.

"Mother. It is time to come back to us. Your dear Hannah is waiting for you."

Taking Mummi's hand in hers, Hannah spoke. "We have lots of cookies still to bake, Mummi. I love the snowman cookies you bake me so perfectly that I can see them in my mind. I fed Nutmeg today. I could tell she misses you. We all miss you. Please wake up. I love you, Mummi. I always will."

A sudden gust of wind pushed the snow up and around the windows. It was so sudden that it caused everyone to look to see what was going on. When the snow settled down, they turned their attention back to Catherine just as she was lifting her hand to Hannah. Everyone held their breath.

"I am here, Mummi. Look what your husband made for you. It is beautiful just like you."

Bringing her other hand up, Catherine called out for Amos. "Where are you? Take my hand, my son."

"I am here, Mother. I will always be here for you."

Amos reached inside the wooden box for the tin heart. Placing it in her hands, he explained. "This is your gift from Father."

Bringing her hands closer, Catherine felt what she was holding. She knew what it was. Opening her eyes, she rejoiced in what was waiting for her.

"Oh, my love made me a tin heart cookie cutter. Just think of the cookies we will bake, Hannah. I want to go home, Amos."

As everyone in that room blew their noses and hugged each other, the doctor took Amos aside. "I must apologize for my abruptness earlier."

"I understand you are busy, Doctor."

"That is no excuse. You and your mother have reminded me why I became a doctor. Sadly I'd forgotten. Your mother is not old as I stated. She's full of life."

"My mother is young at heart. She gives of herself every day. When do you think I can take her home?"

"I would suggest, and it's only a suggestion, that she stay one more day. We can keep an eye on her and check her vitals while you get things ready at home. When you leave, I'll give your mother a prescription for antibiotics and an appointment for a checkup."

"Thank you, Doctor Northrup. I will be sure she continues with the medicine."

The room was full of energy. Catherine looked around, realizing Paul had given her the strength to carry on as she'd asked. When she heard the story of how the tin heart cookie cutter was found, Catherine called Bailey her hero.

"To think this cookie cutter was inside that old barn all those years is bittersweet. While I felt a cutter was missing, finding it on this day of all days is the medicine I needed."

Taking a closer look at the tin heart, Catherine could make out the details Paul had included as he'd done on all of the cookie cutters. But this cookie cutter had that inscription.

"Paul was a skilled craftsman. Even after being subjected to the elements and whatever else in that barn, I can see the work Paul put into this beautiful little cookie cutter. Those two words describe our love. Paul would tell me our love was for keeps. I'm anxious to get back home and make cookies with all of you!"

It was obvious the tin cookie cutter had worked its magic. Despite the excitement, Catherine's vitals were right where they needed to be. Nurses were overwhelmed at what they'd witnessed.

Everyone stayed a little while longer. When Catherine started yawning, they decided it was time to go. Tommy put the wooden box on top of a dresser for safekeeping.

"You get out of here, my Tommy. Don't you have a thing going on tonight?"

"I do have a thing going on tonight, Catherine. When you are strong enough I will bring you to The Tin Cookie Cutter."

"You are special to me, Tommy Morgan. You are all so special to me."

After goodbyes were said and plans were made while standing in the parking lot, everyone headed in different directions. As Claire headed home her phone rang.

"Hi, Tommy. I was thinking about you. Wasn't that some moment?"

"It was an amazing moment. Catherine rebounded right in front of our eyes."

"I agree. Do you need any help getting ready for tonight?"

"No. I think everything is taken care of. I saw Nick earlier. He was asking about you. Maybe the four of us could go somewhere after the gala."

"Well, this is the time of miracles."

"Claire?"

"Yes?"

"I was happy to share that moment in the hospital with you."

"I feel the same, Tommy. I'm glad we were there for Catherine."

"I learned something sitting there listening to Amos talk about Catherine's wedding day. To Catherine, it was like yesterday. Paul has remained in her life over all those many years. Their commitment never died despite his passing. That's true love, isn't it? I've never thought of such things. Too busy doing my stuff I guess."

Claire felt no comment was appropriate.

Once back home Claire changed into her comfortable clothes. After taking a nap she started getting ready for the gala. That red velvet dress looked better than ever.

Chapter Thirty-Eight

TOMMY HAD RESERVED CLAIRE A PARKING space next to his. By the time she arrived it was about the only vacancy available. It was a perfect evening for such a festive event with snow gently falling and the moon behind a haze. Claire noticed limousines with drivers dressed in suits and red ties and long coats waiting their turn to open their doors and escort passengers to the mercantile all decked out for Christmas. Media from around the country were lined up next to one another. Claire was convinced Nick Rossi made certain all the players were in place. When she reached the door, a gentleman in a tuxedo was there to open it. The aromas of those pine trees and wreaths made Claire think of the moment she saw Elizabeth's wreaths nailed to clapboards. It seemed so long ago. With her head down so as not to make eye contact with anyone, Claire hurried to her shop. There she checked her email for orders. After she freshened up, Claire locked the door and headed down the corridor to the party. Everyone who was anyone was present. From politicians to the rich, shop owners to the influential and city officials, they were all there enjoying the food and drink while networking the crowd.

"Claire! Over here!"

It was Nick in the midst of fellow well-off people with recognizable family last names.

"You look stunning, Claire."

"Thanks, Nick."

For a moment Claire wished her father could see her dressed in red velvet with her auburn hair, the shade of his when he was younger. After Nick introduced Claire, he asked if she'd like a drink.

"I'd love a rouge sparkling wine. It has a festive sugar cookie flavor."

Claire had read that in an online article. It stuck with her for some reason, probably because of the sugar cookie reference. While making small talk with Nick's acquaintances, Claire spotted Ari from the TV station.

"It's nice to see you again, Claire. You look lovely in red."

"Thanks, Ari. Did you have any problems with the photos I emailed?"

"They were great. We used them as part of a promo on this morning's news and online. You were given credit. My boss was thinking of asking if you'd be interested in freelancing. You could send us stuff you think might be of interest to viewers. Of course you'd be paid and given credit for your work."

"Think my website could be included?"

"I'm sure that wouldn't be a problem. I'll be in touch."

"Great. Thanks, Ari."

"Making deals, Claire?" Nick asked as he handed Claire her glass of wine.

"When they interest me I do. You must be making deals all the time."

"That's the world in which I travel. In fact, I have a deal for you."

"You have my attention."

"I am going to Vancouver for a week, leaving the day after Christmas. I would love it if you would join me. The photo opportunities would be amazing, not to mention great food and unbelievable skiing. Think about it, Claire. It would be all on me. I can book you a room with a view you'll never forget."

"Are you going on business?"

"It's part business. We'd have time to see the sights."

"I'll think about it, Nick. It might be good to get away. That is if I can get my shop covered."

An acquaintance of Nick's caught his eye.

"I'll be right back, Claire. I haven't seen that man in years."

"Go mingle, Nick. That's what this is all about."

"And I thought it was about slow dancing," said Tommy.

"Where did you come from?"

"I was standing right beside you talking to the Mayor but you and Nick were engrossed in each other."

"Not really, Tommy. He invited me to go with him to Vancouver right after Christmas."

"Are you going?"

"He just asked me."

"Remember, Nick Rossi needs to know the details. If you go I will miss you."

"I'm sure Denise will keep you occupied. Where is she?"

"Getting ready. You look stunning, Claire."

"Thanks, Tommy. So do you in your holiday madras tie."

"Denise kept at me to wear a tuxedo but I couldn't sell my soul to a tuxedo."

"You have to be true to yourself."

"That's what I told Denise when I added this corduroy jacket!"

Claire thought Tommy looked charming. When the orchestra played a slow number Tommy asked her to dance. Setting her glass down, Tommy led Claire into the throng of dancers.

"Velvet enhances your beauty," Tommy whispered.

Claire felt the strength of his arms as Tommy led them slowly through the crowd until the music stopped and the orchestra took a break.

The party was going strong. Everyone was impressed by the work that had been done in bringing the building back to life. A few women asked Claire if she would give them a sneak peek of her shop. They liked what they'd seen in her window displays. Once Claire opened the door, those women did some major shopping. One in particular bought a good majority of her barn prints, explaining she was leaving first thing in the morning and wanted them as gifts to take with her.

"Why don't you go back and enjoy yourselves while I pack up your prints?" Claire suggested.

She took her time readying the order. When finished, Claire put the prints next to the inside of the door before locking it. As she was turning to go back to the party, Denise was walking toward her.

"Hi, Denise. It's nice to see you again. I love your dress."

"I've been downstairs long enough to catch your dance with Tommy."

"We've discovered we both love to dance."

"I'm here now. I'll be doing the dancing. Let me clarify that for you. I will be doing the dancing with my soon-to-be fiancé. We've been shopping for the perfect diamond."

"Congratulations," Claire replied, as Denise turned and went back to the party.

Watching her, Claire decided there was nothing more she could have said. She couldn't lie and say Tommy was a lucky man to be marrying her. Denise getting in her face had turned Claire's stomach. Staring at her gobs of makeup was too much to handle. If there was any suggestion of the four of them going somewhere afterwards, Claire decided she'd pull a headache excuse, although she wouldn't be surprised if she did have a headache.

When things were winding down, Nick asked Claire if she'd like to go for a nightcap in front of Tommy and Denise and a few other stragglers.

"I'd love to, Nick."

After making sure that woman had her prints, the two were out the door but not before Claire gave Tommy a hug. "Thanks for the dance. I heard nothing but compliments on all you've done here."

"See you in the morning, Claire. Ribbon cutting is ten a.m."

The look on Tommy's face showed he wanted to say more but Denise was next to him, her arm wrapped around his in a hold as tight as a wrestler's.

It felt good to be outside. Claire took in the fresh air as Nick explained, "There's a little place right down the street. We can walk there. It even has a fellow playing the piano."

That little place proved to be what Claire needed. Nick ordered a strong Belgian Christmas ale. Claire did the same. After some small talk, Nick brought up Tommy again. Claire didn't have much to offer.

"I must say, Claire. That girlfriend of his is rather unfriendly."

"That girlfriend is about to become Tommy's fiancée."

"Oh," was Nick's reply.

With another busy day ahead, Claire said good night.

"You don't have to walk me to my car, Nick. Stay and enjoy the ale and the music."

Claire took her time. Going by her window displays, Claire experienced a sense of pride in how far she'd come. She remembered when Eric told her she'd never amount to anything. When Claire walked past the door leading to the party she never looked in. Pulling out of the parking lot, the lady in the red velvet dress headed back home. She'd had her fill of socializing for a while.

Chapter Thirty-Nine

SO MUCH HAD HAPPENED IN A short time. Catherine was home, getting stronger every day. She and Hannah even made cookies. Most were heart-shaped. Hannah passed them out at school. While she'd yet to get to Tommy's, Catherine kept saying she'd be there before Christmas. Business was steady at the mercantile. Claire's sales were up 40% over last December and there were still ten shopping days left. Tommy was swamped with special orders. Between the bakery and being the owner of the building, Tommy never got a break. Although she tried keeping her distance, Claire would step in at times, staying late to help him catch up. They made a great team in the bakery. Even customers noticed.

On the day she and Nick were going horseback riding, Claire had to tell Tommy she wouldn't be able to help him that evening. "I'm not sure when I'll be home," she explained.

Claire wasn't fibbing. She had no clue what the day might bring. All she knew was to dress in layers and be ready by eleven. When Nick pulled up, she was out the door in seconds.

"What a perfect day, Nick. I brought my camera."

"I'm certain you'll have plenty of opportunities to use it."

Nick was right. The landscape surrounding what he referred to as his farm was astonishing.

"Even the ride in is spectacular, Nick, with the pines and maples and rock walls and hedges covered in snow. Who put the Christmas wreaths on the rock wall?"

"I did. I wanted that feeling of Christmas even before reaching the homestead. Up ahead is my sugar shack."

"Do you use it?"

"Most every year. I'll give you a quart to take home."

The barn and home were decorated in grand style. Nothing was left undone. A gentleman named Allan had the horses saddled and ready to go.

"Everything is in order, Mr. Rossi."

"Thank you, Allan. It's such a marvelous day. We'll be taking our time."

Walking inside the barn, Nick suggested Claire ride the Appaloosa.

"She's a gentle horse. Loves trail riding. Allan's daughter named her Spots which isn't surprising when you look at her. I'll be on my favorite quarter horse. This is Chestnut."

"She must be named Chestnut because of her color."

"You figured that out right away."

"They are both beautiful horses, Nick."

"Allan has been caring for the horses for years. It's important to find people who understand the value of doing a good job."

"I agree. You are only as good as the people who surround you."

With the temperature close to twenty-five degrees and the sun shining, comfort was no problem as they rode along a well-maintained trail that led to a ridge with a magnificent view. While Claire made good use of her camera, Nick made some calls. On some of those calls, he was wheeling and dealing.

"Everything is so untouched. It's as if we are passing by the home of Mother Nature."

"Love that description, Claire. I often come up here to clear my head when I have a decision to make."

"I can see why."

By the time they got back to the barn it was midafternoon. Allan was waiting for them.

"Another perfect day for riding, Mr. Rossi."

"Yes. But I think the company I was in made it even better."

"Flattery will get you everywhere, Nick."

"I was hoping for Vancouver."

Once Allan had hold of the horses, Nick escorted Claire into what he coined the farmhouse. Having almost lived at her grandmother's farmhouse, Nick's interpretation was far different than Claire's. His farmhouse was more like an estate decorated in a rustic theme.

"How often do you come here, Nick? It's so enchanting."

"I don't get here as much as I'd like to. Please, have a seat. Allan fixed us a late lunch."

A wicker basket full of pine cones and small Christmas balls sat in the middle of a dining room table made of wide pine boards. In one corner of the room a towering balsam decorated in miniature lights stretched to the ceiling. A fire was going in a stone fireplace. Music was playing in the background.

"I hope you'll enjoy a hearty homemade soup accompanied by homemade sweet potato fries, and a cranberry grilled cheese sandwich with a choice of drink."

"Everything sounds delicious, Nick. I'd love a sparkling water."

While they enjoyed their meal, Nick led the conversation back around to Vancouver. "I have some brochures for you to take home and study. Obviously there's much more information online. I would appreciate your decision by the end of the day tomorrow. Then I will make the reservations. Vancouver is a popular destination over the holidays."

"My decision partly depends on making sure I have my shop covered. And then there's Tommy."

"Tommy? What part does he play in your decision?"

"I told him awhile back I'd be around to help bake cookies for New Year's Eve orders."

"Cookies would stop you from going?"

"I told him I would help."

"He has no one else to help bake cookies?"

"Not on that scale. Maybe Catherine will be up to it by then."

"Catherine?"

"The older Amish woman I told you about; the one responsible for Tommy becoming a baker."

"This story of yours is getting more confusing by the minute, Claire. I will await your answer by the end of day tomorrow."

From that point on their time together was a bit awkward. When Claire said she should be getting back, he didn't hesitate to take her. As the sun was setting, Claire was walking through her front door. It never felt so good to be back home. After a shower Claire was going to relax and watch some mindless TV, but after Nick's strange response concerning Vancouver, she got dressed and took off in her car. Something was bothering her. Pulling into the parking lot at the mercantile, Claire noted Tommy's truck.

Since the place was closed to the public it was quiet inside except for some music playing. Claire knew it was coming from the bakery. She knew Tommy would be baking. When she reached The Tin Cookie Cutter, Claire never went inside. Instead she stood and watched the baker, absorbing the moment as he pulled out another sheet of what she perceived to be perfect cookies. Those aromas of cinnamon and nutmeg danced through her soul. It was as if she were looking at Tommy for the first time. There he was, alone but so full of life and meaning, stirring dough he'd be cutting out with tender loving care. He didn't own trains or lodges or barns full of horses or perfectly designed homes or tweed coats or a name that would bring him fortunes. No. He had none of that but what he did have was the stuff that mattered.

Claire left without Tommy ever knowing she was there. Getting back in her car, she turned the radio on and headed to that narrow country road to visit Catherine.

Chapter Forty

IT WAS THE IDEAL EVENING TO be out where the stars and the moon were turning fields into glistening beds of snowflakes. Silhouettes of barns with old rusted windmills, contrasted by homes outlined in strands of lights added a flavor all their own. Taking the now familiar turn onto that narrow country road, Claire kept hoping she wouldn't find a lantern in Catherine's kitchen window. She was in need of the Amish woman's wisdom.

Claire was not disappointed. While there wasn't a lantern in the kitchen window, there were lanterns visible in other parts of that home. Pulling in, Claire noticed a horse and buggy tethered to a post under some maple trees. Catherine already had an evening visitor. That didn't stop Claire. Knocking on the back door, she felt relieved. If anyone could make sense of her confusion it was Catherine. But instead of Catherine answering the door, it was the Bishop standing in front of her.

"Good evening, Bishop. It's nice to see you again."

"It is nice to see you as well, Claire. Please. Come in out of the cold. I was about to leave."

"Is Catherine okay?"

"Oh my yes. The Lord continues to bless dear Catherine. She's getting stronger by the day."

"I hope it's not too late to be visiting her."

"You can be assured if it is too late, Catherine will let you know. Come with me. She's in the front room."

With the moon coming through a window, Catherine, sitting in her rocking chair with Nutmeg on her lap, gave Claire the same welcoming feeling she used to sense when visiting her grandmother. And just like her grandmother, Catherine's smile and open arms were all Claire needed to relax and speak from the heart. Once the Bishop said good night, that's exactly what Claire did.

"How are you feeling, Catherine?"

"I don't want to be wasting our time talking about this old lady. I want to hear about you, Claire. I want to listen."

"I'm confused, Catherine."

"I felt that confusion in the hospital. I will be blunt. I sense you have feelings that you're ignoring. And I would add to that, I sense something triggered them and now those feelings are staring you in the face. Stuffed feelings do not go away. They fester until they can no longer be contained. It's Tommy, isn't it?"

"Why do you say that, Catherine?"

"I too have felt love. Love is powerful. Love cannot be contained. It speaks through our eyes; through gentle touches and sweet nothings. I watched you and Tommy. You speak that language to each other without even realizing it. I witnessed his eyes looking at you. I noted your gentle touches. While you can turn your back on love, you cannot deny feeling love."

"But Tommy will be engaged soon."

"Soon does not mean he is engaged. I know Tommy. I have been thinking of him as I sit here with Nutmeg and look out at the old barn. Tommy is a lot like my Paul. While Paul was a tinsmith, he was a dedicated tinsmith. He put all he had into being the best tinsmith he could be. Tommy is now a dedicated baker after all those years of searching."

"I understand that and I respect his journey and love the cookies that he bakes with such tenderness, but there is another woman in his life."

"Denise has become a habit. She's been someone in Tommy's life but she has never been Tommy's life. There is a difference, Claire. There has never been passion between them. Love is not a habit. Love is fireworks and rapture. Love takes you beyond the stars. Love does not need time to develop. Love is instantaneous. Your heart speaks to you. You sense love. You feel love. When I told you I am still able to smell the wet threads of Paul's long wool coat when he'd come through the door drenched by the rain or snow and embrace me, I meant every word. That smell is forever in my heart. I still remember the first moment I saw Paul. He was thirteen. I was ten and I knew. It is something that cannot be defined. You simply know."

With tears running down her cheeks, Claire began thinking about how to put into words the feelings she'd stuffed away. Catherine was right. Those feelings had festered and she didn't know what to do with them. She'd thought of moving but where would she go. She thought of vacationing in Vancouver with Nick but the reality was she had no desire to go anywhere with him. If it had been Tommy, she'd have her bags packed. Sitting in that home built with the love of a young man for his young bride, Claire confessed her love of a man who'd captured her heart the minute their eyes met on the front porch of that clapboard house with Christmas wreaths on display.

"Catherine—oh, Catherine, I love Tommy beyond the moon and stars. His passion for baking; his passion for Hannah and all the children; his love of life and his smile and his ethic of hard work and his slight beard touching my cheek and his fingers rubbing my hand all send tingles through me. I am in love, Catherine. For the first time in my life, I feel what you felt when waiting barefoot on that front porch right outside that door and I do not know what to do."

Shooing Nutmeg off her lap and pulling back the small blanket covering her knees, Catherine stood and embraced Claire as the moon kept shining, creating those sparkling crystals.

"My dear, dear Claire. The Lord has blessed you and Tommy with a love that is rare; a love full of rapture that makes your toes curl and your heart flip. Now you must pray and be patient. The Lord is at work, my child. It is time for praying."

They stayed in each other's arms as Nutmeg rubbed against their legs and the wind whispered a song of love in the season of hope. When

Claire felt together enough to head back home, Catherine walked with her through the kitchen. That's when Claire noticed the cookie cutters on the counter.

"Hannah is coming over to make more cookies tomorrow. I will tell you a secret. Watch out for some cookies at your doorstep."

They lingered in a long goodbye. Catherine told her she was visiting Tommy at his bakery in a few days. "He doesn't know I am coming. Say some prayers for me as well, my child."

When Claire got back home she found a present with a card sitting in a plastic bag by her front door. Once she'd changed, Claire opened the box and found a quart of maple syrup with a Nick Rossi label on the front and the china teacup and saucer belonging to the Rossi family. The thought of tea inspired Claire to put some water on to boil and take out the box of teabags in the cupboard. Once she'd made her tea in the fancy Rossi cup, Claire sat down at the table and read Nick's note written, of course, in perfect penmanship.

> *My dear Claire,*
>
> *It is with regret that I write this note to you after our enjoyable time together. My intention was never to come across as rude to a most delightful and beautiful woman such as yourself. But the truth is, I was rude and for that I ask your forgiveness. One of my many flaws is the flaw of perfection, which entails, in my case, an obsession in the details. At this point in my life, I am aware I will not change. I cannot change. Details define me.*
>
> *I have planned my trip to Vancouver. I will be leaving the 23rd of December and returning the 10th of January. I've spoken with Tommy concerning the dog I'd requested for my conductor's disabled child. We will be presenting the rescue dog to the boy upon my return. He will be told the dog is a late gift from Santa Claus. My hope is that you will join us. I remember you telling me about the blind Amish girl and how you felt that her meeting another young person with a disability would be a positive experience not only for her but for the disabled boy as well. I would like to work with you to make that happen. I have been blessed by good fortune. I do not take that*

lightly. To give that boy a companion is the least I can do. I believe that dog will become his best friend.

I wish you a holiday season full of peace and happiness. I only ask when you have your first cup of tea in the Rossi teacup that you think of me.

Nick

Any energy Claire had left was used on raising the Rossi teacup in honor of Nick. She felt a huge relief knowing the pressure of going to Vancouver with him was off the table. With so many back orders to deal with in the morning, Claire turned out the light. That's when she noticed splinters of the moon shining on that heirloom gift from Nick.

Of course the moon would be shining on the Rossi teacup and saucer. He is the man obsessed with details, Claire thought, going up the stairs to bed.

Chapter Forty-One

WITH ONLY THREE SHOPPING DAYS LEFT, Claire was thankful Gayle would be working with her full time up to closing on Christmas Eve. It had been so busy Claire found it hard to get out of her shop until it was time to lock her door and drag herself back home. Claire felt bad she hadn't been able to help Tommy in the evenings, but the young girl he'd hired stepped up to the plate.

The day before, while getting a coffee when arriving at the mercantile, Tommy had been in line ahead of her. They talked for a few minutes. All Claire could think of, while he went on about orders and shop owners with problems and a possible snowstorm on Christmas Eve, was her talk with Catherine. She felt his eyes searching hers as the subject of Nick came to the forefront.

"How was the horseback riding?"

"It was the perfect day for it. And once again, Nick had the perfect everything to go along with it. But tell me about the rescue dog you are getting for that disabled boy. I think that is wonderful."

After Tommy filled in the details, he checked the time. "I have a batch of cookies due out of the oven in a few minutes. I hope I see you again before Christmas. Do you have any plans for Christmas Eve?"

"Nothing definite. And you?"

Hesitating, Tommy replied, "Not sure. Depends on some things."

When Tommy gave Claire a hug goodbye, his slight beard brushing her cheek sent those tingles down to her toes. He lingered at the doorway, then turned and hurried back to the bakery. She didn't see him again for the rest of the day.

But that was yesterday. This new day would prove to be another busy one. It was getting down to the wire. Christmas was coming despite Claire's lack of preparation. Midday, she hurried out of her place to do some serious shopping. She'd been thinking about what to get for John and Elizabeth as well as the children and Bailey and of course Catherine. She was aware not to buy anything too fancy or too expensive. Functional was preferred when it came to the adults. Claire had already decided she was buying Catherine an apron. She had her eyes on it. It wasn't frilly. The simple pattern with pockets in the front had caught Claire's attention. When baking with Catherine, she noticed how much use Catherine got out of pockets. After her whirlwind spree was complete, Claire went back to the shop. To her surprise, Elizabeth was waiting for her.

"I am so happy to see you, Elizabeth. What a pleasant surprise."

"Thank you, Claire. I have come to invite you to our home for Christmas Eve. John and I would love to have you be part of our family gathering. The children would be most happy if you could join us. If you are free, come in the afternoon and stay for dinner."

"How kind of you, but you must have so much to do what with the children and Catherine."

"This year has been a little easier since the school's Christmas program was held earlier than usual. So I've had extra time to prepare."

"Then I would love to spend Christmas Eve with you and your family, Elizabeth. What can I bring?"

"You need not bring a thing. We invite you to be our guest."

"Thank you for the invitation. I can't think of any other place I'd rather be on Christmas Eve."

"I took a look at your photographs. You capture our way of life with respect and beauty."

"I appreciate your input, Elizabeth. My goal of any photo I shoot is for that photo to tell its story with dignity."

"And there are so many more stories waiting to be told out on those roads. But for now, I must get going. Mummi is visiting with Tommy. I told her I would come for her when it is time for us to start back home."

Claire hoped Elizabeth didn't notice her reaction to what she'd said concerning Catherine being with Tommy. Watching the young Amish woman walking toward The Tin Cookie Cutter, Claire wondered about Tommy's response, if any, to what Catherine had to say. About half an hour later as Claire was finishing up with a customer, Elizabeth returned with Catherine by her side.

"You are looking well, Catherine," Claire said as she embraced her friend.

"I feel better every day, Claire. Of course I had to try a few of Tommy's cookies. Those ovens of his are something else. I can't imagine using them but his cookies are excellent."

Taking a close look at many of the photographs on display, Catherine praised Claire for the quality of her work. "Elizabeth was correct in telling me how you treat each photo with respect."

Once the two women were ready to leave, Claire walked them to the door. As Elizabeth turned to leave, Catherine took hold of Claire and in a whisper told her to smile. "It is in the Lord's hands now. Tommy listened to all that I had to say. He knows I only speak the truth. Stay strong, my dear Claire. I will see you on Christmas Eve."

With but a few days to go, the shops were staying open until eight. Thanks to an unending stream of customers, time flew by. Claire kept an eye out for Tommy but she never saw him. Once she made it back home, she fixed herself a cup of tea in her Rossi cup and a bologna sandwich with mustard and a pickle on the side. When that didn't do the trick she decided to concoct a fruit smoothie. They always did the trick when Claire wanted something extra.

As she sat on the sofa wrapped in a comforter enjoying her drink, the phone rang. Claire's heart jumped thinking it might be Tommy. To her surprise it was her sister Ellen. As soon as Claire answered, Ellen was crying.

"Thank you so much for that card, Claire. When I opened the envelope and found that pink snowman smiling at me, I sat down and cried. It was a good cry. I realized how much I miss you."

"I cried too when I found it."

"Did I ever tell you why I colored the snowman pink?"

"No, you never did, Ellen."

"I colored it pink because I thought of you."

"What does that mean?"

"That means I considered you to be pretty as pink."

"Knowing that makes the card even more special. How thoughtful you were to me and I never realized it. That Christmas seems so long ago."

"Well, it was, Claire!"

They both laughed, which relaxed them and made the conversation flow.

"I remember every moment of that Christmas. Mom was tired and Dad was really tired and that little brother of ours whined and cried because Santa didn't bring him the race track he wanted. Dad finally put him in his room. I carried your presents upstairs and put them on your bed, then sat waiting for you to wake up. When you did wake up, you had no interest in opening anything so I opened your presents and Dad got mad at me. I can still hear him yelling my name as I ran to my room."

"You can't say many of our Christmases were like the Waltons. But our parents did the best they could. Now when I look back I remember the good times and there were good times."

"Yes, there were good times. I should learn to concentrate on the good. I should do that in my own situation. It would make everything so much easier. But enough of sad old me. Tell me about your life."

Ellen never asked such a question. At first Claire was cautious. She was used to her sister criticizing her every word but this time Ellen listened and commented and gave advice that Claire found insightful.

"So where do you stand with Tommy?"

"I have no clue, Ellen, but I'll keep you informed."

Before they hung up, Ellen asked for Claire's web address. "I will spread the word about my talented sister. And one more thing, I want to come visit you. Let me know what dates will work and I'll be there.

I'm bringing you back your pink snowman. That's probably the best gift I ever gave you, Claire. It came from my heart."

After they hung up Claire kept hold of her phone. She wasn't quite ready to let go of the call.

Chapter Forty-Two

CHRISTMAS EVE BROUGHT SHOPPERS OUT IN droves. Claire never saw daylight until she locked the door at three p.m. Rushing home, she took a quick shower, then threw on a pair of jeans and a sweater. Pulling her hair back, she ran downstairs to gather the gifts. It started snowing when Claire pulled out of the driveway.

With those gifts sitting in the back seat and holiday music playing on the radio, there was something quite enchanting about this Christmas Eve. Claire couldn't put her finger on it until reaching the white clapboard house with corn shocks still standing in a nearby field. Gone were the Christmas wreaths with red bows. Elizabeth had sold them all. Sitting there for a moment Claire realized that enchantment she'd been feeling had nothing to do with gifts. It didn't come with bells and whistles or expensive dishes serving fancy entrees. Rather that feeling of enchantment stemmed from a family with a dog named Bailey and a reindeer named Ginger and a little lamb who slept by a baby named Mary. They'd welcomed her with open arms and invited her to spend Christmas Eve with them in the simplicity and wonder of their home.

Claire recalled the first time she was drawn to this farm with its barn full of sleighs and reindeer and horses and a workshop housing slabs of wood and boards and cans of shellac and varnishes that would be turned into magnificent pieces of furniture and toys. So much had happened since that cold early morning when Claire stopped because her photographer's eye caught sight of fresh wreaths decorated with red bows hanging on the front porch. While she was curious about the Christmas wreaths that morning, Claire had no real interest in Christmas. If the truth be known, she hadn't felt Christmas in years. Oh, she went through the expected motions but Claire felt none of them until now. It had been a gradual turnaround spurred on by that Amish family in the home in front of her as well as learning the art of making Christmas cookies beside a wise, caring woman, and meeting a young man who'd opened her heart to feeling again. What would come of that was unknown but Claire was determined to enjoy every minute of this Christmas Eve. Finding Christmas again was the best gift ever.

Walking down the snowy path and up the steps of that clapboard home, Claire noted the moon breaking through the snow clouds. She could hear the laughter of children and smell the woodstove. Claire only had to knock once and the door opened.

"Claire's here," Frank announced. That's all he had to do. Everyone dropped what they were doing and hurried to welcome their guest. After hugs and Christmas greetings, Claire was inside that home where candles were lit and the table was covered with a festive red tablecloth embroidered with sprigs of holly. In the center of that table sat a simple white candle. Crayon drawings and strings of angels were everywhere. Abraham was sitting on a braided rug playing with his blocks.

"Something smells delicious, Elizabeth."

Welcoming Claire, Elizabeth explained. "It is our traditional Christmas Eve dinner. We are blessed to be sharing this evening with you."

"I wouldn't want to be anyplace else but with you and your family tonight."

Handing Elizabeth her bag of presents, Claire thanked the young mother again for inviting her.

"You did not have to bring gifts, Claire."

"I realize that, Elizabeth. It's a way of showing my appreciation."

"I thank you for your thoughtfulness."

While Elizabeth took the gifts into the front room, Hannah stayed by Claire.

"Mother's Christmas Eve dinner is very delicious."

"I'm certain your mother makes the best Christmas Eve dinner ever, Hannah. Are you ready for Christmas?"

"I have one gift to finish."

Moving closer, Hannah whispered, "The gift is for Mummi. I am sewing potholders for her."

"That is a perfect gift, Hannah. And how is Bailey doing tonight?"

Petting the dog, Claire found herself thinking about the disabled boy soon to be surprised with his own dog. Nick did have a heart. But his obsession with details was smothering.

"Elizabeth. Mary is getting so big."

"Mary will soon outgrow the cradle, Claire."

Coming through the back door with an armful of wood, John welcomed Claire to their home. "When Elizabeth told us last night at the dinner table that you would be coming for Christmas Eve, the children cheered. We have much to be thankful for and that includes your friendship."

"Thank you, John. I told Elizabeth I wouldn't want to be anywhere else but here tonight."

With the lamb standing by the door, Elizabeth told Frank he should take the lamb outside before dinner.

"Yes, Mother." Frank was out the door only to hurry back in and announce Catherine's arrival.

"Mummi's here! She came by horse and sleigh."

Everyone looked out the windows. There she was, getting out of a sleigh with Frank's help.

"Would you take the horse and sleigh to the barn and bring these few bags inside, Frank?"

"Yes, Mummi. Are they presents?"

"I can't tell!"

Catherine was peppered with questions when she walked into the house.

"Sit near the fire, Mummi."

"I feel as if I've come back home after living here for such a long time."

"I miss you, Mummi. I liked coming home from school and having you here."

"I miss you too, Hannah. But I am not far away. Besides, I see you almost every day when you visit me."

"Why did you come by horse and sleigh? Where is Amos?" John asked.

"He was not feeling well, yet he was still going to bring me here. I told him that was nonsense. I sent him home and hitched up the horse and sleigh and here I am. It's been a long time since I hitched up anything, so it took me a while. But once I got going, it felt wonderful to be out there on such a beautiful Christmas Eve with my horse pushing through the snow. It brought back so many wonderful memories."

"I love Christmas Eve," said Frank, back from the barn.

Embracing the young boy and giving Claire a wink, Catherine replied, "Magical things can happen on this night of all nights."

"You should have asked Father to hitch up the sleigh for you, Mummi."

"Your father is getting that horrible cold. He needed to stay home with his family. It feels good to be able to do what I want to do, Elizabeth, although I will admit it wasn't easy."

"Your being stubborn was probably helpful, Catherine."

"Indeed, John."

"Dinner will be ready in about half an hour," Elizabeth announced.

"Can I bring Claire to the barn with me and Bailey, Father?"

"Why do you want to go to the barn?"

"I told Ginger I would bring him an apple on Christmas Eve."

"If Claire wants to go to the barn with you that is fine but we'll have to find her some warm clothes."

"I would love to go Hannah."

"Thank you, Claire."

"I think you should bring two apples for Ginger, then both you and Claire can give him a treat."

"Thank you, Father!" That's all Hannah needed to hear. Once Claire

244

was bundled up, out they went holding hands and a lantern with Bailey by Hannah's side and two apples in her pocket.

"Hear the trees moving in the wind, Claire? Sometimes Bailey and I sit in the field and listen to them. They know it's Christmas Eve. So do the rabbits and deer and that train passing by so far away."

Claire did listen to the trees, something she would have missed if not for Hannah. With that train in the distance, Claire wondered if Nick had made it to Vancouver. She felt like the lucky one. She wouldn't want to be anywhere else than where she was, heading to the barn with Hannah and Bailey as Christmas was stirring in the wind.

That feeling of enchantment was in every corner of the barn. But then it was Christmas Eve and, as Hannah had pointed out, even the animals felt the wonder of it all.

"I can tell Ginger is waiting for me. He isn't making any noise. He is being a good reindeer."

With light from the lantern, Claire could make out Ginger's shadow standing still in anticipation of Hannah's arrival.

Inside the reindeer's stall, Hannah hugged her reindeer while she told him it was Christmas Eve and her mother was cooking their traditional Christmas Eve dinner and Mummi had arrived in a horse and sleigh.

"We have fun together, Claire. Bailey runs ahead in the pasture and Ginger tries to catch her. I don't think he ever does."

With Ginger smelling the apples, Hannah took them out of her pocket. Giving one to Claire, Hannah showed her how to feed an apple to a reindeer.

"Hold it away from you. Ginger will take it out of your hand."

Claire did as Hannah said and Ginger had the apple in his mouth in an instant.

"I will bring you another apple tomorrow, Ginger."

Giving her reindeer another big hug, Hannah asked Claire if she'd like to see her secret spot.

"I'd love to see your secret spot. Is it far?"

"No. It's up that ladder. You go up first with the lantern. Then I'll come up with Bailey."

Claire was going to offer to carry Bailey but she sensed Hannah had it under control. It all worked out perfectly. The three were up in the secret spot in no time.

"Look out the window, Claire. You can see the moon."

Claire looked at the young girl who seemed to know where things should be without being able to see them. Catherine was right. The Lord does provide.

"The moon is beautiful out your window, Hannah."

"I feel it is snowing again. It always snows on Christmas Eve."

"It is, Hannah. The snow is sparkling under the moon."

Moving aside a blanket that Hannah explained was hers, the young girl pulled out a book from underneath a small clump of hay. "I like to read stories to Bailey. This is my book full of Christmas stories. Mummi helped me put them in order. Would you like me to read one to you?"

"I would love that, Hannah."

When Hannah began telling a most beautiful Christmas story, Claire noticed her book was a collection of some of her illustrations. Claire figured she must have memorized the order in which each illustration came in the book. As Hannah went along she told stories to go with the artwork. Hannah's imagination kept Claire's attention to the point neither of them heard the stairs creak or Ginger shifting about the stall. When Claire turned around, she watched John step off the ladder into the haymow. Hannah sensed his presence.

"Father! How did you know we were in this secret spot?"

"Ginger was standing at the bottom of the ladder looking up."

"Such a silly reindeer!"

"I have been sent to tell you it's time for dinner."

"Thank you, Father. We will be right there."

Walking back to the house, Claire remembered when it was Tommy she was walking beside and they slipped on a patch of ice. That's when she told him about the purple tutu and he talked about his father passing and his guilt for not being by his side. Then there was that kiss under the stars and the sound of children giggling behind curtains.

"How is Ginger tonight?" Mummi asked as they came through the front door.

"Ginger was happy to see us."

"Did he enjoy the apples?"

"He loved them, Mother."

While Claire and Hannah had been at the barn, the table was readied for Christmas Eve dinner. Piping hot serving dishes were filled with traditional favorites, from a creamy potato casserole to green beans grown in the garden, to macaroni and cheese and pickled beets and Catherine's banana bread. After everyone was seated, John placed a meatloaf embellished with carrots and onions and slices of yellow squash in the center of the table. Once he sat down, they all joined hands and with their heads down, listened as John said a prayer of thanks.

As they were about to enjoy their meal, there was a knock on the door. Claire watched as John went to answer it.

"Good evening, Bishop. Come in and join us for Christmas Eve dinner."

"I cannot stay, John. I do not mean to interrupt. I was passing by on my way home and thought I'd stop and give you the blessing of the Lord on this most beautiful evening."

"Please. Come in, Bishop. We would love to receive your blessing."

The Bishop didn't linger once he blessed those gathered around the table. "I will not keep you from enjoying your fine meal. Merry Christmas to all. May the Lord bless you."

As the lamb slept and Mary stayed content, plates were filled and the traditional feast began. Candles lit throughout that home added to the moment of family and the season of giving. When they finished their meal, the table was cleared to get ready for dessert.

"We are blessed with Mummi's strawberry eggnog pie and her carrot cake made with carrots from her garden," Elizabeth said as china cups and saucers were placed on the table along with coffee freshly perked. As she was about to slice the desserts, there was a knock on the door. Claire said a prayer as John went to open it.

"Oh my goodness," said Catherine. "What are you doing here?"

Looking up, Claire saw Amos walking in as Elizabeth welcomed her father with Abraham in her arms. "Please stay, Father. I can warm a plate for you."

"I cannot stay, Elizabeth. I wanted to bring Mother this gift to open tonight."

"You should be home resting."

"And so should you, Mother. Did you hitch the horse to the sleigh?"

"I took my time."

"You shouldn't be doing that right now."

"Well, I did. I heard what you said to Elizabeth. You didn't have to come out on such a cold night to bring me a gift."

"I wanted to, Mother. It's Christmas Eve."

Handing Catherine his gift, Amos explained. "After Bailey found the cookie cutter I remembered you telling me some nights Father worked at his bench late into the night. That gave me the idea that other things might have been lost out there over time."

Opening the box, moving paper aside, Catherine's eyes filled with tears.

"Oh, Amos. This was your father's first hammer used for working the tin. I gave it to him as a wedding gift. He used it daily until it went missing. Your father searched and searched for this hammer. Thank you, Amos. Do you have time for dessert?"

"No, Mother. My family is waiting for me."

"I hope you're feeling better tomorrow, my son. Seeing this hammer brings back so many lovely memories. I give thanks to the Lord for blessing me with all of you."

Chapter Forty-Three

AFTER THE DISHES WERE DONE, WATER was brought to a boil as tea-cups were on the tray alongside what was left of the pie and cake. While the women sat down around the table to enjoy a cup of tea with dessert if they chose to have more, John took the lamb outside. He wasn't out there long.

"The wind is picking up. It's snowing again. Maybe you should stay the night, Catherine. Claire, you are welcome to stay as well."

"Thank you, John, but if I take my time I should be okay."

"It would be wise to leave soon, Claire. This road is one of the last to be plowed."

"Even though I'd prefer to stay longer, I will heed your advice and head home," said Catherine.

"I'll help you hitch the horse to the sleigh."

"Thank you, John."

"How will you get the horse unhitched, Mummi, once you get back home?"

"I may be an old woman, Elizabeth, but I can still unhitch a horse and bed him down for the night."

"You're still recovering from pneumonia. I'll follow you on horse-back, get you in the house and make sure it's good and warm, then take the horse and sleigh to the barn."

"Oh John! You're too good to me."

When Catherine didn't argue, John knew it was a plan.

As her car was warming up, Claire thanked everyone for their thoughtfulness. "I am so happy to have been a part of your Christmas Eve. I loved going to the barn and feeding Ginger and listening to you telling stories, Hannah. The dinner was delicious, Elizabeth, as were your desserts, Catherine. I wish everyone a very Merry Christmas."

As Claire was about to leave, Elizabeth asked her to wait.

"John and I were thinking. If you don't have plans for Christmas, we would love to have you join us for dinner."

"Again, you are very kind. I wouldn't want to interrupt any plans you may have."

"We decided it would be best if we stayed home for Christmas. Faith is not well enough to go and Frank's ankle is still sore. So please, come back tomorrow for dinner. We will be singing and playing games and Mummi and the children made Christmas candy to give to any visitors stopping by."

Looking around at the faces smiling and the home anticipating Christmas, Claire accepted their invitation.

"Can I bring something?"

"Nothing, Claire. We would love to share the day with you. Come when you can. Dinner will be at four."

After saying thank you again, Claire was heading out the door when Catherine stopped her.

"I asked him to join us tonight but he must be busy in his bakery."

"I don't think it's the bakery keeping him away, Catherine. I have a feeling Denise is wearing the ring she wanted."

"We do not know what daylight will bring. I will pray for you and Tommy."

"Thank you, Catherine. Will you be here tomorrow?"

"Yes. I will be here. Be safe out there my child."

Snow was falling; the wind was blowing as Claire stepped on the gas and made her way onto the road. What with deer and whiteouts, Claire kept the radio off so as not to get distracted. With nothing going on, she didn't care how long it took to get home.

Unlike the country road, Claire's street had been plowed. Even the sidewalk had been shoveled. The young man she'd hired to clear away the snow had done his job again. It was after seven-thirty when she walked through the front door and up the stairs to change into more comfortable clothes. Back down in the kitchen, Claire poured herself a glass of wine. She thought about going into her studio but instead, she lit the candles under the angel chimes and sat down at the table. Gently moving one brass angel and then another, memories of past Christmases drifted through her mind. Without a doubt the most magical were the Christmases when her grandparents lived in their farmhouse. Those were the ones where her belief in Santa was steadfast. Even the animals in the barn seemed filled with anticipation and the wait between Christmas Eve and Christmas felt like an eternity.

Standing, looking out back where her small garden was buried under snow, Claire remembered Christmas mornings when she'd fly down the front stairs with her brother and sister. Their stockings would be overflowing. Gifts would be piled under the tree. Her mother would be dressed, sitting next to her father on the flowered sofa in the front room. Snow would be falling. The wind would be whispering, making the morning even more wondrous. Now as she thought about those mornings, what struck Claire was the feeling she'd get seeing her parents sitting side by side, smiling as they embraced their children on Christmas morning. Of course there were a few Christmas mornings she preferred to forget, like the few after Eric told her he didn't want children.

As the candles began to move the angels around and around, Claire thought of going through her laptop for any orders she might have missed, but she wasn't in the mood. Nor was she in the mood to play Christmas music, considering it was Christmas Eve and there she sat, alone at her kitchen table without family; without anyone at all. She thought of messaging Tommy but something told her not to.

It was a little after eight when Claire thought she heard a knock at the door. Sitting still, she decided it was the wind moving branches, hitting the roof like they always did, reminding Claire she had to call someone before the branches caused some damage. When that knocking happened again, Claire put her glass down on the table and went into the living room. Without turning any lights on, she knelt on the sofa. Slowly pulling back a curtain reminded Claire of the morning she knocked on the door of that clapboard home and waited for someone to answer. Despite wishing for the same outcome, she didn't see Tommy standing outside her window. In fact, no one was standing there. As she kept looking, Claire noted something flying in the wind. It seemed to be attached to her porch light. Looking closer she noticed faded footsteps in the snow going down her porch steps. Pulling her sweater tight around her, Claire went to the door and unlocked it. She hesitated. All sorts of thoughts went through her mind but curiosity won. Turning the porch light on, Claire opened the door, and that's when those Christmas Eves she'd been thinking about came back at her again as a pink snowman card attached to the porch light by Christmas ribbons flew about in the wind.

Startled by what she'd found, Claire stepped outside and watched the pink snowman do somersaults. It took her a few seconds to grasp what was going on. Just as she realized its meaning, a car door opened across the street and someone called her name.

"Claire! Claire. Merry Christmas!"

That someone was running toward her, running through snowbanks to reach her, to embrace her with tears flowing.

"Ellen! Ellen. Is that really you?"

"Yes, silly. Of course it's me! Your big sister came to wish you a Merry Christmas!"

Chapter Forty-Four

THE COLD DIDN'T STOP A REUNION brought about by a pink snowman on Christmas Eve. Between hugs and tears and laughter, the two sisters stayed out on that porch despite the snow swirling in their faces. A snowplow driver going by brought them back to reality.

"Hey! Ladies! One of you own that car with the door wide open? You better get it off the street before you lose the door and get a ticket. There's an all-night parking ban in effect."

"Oh, I forgot about closing the door once I saw you!"

More laughter went rolling through the night until the snowplow driver started honking his horn.

"Pull in my driveway, Ellen, and hurry. I have so many questions! Oh, it's so good seeing you. Hurry, Ellen! Do you need help carrying anything?"

"No gifts, remember!"

The two kept laughing. While Ellen parked her car, Claire untied the pink snowman card, holding on to it as if it were worth money. Actually it was worth so much more. It was precious to both of them.

Once inside they kept it up until walking into the living room and seeing a photo of their parents sitting on top of a bookshelf. They both stopped as laughter turned to tears.

"Mom and Dad would be so happy that we are together tonight. I still can't believe you are standing here Ellen."

"I was going to call and tell you but decided to surprise you."

"When I saw that pink snowman swirling about in the wind so many memories of so many Christmases when we were growing up came to mind. It didn't sink in right away that you were the one who'd tied that card to the light. When it did, I felt like Christmas had arrived. Thank you for coming Ellen. Having you here in my home is the best gift ever."

The two sisters shed more tears as they embraced one another in front of that framed photo.

A few minutes later as she walked about the living room, Ellen remarked, "Your home is lovely, Claire. But no tree?"

"No time. But I do have a small ceramic one sitting on the kitchen counter. It was made in China."

"Mom would have a fit. We don't have a tree either. The kids are grown with their own lives. Let me rephrase that. They didn't want to come home with Bill out of work and me being my usual unhappy self."

Ellen changed the subject. "Claire! I see a piano. Do you play?" "No but someday I hope to take lessons."

"I remember you sitting with Dad while he played his piano. I pretended not to have any interest but the truth is I was jealous of you sitting beside him. I always thought you were his favorite. If only I could tell him how much I loved hearing him play even though I wasn't in the room."

"I never felt I was his favorite. He never asked me to sit with him. I remember being so intrigued watching his fingers hit the keys making beautiful sounds that I had to get as close to his piano as possible. What I remember the most is the look on Dad's face when he was playing. He'd close his eyes and let his fingers create the music. He was at peace sitting on that piano bench."

"Isn't if funny how we both grew up under the same roof yet we have different interpretations of some of the things that happened?"

"I would think that's normal, Ellen. We weren't the same age. We had different interests. We went through some tough times as a family but I think that's normal too."

Going through the kitchen to a side room, Claire opened a wooden cupboard built into the wall. Taking hold of a bottle sitting in a rack, Claire grabbed another wine glass before shutting the door.

"I never asked. Would you prefer something else to drink?"

"One glass of wine will do it for me. Then I'll switch to tea."

"That's one thing we agree on!"

As Claire was leading her sister through the dining room, sheets of tissue paper with ribbon and tape sitting on the table caught Ellen's attention.

"I remember when Mom would use tissue paper for wrapping gifts. I like the ribbon you chose for accent."

"The gifts have been delivered to a family near and dear to me."

Ellen didn't ask questions. She was in Claire's studio amazed by her little sister's talent.

"You have a way of capturing even the simplest things and making them look priceless."

"That's because they are, Ellen. Come sit next to me."

"I love this window seat, Claire. The view must be wonderful."

"This is my favorite place to sit. There are maple and pine trees out there with feeders attracting birds all year long."

"Remember the mesh bags Grandma would fill with suet and hang out for the birds? I have such fond memories of playing in Grampie's barn and the farmhouse."

"As do I, Ellen," said Claire, pouring a glass of wine. Handing it to Ellen, she continued. "How did you ever get away on Christmas Eve? How long can you stay?"

"It was Bill who suggested I come."

"Really? How did that happen?"

"After you sent me that card, I was a mess. Years of being petty and cold and driven by money caught up with me, and Bill was there to catch me. Imagine, Claire. I'd been so mean and hard on him yet there he was with his arms wide open. It all came out. Every last petty move I made or word I said came out and we are so much better off because of it. I have you to thank. When I opened the envelope and pulled out that pink snowman card, my life turned around. Now I have to work on building some sort of a relationship with my grown children."

"The matriarch of that family I mentioned has helped me realize our parents were good and decent people doing the best they knew how. They loved us, Ellen. Were we a perfect family? No, but I don't think a perfect family exists. I used to. I wasted time holding that against them."

"We've all wasted time holding grudges. You know, sitting there with the moon behind you I am reminded of Mom. You have grown to look like her. The shape of your face; your gentle smile; the way you wear your long hair."

"That is a compliment, Ellen, another beautiful gift on Christmas Eve."

"Does it feel like Christmas Eve to you?"

"It does now that you are here."

"I thought about you the other night when Bill was switching TV channels. He came across reruns of some old Christmas specials. You know, the ones that Mom and Dad used to watch. We popped some popcorn, turned out the lights and watched reruns until we fell asleep."

"It sounds like you and Bill are happy."

"We are for the first time in years. How about you? And Tommy? Right. That's his name?"

Claire didn't have the energy to explain. She changed the subject.

"You didn't answer my question. How long can you stay?"

"Bill told me to take my time but I sensed he was hoping I'd be home for Christmas. Funny thing about that, I want to spend Christmas with him. So I figure I'll stay part of the day with you and head back. But this is the first of many trips I'll be making to see you. Maybe we can get our little brother to join us."

"I called Nathan the other night. He was distant at first but by the time we hung up, he thanked me for calling."

"That's wonderful, Claire."

"I asked him about the three of us getting together. His twins are now teenagers. He'd like them to get to know us before they're too old to care so I think it will happen."

"I can't believe his twins are that old! This is a Christmas of miracles thanks to you, Claire."

The two sisters stayed up past midnight. After enjoying a cup of tea, they went upstairs.

"You can sleep in here, Ellen."

Opening the door to the pale yellow room where Winnie the Pooh sat next to a worn, old, beloved bear, Claire explained it was to have been the nursery.

"I'm so sorry. I never knew Eric changed his mind about having children. You must have been devastated."

"I'm okay now," Claire replied, picking up her old bear and sitting down by the window overlooking the neighbor's yard. "I'm okay."

Pulling up a chair, Ellen spoke in a tone Claire had never heard before. "As your older sister I've let you down time after time and for that I'm sorry. I have no excuse but my self-centered ignorance. But listen to me, Claire. I am here for you. Anytime, I am here for you. This beautiful room with its crib and teddy bears speaks of love. You will find that love, Claire. You are meant to be loved. Please, Claire. In the quiet of this room, tell me about Tommy."

With tears falling on her old bear, Claire opened up to a sister who'd never bothered with her before now. But there she was sitting beside Claire and looking out the window where the children had been making snowmen like they used to do. Now those children were asleep, just like they would be on Christmas Eve, waiting for Santa Claus.

Once Claire began talking about the young man with deep brown eyes and a bit of a beard who loved baking cookies, she couldn't stop. That is until she came to Denise.

"I haven't heard from him. I don't know if he asked Denise to marry him. What will I ever do if he did?"

"I don't have that answer. The one thing I know for sure is you are strong. You are a survivor. And you will find your love."

With her arms around Claire, Ellen whispered as snow gently fell. "Something tells me you've found that love."

Getting up from her chair, Claire went over and turned off the light. Sitting back down she told Ellen to listen. "Do you hear them? There are carolers coming down the street. They're singing 'Silent Night.'"

It's Christmas. Merry Christmas, Ellen. I am so happy you came. I've missed you."

Before they said good night, plans were made for the day ahead. Ellen would follow Claire to John and Elizabeth's. After spending a few hours there, she'd catch the Interstate and be home in time to have dinner with Bill. Claire couldn't wait to take Ellen to that simple clapboard home full of love and family and a reindeer named Ginger and a little dog named Bailey and a lamb that slept next to a baby in a manger, and a young girl who saw the world in her own beautiful way, and the matriarch who taught those around her about life and the fine art of baking cookies with tin cookie cutters made with and given in love. Anything else that might take place at that house on a country road on this Christmas Day was in the Lord's hands.

As she was falling asleep, Claire remembered yet another Christmas Eve. She was sitting on her father's piano bench listening to him play one Christmas carol after another. When he began to play "I'll Be Home For Christmas," the door opened and in walked her mother. The scent of Toujours Moi was everywhere. Her mother never came in the room when he was playing but she did that Christmas Eve with her hair curled, wearing a pretty red sweater Claire had never seen before. Despite being quite young, she remembered her mother sitting down on the bench and putting her arm around her father. It was only a moment; however, it was a moment on a Christmas Eve with tree lights glistening and her mother whispering to her father, "I love you."

Chapter Forty-Five

"DON'T YOU WISH MOM AND DAD could see us having Christmas breakfast together?"

"In my heart, I think they can," Claire replied, looking out the back window at the house where the children had been making snowmen.

"They have to be up by now."

"Who has to be up?"

"Those kids in that house on the corner. They have to be up. It's Christmas morning. Remember our Christmas mornings, Ellen? Forget the chaotic ones. I'm talking about the ones when Mom would cook her special Christmas morning French toast. It was so good and hot and gooey with just enough cinnamon and real maple syrup from what Grampie called, his sap house. If I had all the ingredients, I'd try to make us some."

"I'm fine. Your scrambled eggs are delicious."

"I don't do that much cooking."

"I gave up cooking for a long time but I'm back at it. Bill seems to enjoy what I cook."

"More coffee?"

"Just a touch. I'm........"

Something caught her eye. "Claire! Are these angel chimes the same ones we had growing up?"

"Yes. I was wondering if you'd remember."

"I'll never forget them. Sometimes when no one was looking I'd hurry one of the angels along with my finger. A few times in the process a candle would go out. That's when I'd hightail it away from the table."

"I did the same thing only I'd blow on an angel and a candle would go out."

"I'm so glad you have them on your table for Christmas."

While they finished their coffee, Claire explained how she'd found the chimes in the same box as the pink snowman.

"Funny how two unrelated things stuck in a box on a back shelf in a closet can still hold so much meaning when discovered again," Ellen remarked.

"The chimes and the card make me think of you and me discovering each other again. In a way, I feel like I've been stuffed away in a box on a closet shelf but no more of that. It's time we both embrace life and be thankful for our blessings."

"I agree my dear little sister. Merry Christmas."

It was a little after one when they walked out the door, leaving the pink snowman card on the kitchen table next to the angel chimes. After stopping for gas, Claire made the turn leading to that country road with Ellen following behind. Despite sporadic snow squalls overnight, the road was in fair shape. When they pulled into the Miller farm, the look on Ellen's face when she stepped out of her car was priceless.

"Claire! You never told me your friends were Amish."

"I thought about it and decided what's important is that they are my friends. Their being Amish is a plus."

"Oh, I agree. I find this place enchanting. It feels like Christmas used to feel when we were little, visiting at the farm. I love this, Claire! Thank you for bringing me to meet your friends!"

Ellen didn't stay long. Although snow was not in the forecast, it started in again. After meeting everyone including Ginger, Ellen was back in her car.

"Thanks for everything, Claire. I will keep in touch. Let me know about Tommy. I wish I'd met him. Maybe next time."

"I'm so glad you came. I can't wait to see you again. Give my love to

Bill as well as those children of yours. I'll keep in touch with Nathan and let you know what he wants to do. Love you."

"Take care of that pink snowman!"

"I will. Bye. Love you."

Claire stood by the side of the road until Ellen's car disappeared around a curve. It reminded her of the day Ellen left for college. She waved until her father's car was out of sight.

Elizabeth was busy in the kitchen when Claire walked back through the door. Mary was asleep. John was rocking Abraham.

"Mummi should be along any minute."

"Everything smells delicious, Elizabeth. What can I do?"

"If you don't mind, could you set the table? Faith kept me up during the night and I seem to be behind in my duties. Everything you'll need is in that cupboard. Christmas dinner plates are on the top shelf."

"I don't mind at all, Elizabeth. Anything you need, I'm here to help."

As she went over to the cupboard, Frank asked Claire if she'd like to see what he got for Christmas.

"I'd love seeing what both you and Hannah received."

The young girl was on her feet showing Claire her new rag doll, a new sled, pads of drawing paper, and homemade candy from Mummi. "Thank you for the pretty mittens. Mother told me they are green like the grass."

"You are welcome, Hannah. I bet you can't wait to start drawing with all those pads of paper."

"I can't! I will take the paper to my secret spot and draw."

"You are amazing, Hannah."

Turning to Frank, the young boy told Claire he too received a new sled. "Plus a board game, skates, and look, Claire, a real football. And blue mittens from you. Thanks!"

"Looks like you and Hannah were surprised this morning."

"We were," Frank replied. "Do you like to play football?"

"I grew up around lots of boy cousins and a brother who loved playing football. They got me into playing and I liked it."

Remembering to take the lamb outside before dinner, Frank excused himself as Claire found the plates and dishes she would need to set the table. Frank was only outside a few minutes when he came back through the door.

"Mummi is coming. I can hear the bells you put around her sleigh, Father."

"Mummi is right on time to make the gravy," said Elizabeth.

"I'm horrible at making gravy. I can never get rid of the lumps," Claire laughed as she placed the plates around the table. When she was counting silverware, the door opened and in walked Frank carrying dishes wrapped in cloth. Behind him came Mummi. Putting the dishes down, Frank picked up his lamb and went back outside

"Merry Christmas, everyone! Merry Christmas," Catherine exclaimed.

Hannah rushed to give Mummi a hug and thank her for the candy. As Claire was wishing her a Merry Christmas, Frank came back inside with the lamb.

"I'll be back in a minute, Father. I have to go to the barn with Tommy. He asked me to help unhitch Mummi's horse."

"Tommy?"

"Yes, Claire. Tommy," Catherine replied with a wink. "He stopped at my place early this morning. We got to talking and here we are."

"Look out the window, Mummi. Tommy is taking Frank for a sleigh ride," Elizabeth laughed as she stirred carrots into a casserole.

"Where are they going?" Hannah asked, standing at a window.

"It looks as if they are going around in circles," Catherine chuckled. "They are having fun on this Christmas Day."

Pulling a curtain back, Claire caught sight of Tommy. Her heart quickened when seeing him as the horse kept kicking up snow out in the field.

"He's a kid at heart, that Tommy; a kid who has finally figured it out." Turning to Claire, Catherine whispered, "If you know what I mean!"

"I better get the hot chocolate ready. Those two will be needing some when they come inside."

Elizabeth was right. When the door opened a little while later in they came with their cheeks red, fingers frozen, and eyebrows all snow.

None of that stopped Tommy from going over to Claire and embracing her. As they stood in the kitchen, Claire thought of the story Catherine would tell; waiting on the front porch in her bare feet for Paul's return. And when he did, Paul would run up the steps and embrace her. It never mattered to Catherine if he was all snow or soaking wet. What mattered was Paul coming back home to Catherine's warm embrace. And now, holding Tommy in her arms, Claire understood that moment more than ever. It didn't matter that Tommy was cold and his clothes were all snow and his gloves were wet. What mattered was he was there on Christmas day. He was back home in so many ways.

Chapter Forty-Six

IF EVER THERE WAS A CHRISTMAS gathering where every minute was memorable, it was the one underway inside that Amish home on a country road. The simple setting told the story of the family who lived there. There were no devices, no TVs blaring, no distractions unless you noticed the way Tommy and Claire interacted. Even when passing a dish or platter around the table, it was obvious something was stirring.

"You have prepared another delicious dinner, Elizabeth. The ham with dumplings is unbelievable."

"Thanks, Tommy. It's the buttermilk in the dumplings. Try some hot slaw. It complements the ham."

Passing the dish to Claire, John suggested she try a little.

"Thanks, John. I hope I have room left on my plate. This dinner is so enjoyable."

After taking John's suggestion, Claire handed the dish to Tommy. The touch of their fingers had them saying so much more with their eyes.

Between enjoying the meal and sharing in conversation, dessert wasn't served until close to 7:00. By 8:30 the dishes were done. That's when Catherine surprised everyone when saying she was too tired to go back home.

"I have an idea, Tommy. Why don't you take Claire for a sleigh ride?

It's a beautiful Christmas night to be out there. That empty space at the end of your building is more than sufficient for the horse. You told me you keep some hay in there and it's heated. Come back for dinner tomorrow. Then you can take me home."

"And bring Claire with you. It's the traditional Second Christmas; another day of enjoying our family and a fine meal."

"Elizabeth! That would be my third dinner in a row at this table."

"I think that is wonderful, Claire. You are always welcome at our table."

"Thank you, Elizabeth."

Deciding they would go on that sleigh ride, Elizabeth made sure Claire was dressed for the occasion. "Take these wool blankets, Tommy. They are good and warm."

"Thanks, John. I'll bring them back tomorrow."

Walking down to the barn with the moon high above them, Claire had so many feelings and so many questions. When Tommy told her he'd missed her, Claire couldn't hold back.

"I've missed you as well Tommy. I figured you were busy in the bakery or you and Denise were—were busy."

When he didn't answer, she asked. "Were you busy in the bakery?"

"Yes. I was slammed but that's not why I stayed away."

Claire waited for an explanation. Instead, Tommy held up a kerosene lamp, motioning for Claire to step inside. Then he led her toward the back of the barn.

"This won't take long. Are you warm enough?"

"Yes. I'll be with the reindeer when you're ready to go."

Except for old boards creaking in the wind, the barn was quiet. It was as if the animals knew it was Christmas. With moonlight coming through most of the windows, Claire was able to find her way, remembering to go behind the horse stalls to the door leading to the reindeer. When she opened the door, the sight of those reindeer on Christmas night was breathtaking. Most of them were sleeping. A few came over to greet her. Ginger was there looking for apples. The smell of hay and shaved wood and cans of paint and stain, along with sacks of oats and corn, and grease to keep machinery running, and leftover greenery from making Christmas wreaths made Claire think of her grandfather's barn. She could only imagine what it would have been like if there had been reindeer kept in his barn when she was a little girl believing in Santa Claus.

With so much going through her mind, Claire climbed the ladder to Hannah's secret spot. There was something peaceful about sitting up there in a bed of hay, looking out at the moon. When Tommy came searching for Claire, he knew where to find her. Climbing up the ladder, he sat down next to her. A few minutes later he began speaking from his heart. He had a lot to say.

"I've never talked about feelings with anyone, Claire. Any feelings I had, I kept stuffed away. I've bumbled along being that nice guy with a girlfriend here and there. Any relationship I had, I never put much into it. I never wanted to. I was okay with having just a girlfriend and nothing more. If I felt anyone getting serious, I bowed out. Denise became a habit. Because she lived away from here, I was fine having her come in and out of my life.

Ever since I was a kid, I had this thing inside me. This need to create. For a while my music was the answer. But after I lost my father, music took on a different meaning. Suddenly, there I was—just an electrician; doing a job and coming home day after day after day. The only time I felt alive was when I was with Catherine in her kitchen. But it all changed when that building fell in my lap. Denise was still in my life yet we never talked about where we were going. I own that because honestly, I didn't care. I left her in charge of us while I took care of my creative side. I realize all of this now— because of you, Claire."

Taking her hand as reindeer slept below, Tommy continued. "You woke me up to those feelings I kept stuffed away. You and I have a creative side, making it easier to understand each other. Despite hardly knowing me, you talked me through the guilt I held concerning my father's passing. You love my baking. Love the cookies and the smells from the oven. I enjoy working with you in the kitchen. You're like me, Claire. You enjoy all of it; the mixing, the rolling out and the cutting out and the waiting."

Tommy put the brakes on but only for a minute. "I've never taken the time to think about the next step. I've always jumped right in. But this time, this time was different. As I was about to ask Denise to marry me on Christmas Eve, I thought of you, Claire. I realized this time, I couldn't jump. If I did, I'd lose you. I couldn't let you slip through my fingers."

Moving closer; putting his arm around her, Tommy kept talking. "I've never felt love before I met you. To be honest, Claire, I fell in love with you the minute I found you standing on the porch just up that snowy path. I kept denying it until there I was, sitting with Denise; trying to ask her to marry me and put a ring on her finger that I paid for and never liked. But I couldn't get the words out, Claire. I never could have pledged anything to her because my heart is yours, Claire. Yours now and forever. I can't think of being anywhere else than at this place in this barn on this farm and telling you how much I love you. I love you, Claire. I want to shout that through the barn and over the fields. I love you, Claire Ryan! I've stayed away because I was confused. Spending time with Catherine today made everything crystal clear."

The wind whispering through the trees emulated violins being played as Claire took Tommy into her arms. With her mittens off, Claire moved her fingers about his face; outlining his lips and softly stroking his forehead. Pulling that navy knit hat slowly away, Claire ran her fingers through his hair, bringing him even closer. When his lips met hers, those violins became an orchestra. They became lost in the moment until Ginger let it be known he was still waiting for an apple. That's all it took for laughter to take hold.

"This reminds me of when we fell on the ice."

"And little children were watching us. You don't think anyone's watching us now, do you, Tommy?"

"If they are, I think they're pretty happy for us."

"Oh, Tommy, how I love you. I have since you opened that door. I never thought I could feel love like this but you've made it easy. I love your smile and gentleness; your kindness and creativeness and caring for Hannah and respect for Catherine and your ability to see a building for its potential and not its condition. I love your laugh and twinkle in your eye and the way you dance. You make me happy, Tommy. You make me feel alive again and oh so very happy."

The horse was getting restless. "I think we should get moving on, my love. Are you up for a sleigh ride?"

"I am up for anything with you, Tommy, especially a sleigh ride under a Christmas moon."

"Oh, you are a romantic!"

With the lantern out and the horse and a sleigh full of blankets ready to go, Tommy held Claire's hand as she climbed in and waited for him to be sitting next to her. Taking it slow coming up from the barn, Tommy let the horse know it was time to head out under the stars once they reached the field. Pulling blankets up and around them, they didn't say a word. There was no need. As the horse brought them down a hill and then up the other side, providing a view that took their breath away, Tommy pulled on the reins.

"Perfect! This is perfect!"

Jumping out of the sleigh, Tommy went around to Claire's side. Kissing her tenderly as glistening stars danced above, Tommy got down on one knee in the snow. Claire felt tears falling down her cheek.

"Don't cry, my love. I will forever be by your side."

Reaching deep into a pocket, Tommy pulled out what looked like a small cloth bag. Holding the bag up for Claire to see, Tommy looked into her eyes and again declared his love for her.

"This moment is the moment my life takes on meaning."

Before Claire could say a word, Tommy handed her the cloth bag. Still on his knee, he waited while she opened it. Now he was the one with tears in his eyes as Claire responded to an old tin cookie cutter in the shape of a heart.

"Oh, Tommy! It's Catherine's cookie cutter made by the love of her life."

"This tin cookie cutter is now your tin cookie cutter, Claire. After spending time with Catherine earlier, she went over to the wooden box and brought this to me, telling me to give it to you when I felt the moment was right. I can't think of a better time, Claire. From a love that began so many years ago to our love as we begin our journey, this old tin cookie cutter will always be a part of our story. Will you marry me, Claire?"

"Yes! Yes I will marry you. For keeps, my love."

Once he was back in the sleigh, Tommy signaled for the horse to move slowly through the snow. As they were heading out further in the field, a rabbit jumped out in front of the horse and kept on going. Tommy pulled back on the reins.

"That was one brave rabbit!"

"Rabbit?"

"Guess it was going so fast you missed him!"

"My sister and I had a pet rabbit. We cried for days when we lost him." "The only rabbit I've ever known was Rabbit himself."

"You don't mean Winnie the Pooh's friend, do you?"

"How did you know?"

"I still have all those books. They were some of my favorites!"

"Mine too, Claire. I loved Winnie the Pooh stories growing up. Don't laugh, but I even had my own Winnie the Pooh!"

Claire became quiet. All she could think of was the Winnie the Pooh sitting on a dresser in a pale yellow bedroom. Tommy noticed the change in her mood.

"I've lost you. What is it, Claire?"

That's all it took for Claire to tell her story. When she finished, Tommy spoke softly from the heart as church bells were ringing in the distance.

"I will never hurt you, Claire. I want to grow old with you. And listen to me, I want our children to love Winnie the Pooh like we do."

"Our children?"

"Yes. Our children—our beautiful children."

Putting his arm around Claire, Tommy nudged his fingers underneath her scarf. Then ever so gently his fingers touched her face while pulling her closer as their lips met and passion heightened. Lying underneath the blankets, they became lost in the moment until that rabbit came around again and caught the horse's attention. Off they flew. In a flash, Tommy was sitting up and grabbing hold of the reins.

"Hey horse! Slow down. Slow down!"

The horse finally slowed down. Once Tommy had things under control, he pulled tighter on the reins. "Are you okay, Claire?"

Seconds later, laughter floated through the air and out over those fields.

"I don't mean to be laughing, Tommy, but I can't imagine how we must have looked when that horse took off. Rabbit was listening to you! Oh Tommy, I can't wait to start our journey."

"Claire."

"Yes, my love."

"I have something else you might consider funny. At least, I hope you find it humorous."

"What could it be, Tommy?"

"I have to go to the mercantile. I have cookies to bake for a pick-up first thing in the morning. I'm thinking that could be pretty romantic. We can make the dough—roll it out together and see what happens next."

"I can't think of anything else I'd rather be doing tonight than baking cookies with the love of my life!"

Laughter echoed over the hills and around the hedges on a Christmas night blessed by a curious rabbit and old tin cookie cutter in the shape of a heart made with love and once again, given with love.

"Love is fireworks and rapture. Love takes you beyond the stars."

Barbara Briggs Ward is a writer living in Ogdensburg, New York. She is the author of a Christmas trilogy for adults featuring *The Reindeer Keeper*, released in 2010 and selected by both Yahoo's Christmas Book Club and the Riverfront Library Book Club in Yonkers as their December, 2012 featured Book of the Month. Barbara completed the trilogy with the release of *The Snowman Maker* in 2013 and *The Candle Giver* in 2015. In 2017, her first work of Amish fiction, *A Robin's Snow*, was released.

Her articles and short stories have appeared in the Chicken Soup for the Soul books, *Christmas Magic* and *Family Caregivers*, plus *Ladies' Home Journal*, *Highlights for Children* and *The Saturday Evening Post* online.

In 2018, Barbara's work of fiction, a short story titled, "Sleigh Bells Ring Again," earned first place in Watertown, New York's Jefferson Community College Writing Center's annual Writing Festival. She has been a featured writer on Mountain Lake PBS in Plattsburgh, New York and at Target Book Festivals in Boston and New York.

Barbara invites you to visit her website at www.barbarabriggsward.com. She is on Facebook under The Reindeer Keeper.

CPSIA information can be obtained
at www.ICGtesting.com
Printed in the USA
BVHW072231041019
560317BV00001B/2/P

9 781627 877213